WE WILL
REIGN

USA TODAY BESTSELLING AUTHOR
RACHEL LEIGH

ALSO BY RACHEL LEIGH

Bastards of Boulder Cove

Book One: Savage Games

Book Two: Vicious Lies

Book Three: Twisted Secrets

Wicked Boys of BCU

Book One: We Will Reign

Book Two: You Will Bow

Book Three: They Will Fall

Redwood Rebels Series

Book One: Striker

Book Two: Heathen

Book Three: Vandal

Book Four: Reaper

Redwood High Series

Book One: Like Gravity

Book Two: Like You

Book Three: Like Hate

Fallen Kingdom Duet

His Hollow Heart & Her Broken Pieces

Black Heart Duet

Four & Five

Standalones

NOTE TO READERS

We Will Reign is a dark college, why-choose romance. Please be advised of the following potential triggers:

- Depressive Thoughts
- Bullying
- Assault
- Graphic Murder
- Violence
- Stalking
- Dubious Consent

This book ends on a cliffhanger and picks up in next book of the trilogy: You Will Bow.

For the girls who dream of having their own harem of psychos.

BLURB

Enrolling at BCU was supposed to be my chance at freedom.
An escape from my parents who insist I follow in their
footsteps as a Guardian of the Society.
Keep the members safe—that's what I'm supposed to do. But
how can I safeguard the students when I can't even protect
myself?
Someone has been watching me.
His eyes burn into my soul like a branding iron. At night, he
haunts my dreams and transforms them into nightmares.
And sometimes when I wake, he's there.
Standing at the foot of my bed in awe of my existence. He isn't
the one I fear most, though.
There are others who have their eyes on me, too.
Only their obsession runs deeper than Ridge's and I fear if I fall
under their thumbs, I won't make it out of here alive. *There
once was a sicko who lurked in the mist. He preyed on my soul
baring a closed iron fist. His stare made me itch while his eyes
locked me under his spell. But taking his hand may be my only
escape from this hell.*

.

Playlist
Listen Now on Spotify
Creep by Radiohead
Neurotic by Three Days Grace
Driven Under by Seether
Shiver by Coldplay
Still Frame by Traps
Fine Again by Seether
I Feel Like I'm Drowning by Two Feet
Drift and Die by Puddle of Mud
So Cold by Breaking Benjamin
Save Me by Shinedown
Wasteland by 10 Years
Suffocate by Cold
Dance With The Devil by Breaking Benjamin
We Are One by 12 Stones
Anti-Hero by Taylor Swift
Teeth by 5 Seconds of Summer
Lifetime by Three Days Grace
Tomorrow Comes Today by 12 Stones
Mine by Taproot
Monster by Skillet
The Summoning by Sleep Token
CHECK OUT THE PINTEREST BOARD

"I, Ridge Foster, solemnly swear to keep the secrets, oaths, and promises of The Society. To protect our antiquity and to abide by all rules. I understand that failure to do so will result in my abolishment, never to enter The Blue Bloods' Society again."

It's the quarter meeting for our chapter, and assignments are being handed out to the male members who have graduated from Boulder Cove Academy.

The President of our chapter nods, a smug grin on his face as if he's expecting me to fail at whatever assignment is handed over. "Thank you, Mr. Foster. I trust you won't let us down."

I pick up the small notebook with my name engraved on the front, then I make my way toward the exit.

As soon as I'm out of the meeting room—and in another less tense one—I flip back the black hood of my robe and release all the pent-up air in my lungs.

That shit never gets easier.

Anxiety courses through my veins as I open the notebook and read the first page.

Investigate the death of Sebastian Saint, our former state governor. Report all findings to The Elders.

That's it? That's all I've got to go on?

With only a pen and a mini notepad in my hand, my mission has begun. No backyard training. No clues as to what I'm searching for. We're sent out into the world with only our assignment and the hope that we don't fail.

I read the task again, hoping that something stands out. Anything I can use as a starting point because I've got fucking nothing.

I flip the cover up on the notepad, desperate for more clues, because I will fail if this is all I've got. For the last two years, I've had simple assignments. Track down a couple guys who needed to be brought in for questioning. Deliver a mysterious box. Of course, I was an underclassman at Boulder Cove University. I heard they get harder as you move up, but I guess I was expecting a little more direction.

Fuck it. I can do this.

Pulling out my phone, I type out a detailed email to one of The Blue Bloods—our Society—confidants at the Boulder Cove police department. I suck with words, so I go with something simple.

Send me everything you have on the death of Sebastian Saint.

Of course, I'll get the corrupt files, considering his death was deemed a suicide. That's only because that's what The Elders wanted. Any attention given to The Society is unwelcome, and it's something we avoid at all costs. We make our own rules and outside law enforcement can't touch us. It's one of the many perks of being a Blue Blood.

In the case of Sebastian Saint, and many other members who have lost their lives—justice will *never* be served. At least, not in the way many families would like to see justice served. Instead, we handle everything on our own, and my gut tells me Sebastian's murder was an inside job. The Elders must agree; otherwise, they wouldn't still be investigating.

May the Lord have mercy on the soul who was behind his death.

I slump in a chair of another room, beside my best friend, Maddox.

"What did you get?" he asks, peering over the notepad as I tap the pen to the table.

I hold it up, showing him my assignment. We're not supposed to share this information with a single soul. As a matter of fact, I just took an oath not to do so. Our assigned tasks are done in complete confidence. However, Maddox, Lev, and I have been known to break the rules because of the tight bond we share.

"Fuck, man," Maddox says. "You're like a real detective with that shit."

"Yeah." I smirk. "A crooked detective who is ready to wreak havoc on this case."

"Even better. Weed out those members who have fucked us all. Only then will we, the good ones, truly reign."

"What about you? Do you finally get to do something valuable with your time, instead of learning and creeping on the female students?"

"Nope," he quips, balancing his chair on two legs. "Same as every other year."

"The fuck?"

He holds up his own notepad, showing me the front page. *Watch the Kappa Rho members. Report any malicious acts to The Elders.*

"No shit." I nod, still tapping the pen on the table. "That's all you've got? The Guardians get all the easy shit. Better hope like hell those frat boys fuck up at some point, so The Elders don't think your ass is slacking."

"Watch. Protect. All the saintly acts." He pats his chest, grinning. "You can just call me God."

"Fuck off." I tap his shoulder, gently at that, but it's enough to send him tipping back in his chair. He lands with a thud, and I laugh my ass off.

"What the fuck, you asshole!"

Lev comes through the door, pissed off, as usual. Lev is always in a pissy mood. Our fate for the year is in the hands of The Elders on the other side of that door. Lev doesn't like direction or being told what to do, not that any of us do.

Without a word, he tosses his notepad on the table. I pick it up and read his inscription out loud. "Your target's name will be assigned at a later date. Be available at all times." I flip the notepad closed. "You're such a lucky son of a bitch." I knock his notepad away with my pen. "You get to hurt people and shit."

Lev doesn't push to know our assignments because he doesn't care. In fact, Lev doesn't care about anything at all these days. He just sort of exists in a world that keeps turning while he stands still.

"All right, fuckers," I grumble as I stand up. "I've got shit to do. I'll see ya at home."

Maddox, Lev, and I have an apartment in our small town. Same town we grew up in. Same faces every day. It's home for now, but in a couple of short weeks, we'll be moving back into our dorm at BCU.

It's a short walk from our chapter's meeting center to our apartment. Our Society comprises of thousands of chapters all over the world. We're everywhere. A neighbor, a colleague, a friend. We're an untouchable force you don't wanna fuck with.

The minute I step foot in the door of our apartment, my phone pings with a new email, and it's a response from the confidant I reached out to. Attached is a file, a lengthy one at that, and I'm certain I'm gonna need to open this shit on a computer.

4

I go straight to my room and log into my laptop to start the download. Sure as shit, it's long. But only one thing stands out to me as I begin: the pictures and names of those involved.

One face in particular catches my eye—Riley Cross.

The most beautiful girl I've ever laid eyes on.

Twelve Days Later

"Riley. Riley. Riley." I whisper her name repeatedly, loving the way it rolls off my tongue.

Perched on the branch of a tree beneath gray clouds, I watch as she focuses intently on whatever she's writing in her notebook.

Every now and then, her lips twitch, the pen stops moving, and she stares off into space before returning to her task at hand.

She's perfection personified. An angel sent to me during one of the darkest points in my life. I didn't want to exist anymore. Was ready to leave this world behind and face the new hell I'd entered in my next life.

Then I saw her.

I was certain they fucked me when I got my assignment— prepared to fail. Now, I can't lose because it led me to this flaw- less girl. Even from here, I'm certain I can hear her heart beat and I'm convinced it's beating just for me.

I know what she did. I know all her secrets, but now, they're mine to keep. Fuck the oaths and fuck the promises. My only mission from here on out is to protect the girl who will one day be mine.

I shift my leg, trying to snag my pants off a hook on the branch, when a piece of the wood snaps, falling straight to the ground. With one hand holding a branch above me, I brace myself on the one I'm sitting on, keeping myself steady and secure.

Riley's eyes shoot up from her book, scouring the area, and landing on mine. A smile lifts on my lips, and in that instant, she slams her book shut and snatches it off the picnic table.

Her feet don't stop moving as she scurries away, every few seconds stealing a glance over her shoulder to see if I'm coming after her.

Not yet. But in time.

You can run, but you can't hide. One day, Angel, you will be mine.

CHAPTER 1
RIDGE

WITH MY PREY IN A CHOKEHOLD—HIS back snug to my chest with a gun pressed to his rib cage, right over his heart—I raise his right hand, observing each finger. "Give me the names and maybe I'll let you keep one of these fingers."

"I told ya. I don't know what the hell you're talking about. Look, man. I'm just a normal guy trying to make ends meet. I don't want any trouble."

At first glance, he *is* a normal guy. Mid-thirties, scruffy face with a beer belly. Pretty sure he's even got a wife and kids, which I'll definitely use to my advantage, if necessary. I don't know a thing about this asshole. Don't give a damn about him, either. All I care about are the secrets he keeps. The ones that involve the murder of Sebastian Saint, our former state governor.

Didn't feel much like going to my classes this morning. So I didn't. Might go this afternoon. Might not. With only a couple of weeks left before our chapter's next meeting, when my assignment must be complete, I figured, what the hell, might as well do something worth my time before the party tonight. Which led me here to the riverside park, where I knew I'd find this asshole eating during his lunch break.

Each year during our attendance at Boulder Cove University (BCU), The Elders give the male students a list of assignments. Tests of loyalty, if you will. Each completed assignment brings us one step closer to being an Elder—a member who has completed the training and assignments with advanced knowledge and authority—in which case, we call the shots. Not everyone makes it, but I will. Because one thing I desire in life, above all else, is power for me, Maddox, and Lev. The boys I've climbed every mountain with. One day I will reign over The Society. One day, *we* will reign over The Society.

Then I saw her.

I chose my assignment at the end of the summer during one of The Society's quarterly meetings, not knowing what I was getting myself into with my choice. *Find out who killed our state governor.* He's an Elder and a descendant of one of the founding families. Should've been easy enough. In fact, it was. It took me sixteen hours to find out what happened. I could have handed over the information I got and had a low-key semester, while awaiting my future assignment for the next school year.

But the minute I laid eyes on her beautiful face, I knew I'd do anything to keep her safe, and it was at that very moment, I realized I'd have to be extra careful when carrying out my task because what The Elders want is the truth. And the truth is exactly what I refuse to give them. My new personal goal is to silence those who know what really happened to the governor. I'll betray The Society and twist the truth to keep it hidden, because my obsession with Riley Cross goes beyond any power I'll gain as an Elder.

A Guardian—my angel—killed our governor. And justifiably at that. Sebastian Saint was no leader. The man was a pansy ass who enjoyed fucking with teenagers. The sick bastard preyed on a group of students at Boulder Cove Academy and Riley did what she had to do as a Guardian—a protector of our generational members—and she shot the fucker at point-blank range. Then, she covered up his murder and claimed it was suicide. Being a Blue Blood comes with many benefits. One of them being protection from outside law enforcement. We like to handle our business on our own. And while the cops that were brought in on the case bought the story, because it's the one they were fed, a few of The Elders weren't so receptive to the claim and demanded the truth. They're seeking punishment for the involved members. Over my dead fucking body.

I'm not supposed to know that Riley is a Guardian—as is my best friend, Maddox. Only The Elders are supposed to know who *they* are. It isn't until graduation and our initiation into The Society as Elders that we know who holds what positions. I'm training to be a Sleuth—one who gathers information on cases given to us by The Elders. Meaning, we're all basically their little bitches.

Although we're not supposed to reveal our positions, me, Maddox, and Lev know everything about one another. As for Riley Cross, I know more about her than she knows about herself due to my sleuthing skills.

Raising my prey's hand, I stick his index finger in my mouth and clamp down, biting into his flesh until I feel the crunch of his bone. Right now, I need to hear what this guy knows, and if I suspect it's more than he should, his life will end.

"Fuuuuuck," he howls, while remaining relatively still, out of fear I'll blow out his insides.

I bring his finger farther into my mouth, positioning his nail between my molars. My jaw locks, caging his finger in as I chew like a dog with a bone.

"All right," he cries out. "Fuck. Okay. I'll tell ya everything I know."

Pleased with my ability to break him so quickly, I slide his finger out of my mouth, spin him around with the gun still lodged in his rib, then I ball up the metallic spit on my tongue and shoot it right at his face. It rolls down his nose, and he doesn't so much as flinch as it rests on his upper lip.

I dig the gun deeper, showing him it's still there while giving him one last chance to fess up. "Talk. Now."

His injured finger shakes in the air, his breath hitching. "Mr. Saint—the governor. He hired us to watch some kids at a school on the east side of town. The night he died, we saw them—"

"Who is *we*?" I cut him off, just needing the names, not the details I already know.

"A few guys from the factory he owned, where we work."

I push harder, grinding the tip of the gun against the bone of his ribs. "Names!"

"Robby...Robby Nelson," he stutters. "Andy Porter. And..." His words trail off as he hesitates to give me that last name.

"And...?"

"My...brother, err...Eric."

"That's it?"

His head nods against my sternum. "Better be," I tell him, before pulling the trigger. Splatters of his blood hit my face as I let his limp body fall to the ground. Pleading eyes stare up at me, blood seeping out of him and soaking his sweaty tee shirt.

Pulling out the mini notepad in the pocket of my blood-stained jacket, I add names and cross one off.

~~Dennis Mathers~~

Robby Nelson

Andy Porter

Eric Mathers

I don't even wait until he takes his last breath before coating his clothing in lighter fluid. Then I light a match and toss it down, igniting him in flames.

I know what you're thinking. I'm the bad guy, but he knew too much and that knowledge would hurt my girl.

He had to go. Nothing more to it.

———

Ever looked at something and immediately got locked under a spell? No matter how hard you tried, you couldn't peel your eyes away? Happens to me every time I see her. Nothing else matters. Not the fact that she sees me watching her. Not the people around us. At that moment, it's just us.

God, she's such a fucking toxic beauty. She has the body of an angel, but she walks with the demons. And I bet she loves every fucking second of it. She's deadly, though her appearance would tell you otherwise.

Perched on the cement wall in front of the school, I draw in a long drag of my cigarette. I can't stop watching the way she lights up all the surrounding faces. She's got that ability. A glowing ray of sunshine to everyone she's near.

Her wavy blonde hair, sporting a strip of deep purple in the front, glistens in the sunlight, exposing strands of darker shades beneath the gold. Just like her soul—bright, but with a tinge of darkness.

We're alike in that way—both hiding the dark sides of ourselves. It's painfully obvious we were destined to wreak havoc on the world together.

Sounds of laughter, created by just a few simple words on her part, send me jumping off the wall.

I wonder what she said that was so funny. If only I could be a perched butterfly on the shoulder of her white-knitted sweater.

My feet land with a thud, and I drop my cigarette to the sidewalk, stomping out the lit ember.

I've gotta stop doing this shit. Gotta quit watching her because it only makes me crazier. I fear one day, I'll snap if I can't have her. Be it my mind or her neck, something *will* break if she isn't mine.

"Snap the fuck out of it," Maddox says, knocking me upside my head. Instead of socking him back, I do what he said and come back down to reality, while keeping one eye on her. He dips his chin toward my boot. "Pretty sure you've mutilated the cigarette enough."

The toe of his boot presses firmly to mine, halting my movements. It isn't until he stops, I realize I *have* maimed the cigarette. The tobacco and shredded paper scatter, one with the tiny rocks on the pavement.

"Where the hell have you been all day? You weren't in bio. Didn't see ya at lunch either."

He's still talking, but everything he says slips through my ears as empty words as I watch Crew Vance approach Riley and her best friend, Scar. Crew is Scar's boyfriend, so I'll allow it, but if it were any other guy, I'd be forced to pull her away from the situation.

Maddox must've followed my train of sight because he says, "Look. If you don't talk to her soon, I will. A girl like that doesn't wait around forever for a guy who won't even say hi."

My neck twists, and he stops talking. He knows how I get when I'm around her. Knows about my selective mutism. It's brought on by my anxiety, and nothing makes me more anxious than Riley Cross. It's not something I'd wish upon anyone. It fucking sucks.

"Come on." He throws an arm around my neck, rubbing his

knuckles to the top of my head. "Let's go find you a chick who can actually get words out of you."

I follow Maddox's lead, forcing his words out of my head, because if they linger, I'll lose it. Glancing one last time over my shoulder, Riley's eyes catch mine, setting my body on fire. I stop abruptly, hoping like hell she says something—motions me toward her or comes toward me. Anything. But when her eyes skate away from mine and she continues to engage in a conversation with her circle of friends, my heart thaws and rage consumes me.

It's times like this that I don't like her. Those moments where she pretends I don't exist. Countless times I've watched her and I know she sees me, yet she doesn't acknowledge my existence. What's wrong with me? Why can't she see me the way I see her?

One day she will.

Even if I have to make her.

"The freshman class is throwing a party tonight at Kappa Rho," Maddox says, now getting my full attention. The Kappa Rho House is home to the only male fraternity at BCU. Being a smaller university, they only have one local chapter for each fraternity and sorority. I might loathe the members, but if the freshman class is throwing the party, I'll certainly like one guest.

I step out from under his arm as we walk up the paved stairs to the main campus building. "It's gonna be lit," he continues. "Especially since they're providing the booze and entertainment."

"Which freshmen?"

Maddox's shoulders rise, then fall. "I assume all of them."

If the freshman class is throwing the party, that means Riley will be there. In which case, I'll be there, too. This day just got better.

CHAPTER 2
RILEY

THE PARTY IS in full swing and while I'd love to enjoy it, Scar and I got the shit job of preparing the snack table. Who even eats snacks at a keg party?

I pop a chip in my mouth, then another.

Okay. Maybe the snack table is a good idea.

I steal a glance at Scar, who's looking behind me. "Is he still there?" I ask her and she returns with a subtle nod.

"Yup."

My heart skips a few beats before jumping into an up-tempo rhythm. I'm not surprised. Ridge Foster is always watching me. We're over a month into our first semester here and he's had his eyes on me since I stepped out of my parents' car. We've never talked, but I feel like I've gotten to know him through unspoken words. I've learned to read his facial expressions, his body language, and the way he completely shuts out everyone around him when I'm in his presence.

I've concluded that Ridge is either plotting my demise, or he's falling madly in love with me. I vote the former, considering he's watched me long enough to hurt me, or garner enough information that could destroy me, if he wanted.

Scar dumps another bag of chips into the large crystal bowl,

14

then tosses the empty bag into a box of trash. Hand resting on the table full of snacks, her eyebrows lift. "If you don't say something to that creep soon, I will, Riley. This is getting out of control."

Scar, my best friend and roommate, knows I've been under Ridge's watchful eye. What she doesn't know is the extent of his stalking. As far as she's concerned, he just keeps his eyes on me when I'm around. She doesn't know he's stood outside and looked up at our dorm window more nights than I can count. But the truth is, Ridge doesn't scare me. In fact, I'm grossly enamored by him. Does that make me crazy, too? Maybe it does.

I dump the case of beer into the cooler and move the ice around, making sure each can is covered, then I change the conversation because the topic of Ridge makes me anxious, in a way that Scar wouldn't understand. "This party is such bull-shit. Why should we have to be little bitches to the upperclass-men?" I lift my head from where I'm kneeling, while attempting to hide my skivvies in this hot as sin, gold dress. Looking sexy can be so uncomfortable. A few more drinks and I doubt I'll even care what's on display. My anxiety was in high gear so I had an early start and I'm not regretting it.

"You're deflecting." Scar raises her brows, her lips pressed tightly into a firm line.

She knows me too well, but I don't give up my quest to talk about something else. I smash the box, collapsing it, then toss it into the box of garbage where all the remnants of our hard work is. "Is this gonna go on all year? I mean, these girls who boss us around have to know how torturous it is. They were freshmen once, too."

Scar bobs her head from shoulder to shoulder and sings, "Deflect, deflect, deflect."

Nudging my shoulder against her bare leg, I laugh before

standing up. "Just let it go. If I thought for a second that guy was a threat, you know I'd be screaming for help."

"If you say so." She sighs heavily. "I'm going to get more bottled water, then that should be it. Hopefully, we can enjoy this night a little."

Scar leaves, taking the trash box with her. I watch as she walks away, wishing I had it as easy as she does. The only thing Scar has to worry about is which one of her boyfriends will share her bed that night—yes, she has three, and color me jealous.

As for me, I'm as single as a Pringle with the weight of the world on my shoulders because I have a duty to uphold as a Guardian. Although, I have yet to even do anything as a Guardian. I watch for any odd behavior that might seem suspicious but nothing has really caught my eye. Maybe I'm just too preoccupied with my own life to worry about what everyone else is doing.

A thunderous smack sends a vibration through my body and my heart flees from my chest as I jump back, knocking into the snack table. I clasp my chest and take in a deep breath when I realize it was just a door slamming shut.

For someone who is supposed to protect the students at this school, I am the most cowardly Guardian in existence. In my defense, I've endured more than my predecessors. There are events in my life that I wish I could just forget. If there was a way to erase those days from my memory, I'd do it in a heartbeat. Unfortunately, my actions are now part of me and all I can do is learn to embrace the girl inside of me who, in a split second, took the life of another person.

What I did doesn't mean I succeeded as a Guardian—it means I failed because I reacted and my actions could cost me everything if the truth ever came out. Guardians don't kill. We protect.

The Society—The Blue Bloods—is comprised of different delegations meant to serve, protect, and honor our members. My family comes from a long line of Guardians—protectors, or watchers, rather—and it's in my blood to monitor all members and report any undue findings to The Elders. I know nothing about the tasks and assignments of other students. It's all hush-hush. Sworn secrets. However, I do know that female members, who are not Guardians, don't carry the same weight as the male members.

Truth be told, I don't want this role. I'm terrible at it. There's no doubt in my mind I will fail this series of tests over the next four years and I'll be the first Cross to tarnish our family name as Guardians. And if that happens, it happens. I don't even care anymore. I've got my own shit to deal with and don't have the energy to snoop around, putting my nose in other people's business just to tattle on them to The Elders.

All I want is to have a normal college experience. Drink too much. Lose my virginity, and do the walk of shame a few mornings after a few one-night stands with guys whose names I don't even know. I want to be numb to the rules of The Society. I wanna fuck up and have some regret then pick my head up and keep moving forward because I am so damn tired of trying to be the perfect daughter my parents expect me to be.

Swimming in pity, dark days ahead. Screaming for mercy from the thoughts in my head.

Poetry gets me through the hard times. When I'm feeling an immense amount of pressure, I make up random shit in my head. When I'm in my bed and negativity swims through my mind, I write until it's all out on paper.

Sometimes it helps; other times, it sends me to a different outlet. Much like now. My hand goes right into the cooler full of Jell-O shots. I grab a handful and drop them onto the table. With the top popped off one, I tip my head back, letting the cold, alcohol-infused gelatin slide down my throat. I don't even allow my tongue to get a taste, I just feed my stomach the alcohol it needs to tell my brain to shut the hell up. I wasn't always like this. Once upon a time, I was happy. Now, I'm just the remnants of my mistakes. A broken girl who cannot heal.

Dropping the little plastic container on the table, I grab another and open it, then another. They go down fast and do the job rather quickly, warming my insides. It won't be long until the alcohol mixes with the three straight vodka shots I had when I arrived.

"That must be some good Jell-O." The guy's voice comes from over my shoulder and it's a familiar one. I look down at the table, where three empty Jell-O shot containers lie before turning around.

Face-to-face with Maddox Crane, one of Ridge's tried and true best friends, my tongue drags across my bottom lip. I've never officially met either of Ridge's roommates, and best friends— the other being Lev Pemberley—but I know who they are. It's not like I'd allow a guy to watch me without doing a little digging of my own. Ridge, Maddox, and Lev are juniors this year. At first glance, they appear to be your typical bad boys. More times than not, Ridge has a cigarette perched behind his ear. Maddox is well-dressed, and it's apparent he comes from money, but his looks don't fool me. I see the wildness in his eyes. Lev, on the other hand, I know little about. In the handful of times I've seen him around, he comes off as detached from the world.

My brows waggle, a smirk playing on my lips. "Let's just hope those shots do what they're supposed to."

"Oh, yeah?" He tips his chin, his sterling gray eyes resting on my lips. "And what's that?"

I dart my tongue out, clinging to the attention he's giving my mouth. "Make me forget."

"And what is it you want to forget, Riley?"

It's no surprise Maddox knows my name, and I don't act like he shouldn't. I'm sure Ridge has told him everything there is to know about me. What position I sleep in. What kind of dressing I like on my salad. The fact that sudden noises practically send me out of my shoes. The basic stuff only a very few would notice, Ridge being one of them.

My shoulders rise, locked in position as I say, "Everything."

"Well," Maddox begins, "I've got bad news." His hand, now inside his onyx Brunello jacket—yeah, he's a rich kid with parents who come from old money. As I said, I've done my research—comes out, and he's holding a fifth of a caramel-colored liquor. "Those measly little Jell-O shots aren't gonna touch what you plan to accomplish." He unscrews the top and passes me the glass bottle, but I immediately curl my nose at it. The smell alone makes my stomach turn.

"Oh god, no. I can't drink dark liquor. I wanna forget everything, not spend my night over a toilet."

"Fair enough." He brings the bottle to his full lips and upends his head, taking a long swig while keeping his eyes locked on mine. I gag silently as I watch him.

"I've got the..." Scar's sentence falls short, and she steals my attention as she joins us with a case of bottled water in her hands. "Oh, hello," she says to Maddox, grinning from ear to ear. She leans close, her mouth almost touching my ear. "Who is this?"

Scar knows about Ridge because of how often he's around, but she lives in her own little bubble with her boyfriends—Crew, Jagger, and Neo—so she doesn't have the full scoop on some students here, namely Ridge's friends.

"This is Maddox. He was just offering me a drink, which I politely declined."

Maddox puts the top back on the bottle and returns it to his jacket pocket. "You know my name?" His statement is more of a question and the look on his face tells me he's smitten that I know who he is.

And now, I've just boosted his ego, while making myself sound like the stalker in the room.

"Yeah. I know who you are," I tell him, face flushed. "You're on the football team, right? With Scar's boyfriend, Crew." I nudge Scar, giving her the opportunity to chime in and take the awkwardness away from me.

"Oh yeah," Scar pipes up, "Crew mentioned you a couple of times. You're a defensive top or whatever they're called."

Maddox chuckles at Scar's lack of football knowledge. "Defensive end. And yeah, I know Crew. Outstanding player but he's gotta up his game if he wants the QB position when Octavio leaves next season."

I have no idea who Octavio is or what this defensive mumbo jumbo is they're talking about, and frankly, I'm getting bored. The effects of my shots are taking hold and all I really want is to dance.

Grabbing the case of water from Scar, I drop it to the ground with a thud. Oddly enough, the sound doesn't startle me, but I created it, so it really shouldn't. Wow. My head is fuzzy. And heavy. "Come on," I take her by the arm, "dance with me."

"Ry," she jerks back, halting me, "no one is dancing."

I look around the room, eyes dragging across Ridge, who's sitting on the bottom step of a tall staircase beside the door. I'm surprised to see that he's looking at his phone and not at me, but when I keep watching, his gaze lifts. His eyes flash with heat, as if he wasn't expecting to catch my gaze. My heart flutters, my core catching fire. The rush is too much for me and I'm forced to look away before my entire body goes up in flames.

Scar's right, though. No one is dancing. *What kind of party is this?*

"All right," I tell her. "Then I guess we'll have to change that." I grab her and Maddox by the hands. Surely others will join in.

Maddox resists me, tugging out of my hold. "I'm gonna have to pass. Not much of a dancer."

"Same," Scar says. "I'm sober and I need a good amount of booze before I allow myself to be the center of attention. Besides, Crew, Jagger, and Neo will be here soon and I'm not sure they'd be too keen on me shaking my ass in a room full of horny-ass men." She steals a quick glance at Maddox. "No offense."

"None taken."

"You're both laaaame." I drag out the word as I walk backward into the middle of the room. "She Looks So Perfect" by 5 Seconds of Summer is blasting through the speakers attached to every corner of the room. It's not my typical dance music, but music is music. It's all about the way my body floats through the air. Carrying me away and leaving my troubles behind.

My hands go up and my hips sway to the beat. I keep my eyes pinched shut because if I don't see them, I don't care. I know everyone is looking at me. Those who know me are probably wondering if I've officially lost my mind. Maybe I have.

Scar once asked me if I got a thrill when I pulled the trigger that ended another man's life—I told her no. She then asked me if I was trying to hold on to that feeling. Again, I told her no. Maybe I lied.

Maybe I don't know myself as well as I thought I did.

It all plays out like a slow-motion movie, one I never want to rewind and watch again. The sound of the safety going off is deafening, and one I'll never forget. Only, it's not the gun in Sebastian's hand; it's the one in mine.

My finger trembles over the trigger, and before I can even think about what I'm doing, I pull it back.

He drops to the pavement, blood pooling around his body.

The next thing I know, the gun is being taken out of my hand before getting tossed to the ground.

I look at his face, desperation in his eyes. His mouth opens, but he doesn't speak. Instead of helping him, I watch him slowly slip away, while holding on to the fact that he can't hurt any of us again. This man put us through a year of hell. Sebastian Saint was a fucked-up man, and he got exactly what he deserved.

The song ends, and a new one begins, but I don't stop dancing. This time, it's "Wrong Side of Heaven" by Five Finger Death Punch and the lyrics speak to me. So much so that my body sings along with them.

"Ry," Scar shouts over the music, but I ignore her words and her hand on my waist as she tries to stop me. "Babe, let's get you some water."

I shake my head no, urging her to let me be. I need this.

My eyes shoot open when I'm suddenly swept up in a pair of brawny arms. The palm of his hand pushes my dress up, and he cups my ass.

I lift my head, getting a look at my kidnapper.

"What are you doing?" I ask Maddox as he carries me into the crowd and out of the limelight. "I was dancing."

"Yeah. By yourself."

"So," I huff. "Don't you ever dance by yourself?"

"Can't say that I do."

"Well, that's because you're boring, just like everyone else."

Maddox makes his way down a hall with half of my body thrown over his shoulder. Once we're away from the masses, he sets me on my feet. I stumble a bit, but I brace myself when my back crashes into the wall. Both of my hands rest on the wall behind me and I blow away the wispy strands of hair stuck to my face. Who does this guy think he is? Just because he's loaded and on the football team, he thinks he can pocket my fun. "Why'd you do that?"

"Let me ask you something, Riley. How do you feel?"

My hands fly up, a wide grin on my face. "I feel fucking great," I tell him honestly.

"All that shit you wanted to forget, is it gone?"

"Well, it was," I stammer. "But now that you brought it back up..." I push past him, heading back down the hall we just came from. "I need another drink," I shout loud enough for him to hear me.

I know I look like a train wreck right now. My face feels sticky from my makeup smearing and the cool breeze on my ass tells me my dress has rode up some. I tug it back down, setting it in place.

"Look, I'm just trying to help," Maddox says, now back at my side and looking like a goddamn dream. It should be a sin to look this good. Seriously. He's got the prettiest eyes, the gray color a rarity. His light brown hair is brushed up with natural highlights and a fade on the sides. He's very clean cut, and I'd bet money he pays his barber to drive out here and cut it for him. That's the vibe I get from Maddox—spoiled rich.

My lips twitch with a smile. Instead of ignoring Maddox, I turn to face him and push him against the wall. He's taken aback and now at my mercy. I reach my hand into his jacket pocket, while keeping my eyes on his, and I grab the bottle of liquor he offered me earlier.

Without permission, I twist off the top, hold my breath, and drink.

It burns, but in a way that makes me feel alive.

Sometimes we need a little pain to remind us we can feel in the first place.

These past few months, I've felt dead inside. Like I was the one on the receiving end of that bullet. No matter how hard I try, I can't erase the memory of Sebastian Saint's face as he took his last breath.

I killed a man. A father. A son. The governor and a respectable member of The Society. Was it justified? Yes. Nevertheless, it was still a life.

The events surrounding his death aren't important anymore. He was a bastardly man who did disgusting things. In the end, we all lied to cover it up because he was still *the* Sebastian Saint and there is no doubt The Elders would inflict punishment on me for what I did. Even in death, he would win.

But what has me so fucked up is not the lost life, it's the lack of empathy I feel about what I did. Shouldn't I be sad? Shouldn't I have grieved? Sure, loud noises startle me. I'm constantly on edge, but that's the trauma from that night. In my heart of hearts, I'm not sorry at all.

A good amount of liquid—two shots' worth at least—goes down, and it isn't until my esophagus catches fire that I exhale the pent-up air in my lungs.

Then it hits me. The taste. The smell. The nausea. I choke it all down, ignoring the urge to vomit on Maddox's sleek Neiman Marcus boots.

My reflexes kick into high gear and when I gag, Maddox cranes his neck warily and steps two feet to the right. Out of nowhere, Ridge appears. His hand lands on my waist and he leads me briskly away from Maddox to the end of the hall. I clap my hand over my mouth, fighting like hell to keep down what wants to come up.

There's a line of people outside the bathroom door, but

Ridge shoves the guy in the front aside and leads me in when a girl walks out.

I don't pay Ridge any attention; I don't even bother to look and see if he shut the door before I slide across the floor to the toilet. I drop to my knees, hold my hair to one side, and everything I drank tonight comes out in heaps.

My stomach cramps up and when there's nothing left to expel, I drop backward onto my ass with my back pressed to the wall. My eyes close and I rest my head back against it. It's silent. I can't even hear Ridge breathing, but I know he's there —he's always there.

Hello, consequences, my old friend. If only you'd show your face and punish me for the life I had to end. Maybe then I'd feel remorse or even empathy. Until then I'll hide in the darkness of my insanity.

The sound of footsteps coming toward me has my eyes bolting open. I watch his black boots—they're old and worn, unlike Maddox's. In fact, everything about the two of them screams polar opposites. From their social skills to their choice of clothing, right down to their demeanors. Maddox has shown me nothing but respect in the ten minutes we've actually engaged. Whereas Ridge has never said a single word to me. But for some reason, I'm more intrigued by the quiet one.

My gaze slides up Ridge's holey black denim jeans, to his zipped leather jacket, finally landing on his face. His eyes are soft and in no way threatening. His lips are rolled in as if he's focused solely on me.

"Just had too much to drink," I tell him. "I'll be fine."

He doesn't say anything as he comes closer and closer, until the toe of his boot is touching the three-inch heel of my black suede pumps.

His legs bend and he crouches down, our eyes now level. His hands hang together between his legs, fingers entwined.

Someone pounds on the door and I jolt, scooting back farther until my spine is snug against the wall.

Ridge tilts his head slightly to the left and raises his hand. When he reaches out with an open palm, I elevate my neck, but he doesn't retreat. The backs of his fingers graze gently across my cheek and I blink rapidly, unsure what to say or do.

I watch him intently, his Adam's apple bobbing with each swallow.

"What...what are you doing?" I ask him, doubtful, but curious, if I'll get an answer.

He leans closer, invading my personal space, and when his nose brushes against mine, I turn my head out of fear he's going to try and kiss me. Burying his nose in the side of my head, he draws in a deep breath, cupping my cheek in his hand.

"Ridge..."

There's more pounding on the door, but the dire need of others to occupy this space doesn't seem to faze him one bit.

Moments of silence pass and this is getting more and more uncomfortable. His eyes haven't left mine except for the sliver of a second when he inhaled my scent, which was straight up weird.

Shooting a thumb toward the door, I whisper, "I should get back to the party. I'm sure my friends are wondering where I am." My hands drop to the cold floor, but when I attempt to push myself up, I'm halted by Ridge's hand aggressively pushing down on my shoulder. He holds me in place and my heart rate speeds up.

I gulp, now thinking I pegged him all wrong. Maybe Ridge isn't one of the good ones. I mean, he has been stalking me since I stepped foot on BCU grounds.

"What are you doing?"

More silence, and the longer it drags out, the angrier I get. I

26

push his hand away, but it flies right to my leg, brushing up my inner thigh with the same pressure he had on my shoulder.

"I'm not scared of you." I say the words, hoping to believe them myself.

I grab his hand that's inked in a black mess of tattoos. Different symbols on each finger and a triangular design with an eyeball in the center on the dorsal of his hand. Curiosity has me wondering what else is marked on him, and what they symbolize. I've always been fascinated by tattoos and often wonder what the meaning behind them is. Surrounding the tattoos, there are scars on some of his fingers that look like burn marks and a longer scar that extends from his thumb to his wrist. If I had to guess, that one involved stitches. I turn his hand over, noticing another scar that runs diagonally across his wrist. My heart drops into my stomach and I grab his other hand, searching for the same mark. Sure enough, it's there.

What drove him to do that?

With his shoulders drawn back, Ridge's nostrils flare, and his breaths come rapidly—as if my touch, or this revelation of the pain he's inflicted on himself—has ignited something inside him. I steal a glance between his legs, noticing a massive bulge in his pants.

Oh, my god. Is he turned on right now?

He's still gawking and there's no doubt he knows what I saw. His tongue drags across his top teeth and his lips twist up in a devilish grin.

His unwanted gaze is unnerving. "Why are you looking at me like that?"

Taking my hand in his, he lowers them between his legs.

In an attempt to pull back, I fail, and he only tightens his grip. The expression on his face shifts from confident, to downright wicked.

Curling my fingers, he rests my hand on his erect cock, forcing pressure as his hips rise.

My stomach twists into knots. "What the hell, you sicko." I jerk from his hold and throw his hand back at him. Before he can stop me again, I get off the floor. Now on my feet, I look down at him, a prominent scowl on my face. "Stay the hell away from me."

I'm halfway across the room when his hot breath fans the back of my neck.

I spin around and shove him back a few steps. "Why'd you bring me in here? Why have you been watching me? And why the hell don't you talk?"

Over time, I've learned some of Ridge's expressions. The one he's wearing now—the feverish eyes and strained forearms—that's one of desperation. He wants me and if I don't put him in his place, one day he *will* get me.

Maybe there is part of him that thinks it's what I wanted. I've never given Ridge any inclination that I'm into him that way—or any way for that matter. Sure, he's gorgeous, in a dark and mysterious sort of way. With his black, unkempt hair that hangs over his eyes until he runs his fingers through it and pushes it back. The double hoops on each side of his nose that flare with his nostrils when he's breathing heavily. And his depthless green eyes that show all the emotions he fails to verbally express. Sometimes I look into them from afar just to get a feel for his mood. Oftentimes I dig deep, thinking maybe I'll be able to hear his thoughts. But that's just the wannabe clairvoyant inside me. None of that matters, though. I've never even heard this guy's voice. He's fucked up. There's no doubt about it.

"Jesus," I shout. "Would you just fucking say something?" When he doesn't, I give him another dominant push, showing him I'm the one in control here. His attempt to hold me down earlier was obviously his way of trying to prove that he has all the power, and if I cower, he'll take advantage of me. I won't. I'm not the pushover I used to be back in high school.

"You're just a coward, aren't you? Some sicko who likes to watch girls?" I shove him again, and he falls through the shower curtain. Arms flown back, he braces himself on the wall, quickly catching his balance—the grin on his face never faltering. In a swift motion, he straightens his back and comes at me, shoulders drawn back, chest taut. Ridge's angry eyes deadlocked on mine.

For the first time, I'm scared of him. This is a look I haven't seen before. He's always so in control of his emotions. "Stop," I tell him as I walk backward, but he eats up every step I take, closing in on me. When my back hits the door and the repetitive knocks vibrate through my core, I pinch my eyes shut out of fear of what Ridge is going to do now that he has me pinned.

"Please," I whimper, "please, just let me go."

In one fluid motion, he grabs my waist and jerks my body flush with his. My eyes shoot wide open when he begins grinding his cock against my core. Peering down at the space between us, he groans, and I try to retreat, reaching behind me for the handle, but I can't find it. "Get away from me!'

I suddenly hear the door unlocking and then Ridge pulls the handle and my body comes forward. Once he steps aside, I quickly walk out of the bathroom and away from this fucked-up encounter.

CHAPTER 3
RIDGE

FUCK. I wanted her so bad. Should've just laid her out on the floor, spread her legs wide, and taken what's always been mine. I would've been rough, too. She deserves it for being a little tease tonight. I'll forgive her quickly, though, because I know it was the alcohol pushing me away.

For fuck's sake, I wish she'd just see what's standing right in front of her every single goddamn day. No one will treat her like a queen the way I will. One day she will proudly wear my crown, even if it's drenched in the blood of the men I've killed for her.

For her. Everything I do now is for her.

If only I could tell her. She begged me to say something, but the truth is, I couldn't. My mouth opens, but the words fail to come out. It doesn't happen often with other people, but with her, it's habitual.

Bypassing all the students in the hallway, I search for the one I'm looking for. The one I will take all my aggression out on because he deserves to feel my wrath.

When I spot him dancing with some slut, who's got her tits and ass hanging out, I make a beeline for Maddox, pushing anyone who's in my way.

My blood reaches a boiling point as I grab him by the collar of his pretty-boy jacket, walking him away from his fuck toy for the night.

"Whoa, Ridge," he chuckles breathlessly, hands up in surrender, "what are you doing, man?"

I slam him into the far wall in the living room, rattling a couple frames hanging above his head. With any luck, one will fall and knock his stupid ass out. I lift with both hands, gripping his jacket so tight, my knuckles turn white. "What the fuck are you up to?"

"Just having some fun. No harm in that, is there, *Ridge?*" The emphasis he puts on my name is sarcastic, and it unnerves me.

"You knew I wouldn't interfere when you were ogling her. You fucking knew I wouldn't stop whatever the hell you were doing because I wouldn't allow her to see the monstrous side of me."

That egotistical smirk on his face is the wrong move, and he knows it. I slam his back into the wall, knocking an audible breath out of him. "Answer me, goddammit."

Maddox is three sheets to the wind, and it's no surprise with how much he's been drinking tonight.

His shoulders slump in defeat and the condescending look he was wearing fades from his face. "There were no ill intentions, man. I swear. I was just getting a feel for our girl."

"*My girl.*" I stammer out the words, making it clear that she's off-limits.

"I get it. For fuck's sake, we know. Riley Cross is off-limits. Duly noted."

"Do you? Do you really get it? Why the fuck are you calling her *our* girl? Mine, Maddox. She's fucking mine!"

His eyes widen as if everything I'm saying is coming as a shock to him. Just because me, him, and Lev have shared girls in the past, doesn't mean we'll be sharing Riley. That one is mine, and mine alone.

Maddox and I don't fight often. In fact, his drunken stupidity is the only reason I ever lose my temper with him. He's my family, and I'd fucking do anything for him. But lately, he's been pushing my buttons when it comes to Riley.

Dropping my hold on him, I take a step back while calming myself down. "Just don't fuck with what I have going on. I mean it."

He straightens the collar on his jacket and cracks his neck with his fist pressed to his jaw. "Oh yeah? And what's that? A one-sided relationship?"

"Is that a fucking joke?"

"No, Ridge. Actually, I'm dead serious. Does Riley even know you're into her or does she think you're just some freak who follows her around?"

"It has to be this way for now. You know that." Maddox knows that until I finish this assignment, I can't be with her yet. It's too risky. Flags will be raised and The Elders will question my connection to her, considering she's linked to the governor and the night he died.

"Get your head outta your ass, Ridge. Look around." His arms wave through the air as his eyes dance from person to person. "Look at all the fucking babes here. And you," he jabs a finger into my chest, "have your eyes on the one girl you can't even talk to. Just get over her so someone else can have a shot without you breathing down their fucking necks."

In a knee-jerk reaction, I slap his hand away. "Fuck off."

He's drunk. I have to keep reminding myself of that fact. Maddox would never speak this way sober. He knows how much Riley means to me.

"And what are you gonna do when the truth of what she

did becomes public knowledge and she's banished. Can you save her from that? Do you have the means to protect her?"

"You let me worry about that. It's none of your damn business."

Maddox grows still, aside from his fingers stroking his chin. "Unless..."

Piquing my interest, I lift a brow. "Unless *what?*"

"Unless you let me help you protect her secrets."

"As my brother, my friend, you *will* help me because you know how fucking important she is to me. There's no *unless* about it."

"I don't mean just keeping *your* secret. Think about it. You're one man trying to save her from an international society that's comprised of thousands of members. You really think you're gonna keep what she did under wraps forever? Let me help you."

It's no secret what happens to those who are abolished from The Society. A Punisher will be assigned to the former member and they'll do exactly what Maddox said—destroy. Be it killing them, if it's called for, or just making sure they have zero luxuries in life—no job, house, or security of any kind.

"Help me, how?"

"For starters, I'm a Guardian, too." I've known forever that Maddox is also a Guardian. I'm not supposed to know, but we don't keep secrets from each other—much. Which is exactly why I've also clued him in on my assignment and Riley's involvement. What he doesn't know is the way I'm handling things—on my terms, in my own way. But some things are better left unsaid. "My family has power you don't. Connections. Means. We can throw The Elders off her trail."

While I hear everything he's saying, I don't need his help. "I've got this. Don't fucking worry about it. You've got your own assignment with your stupid fucking Guardian club. Just do your shit and don't interfere with mine. Got it?"

"Not interfering. Just offering to help. And as I said, I was simply getting a feel for the girl. If you ask me, you've got your hands full. Might wanna let someone else hold on to her for a little bit."

My fist lands on the bone of his shoulder and he winces. "Just leave her the fuck alone and quit trying to be her friend— or whatever the hell it is you're doing."

"*When* the truth is revealed, you're going down with her. Might wanna rethink my offer." Maddox clicks his tongue on the roof of his mouth before sliding past me.

My head drops back and I stare at the spinning ceiling fan overhead. Maddox might be right, but if Riley drags me down with her, it means she wants me near her. In that case, *drag me down, baby. Abuse me. Hurt me. Love me.*

When I was eleven years old, my mom told me I needed to get control of my emotions. They rise and fall rapidly, and I feel them too intensely. That same day, my entire life changed in the worst way imaginable.

"Ridge! Stop!" Mom cries out as I raise the bat, bringing it down on her boyfriend of the night's face.

He hit her. No one hurts the people I love, especially my mom. Never again. I lift the bat, bringing it down harder this time.

Mom grabs my arm before I'm able to bash his ugly face in again. "Baby, please."

Her voice steals my attention and the horror-stricken expression on her face puts an end to my episode of madness. With a trembling hand, I drop the bat to the floor. The metal hits the ground with a thud, splintering the ceramic tile. Blood drips from the bat, trickling between the fresh crack.

34

Two arms wrap around me from behind. They're warm and safe and allow me to forget for a minute.

"Oh, Ridge. What have you done?"

I open my mouth to speak, but my words fail me. No matter how hard I try to tell my mom what I did, I can't. My throat isn't restricted. I'm still breathing. So why can't I speak?

Say something. Tell her why you did it. Tell her why you'd do it again and again if needed. For her. To protect her. Always.

Mom turns me around, her hands now holding on to both of my arms. She drops to her knees, resting in a pool of blood. Tears stream down her cheeks and the sight alone has me crying, too. Words fight to climb out, but they're stuck somewhere deep inside me.

I raise my hand, swiping my finger under her swollen eye and catching her tears.

"Oh, sweet boy," she cries out, pulling me into safety again. Her hugs are my happy place. Mom makes everything better.

When I say nothing, she hugs me tighter and whispers, "I understand."

She knows. I don't need my voice because she knows.

"You have the biggest heart, Ridge Foster. You love fiercely. But you need to get control of your emotions. The rapid rise and fall will get you in trouble one day, if you let them. Now go to Maddox's house next door and don't say a word about what you did, Ridge. Promise me? Let me do this."

I gulp, my head immediately shaking no. "No," I finally say the word, and it's a song to my ears because it's reassurance that I'm not permanently broken.

"I have to do this, baby."

"No," I shout. "No!" It's all that comes out, but it's something. I can't let her do this. I killed him. Not her.

"Ridge," she presses, "The Society will protect me. I promise, I'll come home to you. Now go next door and stay with Maddox

and his family until I call." She pulls me in for one last hug. *"I love you, Ridge."*

"I love you, too, Mama."

Mom was right, The Blue Bloods protected her and cleared her name for a murder that I committed, and she walked away scot-free. Until she wasn't free anymore.

When someone helps you, they always want something in return.

Four days later, I saw her beautiful face for the last time. That's the day I began my path down a road of complete fucking insanity. I killed a man when I was only eleven years old, and when I saw his face as I was beating the life out of him, I knew he wouldn't be the last.

The world is full of evil people, and my secret is, I'm the worst of them all.

CHAPTER 4
RILEY

"UGH," I grumble, dropping on my bed in the same dress I had on at the party. My fingers weave through my hair, massaging my scalp. "If this headache is the start of what I'll face in the morning, I'm never drinking again."

Scar pulls my light pink comforter up to my chest, tucking it in on both sides of my body, just the way I like it. She rests half of her ass on the mattress beside me. "Did you have fun?"

"Eh," is the sound I choose for that question.

"Oh, come on, Ry. You danced, you mingled—which is your favorite thing to do. You had to have enjoyed yourself a little."

I roll to my side, tugging the comforter over my shoulders. "It was all great until I drank Maddox's whiskey, or whatever the hell it was."

"*You* drank whiskey? That doesn't sound like you."

That's because I'm not me anymore.

I've only known Scar for a little over a year, but in that year, we've gotten close. Sometimes I feel like she knows me better than I know myself.

"What's up, Ry? Talk to me."

Did I mention she can also read me like a book? It's true,

and most of the time, I hate it. But tonight, I feel the sudden urge to speak my heart out and who better to hear what my heart has to say than my best friend.

"I really miss the person I was." I spit out the words before my brain tells me to choke them down. Now that they're out, I feel the sting they left behind. It's been so long since I've openly admitted how much I hurt inside. And even then, I half-assed it and only gave the pitiful version of what I truly feel. Talking about it too much brings all those painful feelings to the surface and I just want to push them down and forget.

Scar drops to her side on my bed, her head propped up with her hand, her face aligned with mine. Her fingers sweep through my hair, pushing stray strands off my cheek. "You're still you. Even after what happened, you're still Riley."

Talking to Scar about this might be my best option, but it doesn't mean she'll understand. I'm not sure anyone can unless they've done what I did.

"I still have the same name, and the same body, but I'm not the same person. Don't pretend you haven't noticed. It's impossible not to."

"I mean, yeah, it's apparent that you're not as bubbly as you used to be. You drink a little more, and don't get me started on this." She flips the streak of purple in my hair. "Dark purple, Ry. Really? What happened to *everything* pink?"

I laugh because it's true. Before the incident, I lived in pink. I basked in everything bright and glittery. Once upon a time, I radiated positive energy.

"Everything just feels so dark lately." Saying it out loud makes me realize how depressing I sound. All I do lately is over-think and wallow in self-pity.

"Babe, it's normal to feel that way. You went through a lot last year. It's not uncommon to have trauma after going through something so...traumatic. You'll find yourself again."

I wanna believe her. I'd like to think that eventually I'll be able to sleep through the night again, or wake up with a smile on my face in excitement for what the day has in store for me. She doesn't know the whole truth, though—that I don't regret what I did. That I'm scarred by the sounds and the face of the man I killed, but I'd do it again if it meant protecting my friends.

How would Scar feel if she knew part of me is proud of what I did? Would she think I'm some whack job who takes pride in ending lives? *Is that who I've become?*

I'm a Guardian. It's in my blood to look after members, but that doesn't involve murder. I shouldn't be proud. I should be ashamed of myself.

"You're right," I finally tell her, even if I know she's just trying to make me feel better. I know she cares and I know she'll always hear me out. "I'll be fine. Just need more time."

Scar leans close and kisses the top of my forehead. "You most definitely will. Now tell me about this Maddox guy." She waggles her brows. "He's cute."

I bite the inside of my cheek, holding back a smile. "He is cute, isn't he?"

Her response is a profound nod. "Hell yeah, he is. And well-dressed."

Maddox made the party tonight more manageable, even if we only hung out for a short time. He's definitely nothing like his friends. Ridge is...Ridge, and I don't know much about Lev, other than he's not very social. I've never seen him at a party. Rarely see him out at all for that matter.

"Keep me updated on that developing situation," she says before smoothing out the blanket around me. "Now, are you gonna be okay if I leave with Neo?"

"Oh, shit. I'm sorry. I totally forgot Neo was waiting outside. Yes." I shoo her away with the one hand that's not tucked under the blanket. "Go. I'm gonna try to sleep while praying to the lords above that this headache is gone when I wake up."

Scar's leg swings over the bed. "I'll be back in the morning with coffee and donuts. Sound good?"

"Sounds perfect." She's halfway out the door when I holler, "Hey, Scar. Thank you."

"Always, babe."

As soon as the door closes, I reach over and grab my journal. It's wrapped in pink leather with a clasp and a matching pen with my name engraved on it. My mom gave it to me for my sixteenth birthday and I've almost filled it with short poems and random quotes.

With the pen to the paper, the dusky thoughts in my head break free.

I touched the flames, and I liked it.
I tasted sin—so bitter, so tart.
I reached into the fire and got warm.
I sat alone as the embers burned out in the dark.

———

My long lashes flutter open when I'm startled awake. I slap my hand to my nightstand until I find my phone. Once I've got it, I hold it up to check the time—*three-thirteen.*

"What the hell?" I've only slept for two and a half hours? I drop my phone down beside me. I suppose two and a half hours is better than some nights, where I only get an hour of sleep at a time in between waking up. Part of me was hoping the alcohol would knock me out until the sun woke me up in the morning.

My head isn't pounding as hard, but I definitely still feel the effects of the alcohol I drank. Everything is fuzzy—like a dream.

I shift onto my back, eyes wide open and plastered to the ceiling. My body shivers, a strange feeling washing over me. The notion that someone is watching me. It's happened before and my intuition was right. Only this time, it's in my room. My safe place. My sanctuary.

I turn my head slowly, while keeping my shoulders pinned to the mattress. I grab my phone at my side and grip it tightly, while keeping it low, so it's not visible to anyone who might be in my room. When I see his shadow from the closet light dancing on the wall, my heart jumps into my throat.

This isn't just a bad dream. It's a nightmare.

Rooted to the bed, my eyes drift around the room in search of him. Maybe I've been too trusting to think Ridge would never hurt me. Is that why he's here? To hurt me?

Turning my head toward the door, I stop halfway when I catch him standing tall at the foot of my bed. I yelp at the sight before me. My hand slaps over my mouth and I swallow down the urge to scream.

Ridge trails his fingers across the comforter over my feet as he walks slowly around the side of the bed. My heart races at the same tempo as the pounding in my head.

I don't take my eyes off him, and he doesn't break his gaze on me. The sound of something jiggling in his hand has me elevating my head slightly.

In the dim of the light, I'm able to see what he's holding—a bottle of some sort. He twists the top off and shakes it over his hand. A couple pills drop out and he brings them to my mouth.

I gulp, choking on my words. "What is that?"

Hesitantly, I scoot until I'm sitting. Instead of taking the pills from him, I go for the bottle he's holding. I hold it up to inspect what he's trying to feed me and, sure enough, it's my prescription sleeping pills that were in the drawer of my nightstand.

Ridge takes the bottle back, puts the top on, then sets it on the table. I watch every move he makes intently, each finger bend, each flinch. And when he reaches for my hand, I let him take it. He's got manly ones—strong, rough, and calloused. Flipping my hand over, he sets the pills in my palm before raising my hand to my mouth.

I hate taking medication and those pills are a last resort, but I'm so tired and really need a good night's sleep, but I can't accept anything from him. I can't trust this guy.

Why am I letting him do this? Throw the pills and run!

But I don't stop him. My heart pounds recklessly, reminding me I'm not only awake, but alive. Suddenly, I'm mesmerized by him. Under a spell that I can't get out of. This dark shadow of a figure entered my room, uninvited, and here I am, holding on to the fact that he's also enamored with me. He has to be. Why else would he spend so much time studying me?

Ridge has a way of captivating my mind. It's like every logical response to his behavior vanishes and I'm left to my own devices, which is never a good thing. The little girl inside me, starving for attention, is drawn to him because attention is what he gives me.

The pills roll around, some of the coating seeping onto my taste buds.

I watch closely as he picks up a glass of water I had on my nightstand and brings it to my mouth. I don't take control; I just tip my head back and swallow down the water with the pills.

I'm not sure why I take what he's giving to me. There's a part of me that resorts back to my childhood when my mom would care for me when I was sick. It gives me a feeling of security knowing someone cares.

The glass clinks against the table and Ridge takes a few steps back until he's sinking down on my pink, velvet wingback chair that's angled toward me. His forearms lay flat on the armrests and he leans back, getting comfortable.

There's no point in asking him why he's here, or what he wants. I'll get no response. Instead, I lie still and allow my mind to focus on his presence, rather than the dark thoughts that invade my head any other night.

He's a distraction, and while it's fucking insane, it works because the next thing I know, I'm fading away.

CHAPTER 5
RIDGE

NOTHING IS MORE painful than losing your voice when you have so much to say. If I could speak right now, I'd be by her side, where she's asleep, kissing her forehead and whispering, *You are worth the mess I've made.*

I'm in over my head with this girl, but it doesn't even matter. Nights like this, alone with her, make me realize *nothing* else matters.

I lean forward, pressing my elbows to my knees, my eyes never leaving her beautiful face. I could close my eyes and still see it in my head. Her face—her body—it's all tattooed to memory.

She's on her side, facing me. As if she fell asleep in that position, just so I could watch her. Her mouth parts slightly, shoulders rising a smidge with each breath she takes.

I drop my elbows and stand up while keeping my calves anchored to the chair. If I get too close, I might lose control—and control is not something that comes easily to me.

My chest heaves before tightening. Palms sweating, I stretch my fingers and step forward before stepping right back.

Don't do it. Don't go near her.

How can I not, though? She's so close. So attainable.

And she's not waking up now that she took her sleeping medication.

Creeping slowly to her bedside, I keep my arms at my sides.

Just one touch. One touch, then I'll go back to the chair.

With a trembling hand, I stroke her cheek gently. Being this close is painful. My body is packed with emotions that are ready to slice me open and spill out all over her angelic body.

I've always felt deeply, but I've never felt *this* deeply. It's almost unbearable. The agony is too much to handle.

I should leave.

I can't leave.

Get the fuck out of here, Ridge.

Don't go.

I jump back as thoughts consume my head, screaming to be heard. I'm constantly battling different voices telling me to do different things when what I really want is to be near her. Always. Forever.

Minutes pass. Lost staring at the masterpiece in front of my eyes. I sigh heavily as I rejoin her. And when I'm there, I shut off the voices and follow my heart. Slowly, I peel the blanket down, exposing the milky skin of her shoulders. Once they're free, I keep going until the blanket rests in a mound at her feet.

It's not like I'm trespassing. She knows I'm here and willingly went to sleep in my presence. She trusts me.

She shouldn't.

My fingers move at a featherlike pace up her leg, and she twitches at my touch, arousing something inside me as I see her unconsciously react to me. When her leg lifts, knee bent at her side, my eyes crawl between her legs, resting on her white cotton panties.

Self-restraint eludes me. My mind is unstable. Rationality swims in the murkiest of waters and I cannot stop myself. I just can't.

Before I can even consider an alternative, I unzip my jeans and push them down along with my boxers.

I won't touch her while she's sleeping, at least, not yet. But fuck if I won't touch myself with dreams of her in my head.

Fisting my swollen cock, I stroke it while leaning closer and closer to my sleeping beauty.

"This could be your hand, Angel." I whisper my words into her hair as I draw in a deep breath of her intoxicating scent. It's a smell I can never get enough of and one I stroke myself to every night. Last night, it was her underwear that I took out of her bathroom trash last week. She was just coming off her period and there was a bloodstain on them. I buried my face in those panties and came within a minute.

Right now, I might not even last a full sixty seconds.

My knees press to the bed and I climb up, hovering over her face. I pump faster and faster while watching her mouth, wishing I could slip my cock between her soft, pink lips.

I could.

I could do it. Gag her until I come down her throat. She'd probably wake up and take over, sucking me off all on her own.

My heart rattles against my rib cage as I fight temptation.

Do it. Fuck her mouth.

Don't do it, Ridge.

I won't.

But I hold tightly to the thought as I release, spilling all over her dress.

"Fuck, Angel," I grumble. "You see what you do to me?"

I give myself one final pump, making sure I give her every last drop.

Before pulling my pants back up, I sweep my finger across the wet semen on her dress and bring it to her mouth. Dragging it across her lips, I lean down and whisper, "Here's a little taste of what's coming."

CHAPTER 6
RILEY

YOU KNOW that feeling when you wake up and you're certain that you either slept too late or forgot about something? That's how I feel when my body springs forward. My chest is literally vibrating from my rapid heartbeat. So much so that I put my hand over it, trying to slow the rhythm to no avail.

How the fuck is the sun up? That's what has me all anxiety-ridden. It's been months since I slept through the night. Granted, I did wake up once, but...

My eyes shoot to the chair where Ridge sat last night...but he's gone.

When did he leave?

Was he ever really here?

My God, how drunk was I?

Something feels off. I look to my left and...I smell him. My face drops on the pillow beside me and I inhale the scent of anise and cedarwood.

Was he in my bed?

The door flies open, and at first thought, I think it'll be him. But when I see Scar, I drop my hand from my chest and breathe a sigh of relief.

She walks in carrying a drink holder with two to-go cups of coffee and a brown paper bag sitting on top. "Morning, babe."

"G-good morning," I stutter, eyes searching the room as if I might actually find him in a corner.

He *was* here. I saw him with my own two eyes. He walked beside my bed, even touched it, then sat down in my chair.

I toss the blanket off me and jump out of bed, my dress from last night riding up my ass and exposing my white panties. I run my hands down the sides and feel a clump of dried goo. I must've been totally wasted last night and spilled something all over my dress.

Dammit. I hope I didn't make an ass of myself. Better yet, I hope I didn't do anything stupid when Ridge was here. I was pretty pissed at him last night, that I remember.

My dry lips smack together as I search haphazardly for any sign that I didn't imagine him coming into my room. Dropping to my knees, I look under the chair, and when I find nothing, I crawl around it.

Scar sets the carrier on the small round table by the door and her feet move toward me. "Umm, Ry. What in the world are you doing?"

Once defeat settles in, I drop onto my ass on the floor and crisscross my legs, not giving a damn that I'm baring everything under my dress to Scar—she's seen it all before.

"He was here," I whisper to her, or maybe it's to myself because I need to know I'm not completely losing my mind. "I know he was." I turn my head to look at her and the puzzled expression on her face proves she is on board with the assumption that I'm crazy.

Her brow lifts, and she kneels down beside me like I'm a child who needs eye-level interaction. "Who was here, Ry?"

No. She'll ask too many questions. Then she'll hunt Ridge down like he's a predator and grill the hell out of him. No. I can't tell her. "No one. I just...had a really weird dream, that's all."

Her perplexed look shifts to one of sympathy. "About him?"

She's referring to Sebastian Saint, naturally, considering he's in my dreams every night. *Except last night.* In fact, I don't even think I dreamt last night.

I get off the floor and Scar does the same. "No," I tell her as I pull my dress down. "Actually, it wasn't a bad dream this time. Just weird." I hate lying to her, but there are some things we just have to keep to ourselves until we're able to figure them out.

Such as my fucked-up emotions. Not just figuring them out for myself, but with Ridge, too. I swear the guy gives me whiplash and he hasn't even spoken to me. I can't quite figure out how he makes me feel. Sometimes he's hot, while other times he's cold. Any sane person would report his behavior to the dean immediately, but for some reason, I haven't.

"Well," she drags out the word as she lifts a cup of coffee out of the carrier. "This should help you survive the day." I take the coffee from her and flip the little tab on the top before blowing into it. "How's your head this morning?"

"Good," I say honestly. "Great, actually." Then it hits me. The sleeping pills. No wonder I slept so well. Ridge fed them to me and I accepted. My God, I am such an idiot. He could have drugged me with something else, but in my semi-comatose state, I accepted them. Of course that means I'm going to feel groggy today, on top of my hangover. It's why I rarely ever take those damn pills in the first place.

I set my coffee on my nightstand while Scar shuffles through her drawers on her side of the room.

Picking up the bottle Ridge sat on my nightstand last night,

I tap it against my palm, rattling the contents. I knew I didn't imagine him.

"I hope you're feeling better, Ry," Scar's tone shifts abruptly to a more serious note, "because I have something to tell you."

"What happened?" I set the bottle back down and sit on my bed. Flicking tiny gold specks of glitter on the sheet from my dress, I prepare myself for the worst because Scar only uses that tone when it's something big.

Her shoulders slump, and she tosses a pair of dirty jeans in her laundry basket. "We have cleanup from the party last night."

"Son of a bitch." I drop back down on the bed, resting my head on my pillow. "Of course we do." Cleanup is nothing like what I thought she was going to say, but I'm still not happy about it.

I swear the upper-class girls hate us. We're constantly given tasks, and while I'm certain they're nothing like what the guys have to do, it still sucks.

Reaching over to my nightstand, I grab my coffee and scoot up so I can drink it down before jumping in the shower. Mmm...black and bitter, just the way I like it.

"How many of us?" I ask, hoping like hell we have a large group of girls to help clean up.

"Not really sure. Elena sent out a text, didn't you get it?"

"Haven't checked my messages. And right now, I wish you hadn't either."

Elena is a sophomore and like a peer advocate with a whip. She tells us what to do and when to do it. But she also has a junior ahead of her telling her what to do. The senior girls basically hold all the power over us and if there is one thing I hate more than anything, it's being told what to do.

Dragging my ass out of bed, I grumble repeatedly, making

my disdain for this situation clearly known. "Going to shower. I'll be back." I grab some clothes and make my way down the hall to the communal bathroom. Once I've washed away a night of heavy drinking, I put on a pair of gray sweatpants and a pink hoodie with a bitten donut on the front. I toss my damp hair up in a clip and don't even bother putting on any makeup. The old Riley wouldn't dare leave the dorms without a fresh layer of foundation, but this is the new me and my new motto is: Don't like it, don't fucking look.

I'm back in our room, slipping on my white sneakers, when Scar's voice hits my ears. "Oh yeah. I forgot to tell you, there's a bonfire at the hot springs Friday night. The guys are forcing me to go with them, in which case, I'm forcing you."

"Nooooo." I drag out the word. My head falls back and the pushover inside of me begs the new me to step in. "Not another party, Scar. Please."

"Come on. You've bailed on all the good parties already this year. Even the one Maddie and Jude attended."

"But I went last night."

"You had no choice last night. The freshmen threw the party."

Maddie is Neo's—one of Scar's boyfriend's—twin sister and also a good friend of ours. Jude is Scar's half-brother and one of our other best friends. Jude and Maddie don't attend BCU, but they came for a visit a couple weeks ago, and I missed seeing them. Now, Scar will use that as bait to get me to go to, yet another, party.

"It's not for a few more days," Scar continues. "So I've got plenty of time to convince you."

"We'll see," I grumble in defeat. "Is that good enough?"

Scar hooks an arm around my shoulder and leads me out of our room, closing the door behind us. "For now."

We make our way down the hall that reeks of a dozen

different fragrances of perfume with a musty stench that seeps from the gray carpet. There's fifteen rooms on our floor that house two girls in each room. Upstairs are the three-bedroom quarters. Scar and I are in the very last room; therefore, our trek to the only staircase on the other end isn't a quick one.

We pass by three girls, one of which lives on the same floor. She's quiet for the most part and I've got no issues with her. As for the other two—Melody and Hannah—they live at the Delta Chi House, the girls' sorority, and both are major bitches.

As we pass, Melody sticks her nose in the air in an attempt to prove she's above us.

Scar flips her hair over her shoulder, mocking Melody's prissiness, and I laugh. "Some bitches never change," Scar says, loud enough for the girls to hear.

"And some hellions stay the same," Melody tosses the insult back at us.

Scar and I have quite the reputation for raising a little hell in high school. Well, not so much raising it, but sort of existing in it. We hoped the drama wouldn't follow us to BCU, and so far, it hasn't been too bad.

I steal one last glance at the girls' backsides. "Is it just me or does it seem like Melody and her clique are never doing any of the dirty work we have to do? Granted, I know they're in the sorority, but it shouldn't negate their responsibilities as a member of The Society."

Scar grumbles, "Oh, I'm sure Daddy bought her out of her chores. If only mine would do the same. Apparently, it's important that I have the full college experience as a Blue Blood." She fakes a gag, then impersonates her dad with a deep voice. "It'll strengthen you in the long run."

"Pretty sure my parents have the same mindset," I tell her. My dad's made generous donations to the school, but I guess it wasn't enough to get me out of the party setup or cleanup. We're not rich, by any means, but my parents do well for themselves. My father is a private investigator, which pairs nicely with his investigative skills as a Guardian in The Society. And my mom's a well-known reporter for our local newspaper. It's not required to have a career that correlates with our roles as Guardians, but it's definitely useful. I chose to pursue a degree in journalism and it's actually a choice I made on my own. I love writing, even if it is just poetry, and the skills I learn as a Guardian will, no doubt, assist me in doing the research for my articles.

We jog down the steep staircase to the first floor and the cold air from the open door hits my chest, puckering my nipples. "Holy hell," I shiver, hugging myself. "When did Mother Nature decide to spring winter on us? It's only the first of October."

"We're in the Colorado mountains, babe. Aren't you used to it by now?"

"Nope. And I really hope this chill in the air isn't a sign that we're skipping fall and going straight to winter."

There's a guy holding the door open that I don't recognize. My only assertion is that he's here to meet up with one of the residents. But when Scar and I step outside and I thank him, he allows the door to close and heads down the concrete steps behind us.

"Don't you worry," Scar says. "I'm sure we'll get the full fall experience. Ghosts, goblins, witches brew, and all."

"I sure hope so." For as long as I can remember, I was always on my schools' decorating committees that would set up for seasonal events, dances, and any social event. This is the first year I haven't signed up to partake in any festivities because at BCU, the Delta Chi girls are in charge of planning.

Maybe that's what I need to do...start getting involved again. Maybe I could offer the girls in the sorority my help.

They can't all be as bad as Melody. Forcing myself out of my room, while surrounding myself with people, could really do me some good. Obviously this 'dwelling on my past' thing isn't working. After all, what more can I possibly lose, besides my dignity, if they say no?

One thing I *am* certain of is that Scar and I are going to have the best damn legs around after this school year. All this walking is surely good for our calves, especially when they burn this badly.

Fifteen minutes later, after walking in the chilled temps, we arrive at the Kappa Rho House. It's astonishing how different it looks in the daylight compared to the night.

Hidden among blue spruce and pine trees is a mansion-sized white house that homes over a dozen men who, for reasons unbeknownst to me, joined this fucked-up fraternity. We've already got enough going on with The Society and school, so why in God's name would anyone want to take on added responsibilities during what are supposed to be the 'best years of their lives'? Not to mention the things they do to each other are deplorable. Those poor freshmen boys have to walk through fire just to get into this fraternity, and once they are in, they're tortured for an entire school year.

During the cold months, Kappa Rho and Delta Chi are where most of the parties are held since both sit deep in the woods. There's also more social space since they're actual houses, as opposed to the dorms which have only a bunch of rooms and a small lounge on the basement level.

The fraternity and sorority houses on campus are the only ones not named after a founding family. My family, the Crosses, aren't a founding family, but I like to think our roles in The Society have baptized us as vital members.

I stop walking directly in front of the tall staircase. "You sure you don't want to ditch cleanup and go drink coffee in front of the fireplace at the student center?"

Scar furrows her brow then gives me a playful shove. "Move it, girl. If we ditch our chores, they'll make us do something much worse next time."

I grumble in defeat as I drag my ass up the stairs, shoulders slumped. Scar reaches for the U-shaped handle on the door, but before she can pull it open, the mysterious guy from Willamette House—our dormitory—steps in front of us, sporting a rather impressive smirk. "Allow me."

He's not bad-looking, if you're into the preppy-boy type, which I am. Blond hair, arctic blue eyes, and some weird connect the dot symbol tattooed to his arm. Although, I'm more concerned about his body temperature because it can't be over forty-five degrees out here and he's sporting a short-sleeved white polo shirt.

Scar steps inside with a scowl on her face and I know her protective side is kicking into high gear. If I had to guess, she wants to know why this guy was at our dorm and why he's here now. I, too, should be curious, but now I'm looking at that tattoo again and I wanna know what it means.

See. I'm a terrible Guardian. The worst.

There is no doubt in my mind that I'm too trusting. No matter how hard I try to change that flaw, I continue to search for the good in people. It's the one thing about myself that hasn't changed, yet. Let's hope no one takes away that innocent side of me.

I lean my shoulder into the building and drag my eyes from his crotch to his face. "What's your name?"

Another flaw: I suck at flirting. Abso-fucking-lutely suck. I never cease to embarrass myself, much like right now.

The wind picks up, blowing strands of hair out of my clip and into my face. Butterflies swarm my belly when Strange

Guy brushes his fingers across my cheek, sweeping the hair away. With a wide grin, he holds his head high, displaying his sheer abundance of confidence. "Cade. And yours?"

"I'm Ri—"

The next thing I know, I'm being jerked by the arm through the doorway. Once I'm in the house, Scar lets go of me, and as I rub my arm, I give her a sour look. "What was that for?"

She slams the door closed with Cade on the other side. "He's a Kappa Rho and a creep. Stay away from him."

Makes sense why he's here. This is his home. Doesn't explain why he was at our dormitory, though.

"All right, Mommy. What makes him a creep?"

"The guys told me he once slipped some pills in a girl's drink and took advantage of her. They all warned me to steer clear of him."

"Okaaaay." I tow the word. "This is all hearsay, Scar. You can't believe everything someone tells you."

Her nostrils flare and she huffs in defense. "Why would they lie about this?"

I turn around and walk farther into the house, kicking plastic cups out of the way and other articles of trash as I mutter under my breath, "I guess I just don't think it's fair to judge someone based on what others say."

"You're such a pain in the ass. Just be careful, okay?"

Exhaling profoundly, I drop my sarcasm. "Fine. Thanks for destroying my dreams of *finally* meeting a decent guy."

"You're welcome for being saved from a not-so-decent guy."

I know Scar means well. And most of my bitching really was sarcasm, but I was also being somewhat serious because I can't find a good guy around here for the life of me.

Part of me is a little envious that she doesn't just have one boyfriend, but three. I want three boyfriends, dammit.

Letting go of the possibility that I'll find Mr. Charming tonight, I get to work on cleaning up this hellhole. The amount of trash in this house could overflow a landfill.

I start in the living room, while Scar works in the kitchen. About thirty minutes in, I realize I haven't seen anyone else here. Not a single person. It's pretty strange, considering a dozen guys live here. Not to mention, Cade just came home. Now that I think about it, I'm not sure he even came inside, unless he used a different entrance.

"Hey, Scar," I call out, knowing she'll hear me since she's just on the other side of the wall.

After putting a few more cups in the large black trash bag, I take off my yellow rubber gloves and toss them on the back of the couch. "Scar," I try again, but it's still eerily quiet.

I bypass a couple of full and tied bags and what appears to be a pool of vomit on the floor, which makes me scrunch my nose. *Disgusting.*

"Scar. Where the hell are you?" I step into the kitchen, but there's no sign of her. It doesn't even look like she's cleaned anything in here.

Where did she go?

Reaching into my pocket, I pull out of my phone and see that I have a few messages. Some of which are from last night and it's a reminder that I haven't checked my phone since the middle of the night, before Ridge showed up in my room.

One is from an unknown number, but the first four words of the message sent at six this morning grab my attention.

Sleep well, Angel. And...

I click on it and keep reading.

> Unknown: Sleep well, Angel. And don't worry, I'll keep the monsters away.

"*What. The. Hell?*"

How did he get my number? And I say 'he' because I know exactly who this is. It has to be Ridge. There is absolutely no one else who would send this message.

I quickly type a response, unsure if my rapid pulse is due to excitement that he finally said words to me, or horror that he's gone as far as to find my number.

> Me: How did you get my number?

As I wait for a reply, I save his number in my phone.

Long minutes pass, and he doesn't respond.

Each interaction with this guy, be it a visit in the middle of the night, or a run-in at a party, is beyond fucked up. There's no doubt in my mind he's read my message by now, so why isn't he responding? Why is Ridge so vague and mysterious?

"Shit." Suddenly, it hits me that Scar is still missing.

What if this was just a distraction to buy time and he's done something to her?

Horrified at the thought, I manically search the house. I'm opening and closing doors to bedrooms, closets, bathrooms. I didn't realize until now how big this place really is. Then again, it houses quite a few guys so I'm not sure why I'd expect it to be small. There's at least six bedrooms and four bathrooms and I haven't even started my search of the basement.

"Scar," I call out, hoping like hell I get a response this time.

I'm on the second floor, tearing open a shower curtain, when I hear a door close downstairs. My body can hardly keep up with my feet as I flee from the bathroom and down the stairs. Slipping on one of the hardwood steps, I grab the banister and catch myself before I bust my ass.

"Scar? Is that you?"

By the time I make it back into the living room, I'm breathless, and now in a state of confusion when I see that the front door is open. My eyes are wide and alert as they skim the room with each cautious step I take toward it.

"Scar," I say again, this time my voice almost a whisper.

A gust of wind ripples through the door, and the cool air hits my face. I pick up my pace, crossing the room to the door. Gripping tightly to the handle, I lean forward and look outside, only to find nothing. I slam the door shut and take a step backward, until I bump into something, or rather, someone.

At first thought, I assume it's Scar, but when I fall back into the stranger's arms and look up, I see that it's Cade. He reaches around me and clicks the lock on the door, the sound deafening, like a prison gate closing. My breath catches in my throat as I steady myself and come forward onto my feet.

I spin around and plant my hands to his chest. Shoving him back a few steps, I hiss, "What the hell are you doing here?"

Unaffected by my outburst, Cade rubs his chin. "Because it's my house. Why the fuck are you here?"

This is a complete one-eighty from how flirtatious he was earlier and I'm completely turned off right now. "I'm on cleanup, asshole."

"Then quit snooping around when you should be cleaning up this mess." He kicks an empty can that rolls across the living room floor.

"Please tell me why you think it's any of your business what I do?"

He reaches for my cheek, a cocky grin on his face, but I slap his hand down aggressively.

"Don't touch me. I don't even know you."

A subtle laugh climbs up his throat, and he glances away, tracing his mouth with his fingers. "Oh, I see how it is. You like to play? All right," he holds his hands up in surrender, curling his fingers toward his chest, "we can do this your way. Come here."

Everything Scar said about this guy is right. He is a creep. My shoulders tighten, the tendons on my neck standing out. "Scar!" I shout loudly before walking toward the kitchen again.

I'm stopped halfway when Cade throws his arm around my waist. "Whoa. Whoa. Where do you think you're going?"

A loud knock at the door has my soul practically jumping out of my body. "Calm down, baby girl. I've got you."

In an attempt to shove Cade away, I fail miserably when he only tightens his hold on me. Spinning me around, my chest is flush with his and he holds me with both hands, wrapping me in a tight hug.

"That's the problem. I don't want you to have me." I raise both hands to his chest and push hard, but, once again, he shows he's the dominant one here.

The knocks grow stronger and louder and I'm hopeful it's someone who would help me. Scar—maybe even Ridge.

Scar is obviously gone and it wouldn't surprise me one bit if Cade got rid of her somehow, just so he could have me alone in this house. With my options limited, I call for help from someone else. "Ridge!" It's not a longshot, considering he's everywhere I am.

"Ridge?" Cade chuckles. "Ridge Foster? You mean Freakshow? What do you want with him?"

"Far more than I'd ever want with you," I grind out. "Now, let me..." I shove him again, this time making headway. "...the fuck go!"

And I'm free. Wasting no time, I go straight for the front door so I can get the hell out of this house. Clicking the lock first, I pull open the door. "Scar?"

She walks beside me, avoiding eye contact, while combing her fingers through her hair. "Why'd you lock the door?"

"I..." My words trail off because she needs to answer my questions first. "Where were you?"

Her eyes wander to Cade before coming back to me. She leans close and whispers, "Neo sent me a text to meet him in the shed out back." Her eyebrows waggle and I make a note to shave them off when she's sleeping.

"You left me here alone..." My voice rises with each word that leaves my mouth. "...to go have sex with Neo in a shed?"

"Ry," she whispers. "Would you quiet down? There are people here."

I follow her gaze over my shoulder and see that Cade has been joined by two guys and a girl—that girl being Melody.

Where the hell did they come from? Must've come through the back door because I searched this house high and low and no one was home.

Cade tosses an arm around Melody's shoulder and pulls her close. "Don't quiet down on our account. This was just getting good."

Melody bursts out laughing, taking advantage of this opportunity. "As I said earlier, ladies, some hellions never change." Her words are directed at us and I'd love nothing more than to shove them back down her throat.

"Fuck off, Melody," Scar snaps.

Melody crawls out of Cade's arm and walks toward us, one foot in front of the other as her heels clank against the hardwood floor. "The shed? Really, Scarlett. Are you and your boyfriends really that trashy?"

"Fuck off," I snap at Melody. "At least we don't associate ourselves with rapists." My eyes land on Cade's, but no one seems to notice except him. I'm not even sure if what Scar told me is true, but after today, I'm almost certain it is.

"Rumors like that aren't taken lightly around here," Melody warns. "Might wanna keep your mouth shut before someone shuts it for you."

Scar lunges at Melody, but I grab her by the waist. "Scar," I warn. "She's not worth it, babe."

She puts up some resistance but allows me to drag her to the door before she does something she'll regret. There isn't a doubt in my mind that she'd demolish Melody's face, if given the chance. Scar is feisty, and someone you don't want to piss off.

Once we're out the door, I kick it shut and Scar curses at the sky. "That stupid fucking bitch. One of these days..." Her hands grip both sides of her head in frustration. "...one of these days I am going to destroy that girl. Should've done it back at The Academy when there were fewer witnesses."

While she's going on about Melody, all I can think about is Cade's grubby hands all over me. If Scar hadn't come when she did, he could have dragged me up to his room and raped me. Chills skate down my spine at the thought.

I'm learning really fast that the guys here don't fuck around. If they want something, they take it.

After Scar has calmed down and I've pulled her back three times from trying to get into the house and kicking Melody's ass, we head down the campus bike trail and back to our dorm.

We're five minutes into the walk, and Scar has finally stopped ranting about Melody. After a minute of complete silence, she finally says, "What happened with you and Cade while I was gone? He didn't try anything with you, did he?"

I'm sort of at a loss for words because if I say yes, I know Scar will tell Crew, Jagger, and Neo and there's no doubt they'll raise hell over it. The last thing I want is for the student body to think I'm a problem starter. "No," I lie, "he didn't try anything."

Stepping onto the paved part of the trail and out of the woods, the snap of a branch grabs my attention. When I follow the sound, I meet Ridge's gaze. He's leaning back on the trunk of a large tree with the hood of his sweatshirt pulled up. One leg is kicked up behind him, and in his hands are two broken branch pieces. He drops them to the ground before reaching up and grabbing another. His eyebrows cave in, nostrils flared, and he snaps the branch in two, my body jolting right before I break the stare and keep walking.

Cade is definitely a creep, but maybe he was right about Ridge. What if he is a freak? A freak I let enter my room and watch me sleep.

CHAPTER 7
RIDGE

WITH THE BLADE pressed to my prey's neck, I drag it across his flesh with enough pressure to slice through his vocal cords.

Even if he survives this, he won't be talking.

Contrary to how it seems, I don't enjoy taking lives, but it's an outlet when Riley pisses me off. Much like today. I saw her talking to Cade in front of Kappa Rho. She was flirting! My girl was fucking flirting with another guy right in front of me! I had to get away before I did something I'd regret, and this life that I just took had to be taken, regardless. What better time than when I'm feeling vengeful?

With a body at my feet and blood on my hands, I drop the knife then reach into my pocket and pull out my phone.

Riley texted me earlier and I've re-read the message over and over.

Suddenly, all the anger I feel toward her dissipates. As quickly as she pisses me off, she calms me just as fast.

I want more than anything to text her again. The thing is, I should have never texted her in the first place. It's too much of a risk. Things could go very bad if The Elders find out we're in a relationship.

I read her message again...

65

> My Angel: How did you get my number?

I wish I could tell her I've had her number since the day I first saw her. The weeks that followed that monumental moment were filled with copious amounts of research and digging so that I could find out everything there is to know about Riley Cross. Even when I knew I wouldn't be able to hand over the information I garnered to The Elders, I continued to search because I needed to know all about her for myself.

Where she was born. What size bra she wears. I know she has a small scar on her abdomen from having her appendix removed when she was only six years old. My heart pangs with agony at the thought of Riley enduring such pain as appendicitis.

If only I could go back and love her from the second she was brought into this world, I would have kept her safe from all pain, even if it meant us leaving this world together to escape it.

I read the message again, my back pressed firmly to a tree.

> My Angel: How did you get my number?

I pop the button on my jeans and reach into my pants, getting a tight hold on my dick.

With the dying man at my feet, I stroke myself. He gasps for air, holding tight to his neck while blood seeps out. The same blood that's on my hand, lubing up my cock.

Ignoring his presence, my thoughts go to her—to us.

With my phone gripped in one hand and my cock in the other, I imagine Riley naked in bed when she sent this message to me. I bet her fingers were buried in her pussy when she sent it. I know Riley likes to pleasure herself. I've watched her countless times, and in my head, every time her lips parted, she was moaning my name.

I imagine her soaked fingers running up her smooth stomach before pinching her pink, hard nipples. Then she'd stick them in her mouth and taste herself. I bet she tastes so sweet.

One day I'll find out how sweet her arousal really is.

I envision her hips thrusting into the air while tapping slowly into the phone.

Once she got the words typed out, she probably gyrated the phone against her pussy while pretending it was my cock.

I push my pants down farther, springing my cock free, then I pump myself faster, head resting back against the tree as I look at her words on my screen.

"Fuck, Angel. I need you so bad. Need to feel you. Taste you. Hold you."

My entire body flushes with heat and a dire need to combust. I keep stroking as cum expels from my cock all over the dying man at my feet.

"Motherfucker," I grumble as a text from Maddox comes through. I stuff my cock back in my pants and zip them up quickly.

He's lucky I finished when I did.

> Maddox: Where the hell are you? 10-33!

10-33 is our signal for an emergency, or something important, but lately, Maddox uses it when he so much as needs one of us to bring him a roll of toilet paper to the bathroom.

With a sticky hand, I drop my phone back in my pocket. I'll talk to him when I get home. No sense in wasting time.

Two desperate eyes look up at me and the son of a bitch is

still alive, fighting like hell for his life. I rub my hands together, using his blood and my semen as lotion for my dry skin.

The bastard mouths the word 'help,' and I laugh, bringing my hands to my chest.

"Me? You really think I'm gonna save you? Look," I kneel beside him, "I know what you're thinking. I'm fucked up. But love makes you do crazy things. And I, Ridge Foster, am madly in love with Riley Cross."

Wow. I never said that out loud. It's got a nice ring to it.

Reaching over, I grab the knife and stick it into his chest, ending his life.

Vacant eyes peer up at me as I pick up the bottle of lighter fluid and douse him. Once I'm sure he's covered enough, I take out my matchbox and strike one up before throwing it down. His body goes up in flames—taking my fingerprints along with it.

~~Dennis Mathers~~
~~Robby Nelson~~
Andy Porter
Eric Mathers
Two down. Two to go.

———

"What the fuck was the emergency?" I slam our room door shut and drop my keys and phone on the round table. "And I swear to the sky, if it's some dumb shit, I'll never respond to that code again."

Maddox is pacing the small space, eyes down, hands in the pocket of his jeans.

"Where's Lev?" I ask as I walk to the small sink in our kitchenette to wash the dried blood from my hands.

Maddox stops walking as if he just realized I was here. "We

gotta fill him in on this shit with Riley. Your assignment. All of it."

He pays no attention to the red water running down the drain, and I make no attempt to hide it.

"No." I shake my head. "Fuck no. We had a deal."

"He's gonna find out. Secrets aren't as safe as we think in The Society. And when he knows you—we—kept this shit from him..." He's cut off when the door opens and Lev walks in, in true Lev fashion with slumped shoulders and a desensitized expression.

Lev isn't like normal people. Not that any of us are. Then again, what is normal anyway? If I had to choose, I'd say Maddox is the most normal of us all. He comes from a nice home, usually makes good choices, until now.

What the hell is he thinking telling me we 'gotta fill him in'? It's asinine. Maddox of all people knows how unpredictable Lev can be. Being an apathetic person, paired with his future position in The Society as a Punisher, we have to be very careful with Lev.

While these years are all about training for our future roles, we still take them very seriously, and Lev is no different. Punishers do exactly that—they punish.

While I love the guy and I'd do damn near anything for him, Lev is a loose cannon. Our freshman year of high school, he endured some shit that left him fucked up. His doctors call it alexithymia and say he lacks empathy. Lev can feel emotions; he just doesn't know what it is he's feeling. Now, the only way he expresses his feelings is through anger. He's on medication that keeps him in check, but he's completely zomb-ified on that shit. He tells us he just doesn't give a fuck, but we know better. Somewhere inside the shell of the guy Maddox and I grew up with, is the boy we once knew; he's just hiding until he knows it's safe to come back out. I've got faith he'll come back to us one day, but until then, Maddox and I will be right by his side.

Lev looks from me to Maddox. "Who died?" He closes the door and peels off his down winter coat. I can't help but wonder if it's a serious question, or a joke. But there's no way he knows. No way anyone knows, including Maddox.

Maddox and I share a look packed to the brim with unspoken words. He wants me to tell Lev about my task of finding out what happened to the governor. I shake my head at him sternly, eyes narrowed.

Maddox pipes up, breaking the awkward silence. "Where the hell were you?"

Lev drops on the couch. His head falls back, eyes closed. "Had a meeting."

A meeting means he met with his therapist. Lev has had the same therapist since 'the incident we don't talk about' and it's the only one he'll talk to, so now, his therapist drives two hours to come here twice a week for a one-hour meeting.

"And," I begin, grabbing a towel off the table and drying my hands, "how'd it go?"

Lev lifts his head and his eyes pin to mine. "What did you say?"

Lev doesn't talk about his meetings. Or much of anything at all for that matter, so it really was a stupid question.

"Nothing," I say, dropping the subject. "I've gotta go take care of some shit." I glance at Maddox. "So if we're good here..."

Maddox walks past me, his shoulder bumping mine before he snatches his coat off the hook by the door. "I'll go with you."

"No. No, you won't. I said I've got shit to do."

Last thing I need is Maddox on my ass again, feeding me more bullshit about how we need to fill Lev in on the governor situation. Lev doesn't know my assignment involves Riley. Lev doesn't know Riley's a Guardian. Hell, Lev doesn't even know Riley. We might be best friends, but seven years ago, we learned that some things are better left unsaid when it comes to Lev. The less stress for him, the better off we all are.

"Hey," Lev calls out as he reaches for the remote control beside him. "Where're you guys headed?"

I look at Maddox, who's wondering the same thing, before telling Lev, "To the student center to grab a pizza."

Lev spreads his legs and narrows his eyes at us, as if he suspects I'm lying. "All right," he finally says. "Bring me back some. I'm fucking starving."

Eyes rolling, I pull open the door and try to close it quickly behind me, but it's halted by Maddox who comes rushing out.

As soon as the door closes, I tear into him. "What the fuck, man?" I grit out. "Told you I had shit to do."

"He's gonna find out, man. We gotta tell him."

"Quit repeating that and just tell me what the fuck this is about. Time is of the essence right now."

"I got a call this morning from my dad. Some guys have gone missing..." His words break off and I wave my hand through the air, moving this conversation along. "There've been two men in the last twenty-four hours who were reported missing. Both were employed at the late governor's factory. Now, I know damn well the dead governor isn't behind it."

I blow out the pent-up air in my lungs and sweep this conversation under the rug. "Boulder Cove isn't some small town. Shit happens." I'm walking down the hall toward the staircase when I realize he's not following. Annoyed, I spin around. Really didn't want him to come with me, but now I'm wondering why he's suddenly not. "What are you doing?"

"Shit happens? Are you kidding me right now? This whole thing is gonna blow up if more men go missing, especially if it has anything to do with the governor's death." He grows still, lips pursed. "You wouldn't know anything about that, would you?"

I could tell him. After all, this is Maddox. I trust the guy with my life. But I won't drag him into my mess. Especially with his father being such a hard-ass on him all the time. Maddox might feel some sort of obligation, or even try to assist him, just to earn some sort of validation from his old man by bringing him pertinent information. Either way, what I did stays with me—and only me.

I tip my chin, surprise on my face. "You're serious? You think I'd hurt these men? If they were in any way connected to the governor, I need them alive and well in order to interrogate them for my assignment."

He lifts a brow, making strong eye contact. He doesn't have to use words. I know what he's insinuating.

"Fuck off," I grumble, "I was just a kid when I beat that bastard with a bat. And he deserved it. You really think I'd kidnap grown-ass men? Or murder them?"

"Never said anything about murder, Ridge."

"It's what you're insinuating, am I correct?"

He shrugs his shoulders and keeps quiet, giving me my answer.

Still not saying anything, he just looks at me, waiting for me to burst at the seams with the truth. We're at least six feet apart and I don't close the space between us to finish this conversation. Instead, I say it loud enough for anyone with ears in our vicinity to hear. "People go missing every day." My hands go up in the air, my way of saying, 'it is what it is.' Then they fall and I get back on track to deal with something—or someone, rather —that needs to be dealt with. Maddox believes I could do it because he knows me better than anyone. And he'd be right—I am fully capable.

When I reach the stairs, I steal a quick glance over my

shoulder to see if he's coming. Sure enough, he's headed my way. I make my way down, taking two steps at a time.

"All I'm saying is, this shit's gonna get around, and if Riley is connected to these missing cases in any way—"

"Whoa. Whoa. Whoa." I stop him at the bottom of the staircase. "Riley has nothing to do with this. Don't you dare drag her name into this shit."

"Can you really be so sure? Look at the facts. The girl killed our state governor—"

"Would you keep your fucking voice down!" I look over my shoulder, up the stairs, and out the front door. He's lucky no one is around to hear what he just blurted out.

"Would you stop interrupting me every time I try to say something? Jesus Christ, just hear me out."

Stepping out the open door, I cup my hands around my mouth to warm them.

We're walking again, and while I don't give a shit if he comes with me, I might try to lose his ass if he doesn't drop this shit.

"Hard to do when I think my best friend is—"

"Drop it, Maddox," I say sternly. "It's in your best interest to just let this go." I hate when my emotions surface like this. Hate it when they take control of my body. Sometimes I think it'd be easier to feel nothing, like Lev, than to feel so strongly about a girl. One that I've killed for. I'm a monster. He knows it. I know it. And one day, she'll probably know it, too. But she's worth it. I swear to fucking God, she is worth it.

"What about Lev...?"

My neck snaps to the left, where he's walking beside me. "Lev can't know anything. Not about my assignment. The governor. Riley. Nothing. Not yet." I make myself clear, hoping he realizes how important this is to me.

"Ya know," he says, after a moment of silence, "you're really putting me in a fucked-up position between you two. I don't enjoy taking sides."

"No one's asking you to take a side. This is all for Lev. Look," my voice shifts to a high note, "if it makes you feel better, we'll just say I owe you one." I turn to face him, holding out my fist. "Deal?"

He bumps it back, sealing the deal, and his eyes roll. "I'm holding you to it, but you better not fuck us all in the process. What's our motto?"

I slap a hand to his shoulder and lead him up the staircase. "We will fucking reign."

"Damn straight we will. And no one," he presses, "absolutely no one, will interfere with our plans."

We walk up the stairs of the Kappa Rho House and it's not until I kick open the front door that Maddox even realizes where we're at. "What are we doing here?"

"Reigning, man. Starting with this university, then we will fucking reign over The Society."

That's our endgame. Maddox, Lev, and I made a pact our freshman year of high school after The Society royally fucked me, then Lev and his family. They're the reason we're so screwed up. We also learned, not only the power we might hold in The Society, but also the power we could strip from some Elders who aren't deserving. If we play our cards right, we could sit at the top with everyone else beneath us as our little pets.

I walk through the house, ignoring the flirtatious looks from a few girls on the couch. Although Maddox has no self-control and positions himself right in the middle of them all.

It's better this way. He's not gonna like what I'm about to do. Maddox is one of the good guys. Not much of a rule bender, unless it involves pot and booze. He's a little pretentious, but he's got good intentions, and he's loyal as fuck.

Letting him do his thing, I walk up the stairs, my boots resounding heavily with each step I take.

It doesn't take me long to get to Cade's room, considering I know exactly where to find it. I've attended a few parties here and I've done my share of snooping around. It's not that I'm nosey; I'm just very aware of my surroundings.

I kick open his door in the same fashion as our entrance into the house. Only this time, the toe of my boot goes through the door and I have to jerk it out of the splintered wood. Hopefully, the hole serves as a reminder to Cade that I'm not fucking around. Although, I'm sure he'll get the message nice and clear in about two seconds.

His eyes shoot over his shoulder, his pasty pale ass on display as he's kneeling on the mattress of his bed.

"What the fuck?" he growls. Yet, he doesn't stop. Just keeps rocking his dick in and out of the chick bent over in front of him. He points a stern finger at the door, angry eyes locked on mine. "Get the hell out!"

Ignoring his demand, I walk steadfastly toward him, grab his pointed finger and bend it back just enough to keep it intact, but far enough to cause him immense pain. "That's for using this finger to touch what's mine."

"Fuuuuuuck!" he cries out, like the little bitch he is.

Erica, I believe is her name, wisely slides away from him and grabs a sheet to cover herself.

"Oh my god! You're gonna break his finger!"

A devilish grin makes its way on my face and her eyes widen before she bunches the sheet in her hands and scurries toward the door.

I'm not even sure if she's gone before I drop Cade's hand, clench my fist, and plant it right on his nose. He loses his footing and falls back onto the mattress, blood running down his hands that swaddle his face.

"You're gonna pay for that, asshole." He gets up quickly and charges at me with his pants hung around his ankles, limp cock flapping around.

Swerving to the left, I dodge his lunge and spin around, grabbing him by the waist before throwing him onto the floor.

Adrenaline courses through my veins and my rationality eludes me as I lay one punch after another on the gory flesh of his face.

His hands rise between us to shield my blows, but I punch through them, landing six out of ten shots.

"Ridge!" I hear Maddox's voice before I see him, and it isn't until I'm pulled backward that I even comprehend what's going on.

"Get the fuck off me!" I shout at Maddox. The second I'm free, I lunge forward at Cade, who's got a shirt to his face, soaking up all the blood, but I'm pulled right back.

"Calm the fuck down!" Maddox snaps back at me, wrapping his arms around my chest to hold me in place.

"He was trying to get with Riley earlier," I tell Maddox, in hopes he'll understand and free me from his death grip. I turn my attention to Cade, whose bloody mouth is curled up in a smirk. "You stay the fuck away from her, or next time, you won't be so lucky."

Maddox lifts me up, leading me toward the door, but my eyes never leave Cade's. "I mean it, fucker. Stay away from her or I'll fucking kill you."

"Out!" Maddox gnashes, tossing me out of the room.

He follows behind me, but before he closes the bedroom door, I hear Cade shout, "I've always craved what I'm told I can't have, Ridge. Challenge accepted."

Something violent snaps inside me. Hot blood flows through my veins, filling my face with insatiable heat. The urge to go back in that room to finish him off is damn near suffocating. As if my lungs have been depleted of air and I'm unable to fill them again until I'm certain he'll never touch her.

Today is not that day. Not with my best friend here to witness the horrendous act. He doesn't deserve a lifetime of that trauma. But Cade better heed my warning. If he goes near her again, I will be back.

"Jesus Christ, man. You could have killed him. Are you sure she's worth all this?"

"This and more."

This and more.

CHAPTER 8
RILEY

"HOLY SHIT." I stop in the middle of the student center, surrounded by people, but my eyes are only on one person.

Scar follows my line of sight, finally finding it. "Who is that?"

"Is that Cade? The guy from the Kappa Rho House?" I ask her about the guy sitting at a round table with a splint on his nose and two yellow eyes.

She takes a few steps forward, getting a better look. "I can't tell, but he's with Melody and Hannah, so it could be. If it is, what the fuck happened to him?"

His mischievous eyes wander away from the conversation being had between the girls, and land on mine. I immediately snap my gaze away and grab Scar by the arm, pulling her in the opposite direction. "It's him," I tell her. "I'd know those evil eyes anywhere."

"Well, someone got a hold of him, and it doesn't look like they were too happy with him."

Stealing a glance over my shoulder, I catch his stare again. Only this time, he's not sitting on the table anymore, he's coming toward us. "Not our problem," I tell her, picking up my pace and dragging her along with me.

"Ry. Slow down." Scar jerks back. "We still have twenty minutes before our first class."

"He's following us," I grit between my teeth. "Just keep walking."

Really don't feel like starting my Monday off with drama from Cade. And if I know him like I think I'm starting to, he bathes in it. It's just a vibe I get from him. My first conversation with Cade felt like a meet-cute, but the second encounter, I saw the depth of his arrogance. Had Scar not shown up when she did at his house, I have no idea what he would have done. Add that to what I heard about him drugging a girl and taking advantage of her, I have no interest in getting to know him.

"Yo, Riley." His voice comes from behind me and the words reverberate through my chest like a drum. Or maybe that's my heart. Either way, I don't like it.

I walk faster, keeping my eyes in front of me, hoping he'll think I don't hear him and goes away.

Leave it to Scar to look over her shoulder, and when she does, she stops walking. "Go away, asshole," she hisses.

I could continue to ignore his presence, or I could quit being a little bitch, who lets her best friend speak for her, and turn around to face him.

"What do you want?" I pivot on my heel and lock my arm tighter around Scar's.

Seeing his face up close like this is so much worse than from afar. Someone definitely broke his nose. I cringe at the sight, imagining how painful that must have been.

His eyebrows pull together in a heavy scowl. "You can quit staring at it now. We're all well aware that my nose is broken." His fingers run down the length of his nose. "Had a run-in with a wall."

I call bullshit, but I don't say it out loud. He can tell whatever story he wants, but I'm certain it was either a guy he pissed off, or a girl he tried to get with who wanted nothing to do with him.

"If that's your way of starting a conversation, it's not a good one. Now say what you need to say so Scar and I can get to class."

His glare on me relaxes before his mouth tugs up in a smile. "I wanna take you out."

"You...wanna take me out?" I can't help the laugh that follows, but it quickly disintegrates, washing away any humor from my face. "Fuck off, Cade."

"Ouch." His hand slaps over his heart. "Way to kill a guy's ego."

"Oh, I'm not worried," I tell him, "I'm sure it's inflating again as we speak. In fact," my eyes wander to the left, where Melody and Hannah are watching us intently, "I see some girls checking you out right now. Better luck with them." I pull Scar along, leaving Cade behind us.

We're at least six feet away from him when I hear him holler, "I don't do well with rejection, babe. But you'll come around. I can guarantee it."

"What. The. Actual. Fuck?" I mumble as we round the hall corner toward the first-floor classrooms.

"Yeah. That was downright weird." Scar drops her arm from mine and reaches into her buzzing pocket. "It's Jagger. I'll see you in class."

I nod in response and continue on my way to creative writing—my favorite class of the day. Not only because it's my only class with Scar, but also because I love being creative, and I love writing.

Ridge is also in this class, which is odd to me, since he's a junior. I can only conclude he either needed the extra elective, or he signed up because of me.

Ugh. Don't be that person, Riley. Don't let your head get as big as Cade's.

Chances are, there is no coincidence at all.

I step into the classroom, then step back when I see that Ridge is the only one sitting there, in the same seat he's always in, directly behind me.

Well, this is awkward.

Probably should have dragged out the conversation with Cade a little longer to avoid being so early. Now Ridge probably thinks I'm some sort of book nerd, or teacher's pet. Which I am, but that's beside the point. Then again, he's here early, too. I wonder if he's always this early. I guess I've never really paid much attention.

Biting my bottom lip, I take in a deep breath and fully enter the classroom. Flashing Ridge a half-smile, I slide between the tables then pull out my chair. With my bag resting at my feet, I sit down and pull out my MacBook.

It's so quiet.

Am I sweating?

I wipe my forearm across my forehead.

Yep.

At least I'm in front of him, so he can't see. Not that I care. Ridge is nobody to me. Just a guy who stalks me...while I let him.

My body jolts when a hand smacks the table beside my laptop. My spine stiffens, shoulders raised. The eyeball of his tattoo peers up at me and it's the first time I've noticed the single tear beneath it. But what's more concerning is the fresh cuts on his hand.

Could it have been him that broke Cade's nose? But why?

Turning my head slowly, I raise my chin. "Can I help you?"

Cold eyes look down on me, as if I've offended him in some way. His mouth opens and my heart jumps into my throat. At least, that's how it feels with how fast it's beating. So many unspoken words, and finally, he's going to say something.

But when his shoulders drop and his mouth closes, there's a pang of disappointment in my chest.

Turning back around to face the front of the room, I give up. There is no point in trying with this guy. It's obvious he has nothing to say to me. I know he talks. I've seen his mouth move many times while he's conversing with his friends and doesn't know I'm watching. Ironic, isn't it? Sometimes I watch him, too.

Ridge slowly lifts his hand, exposing the pen beneath his palm—my pen. I must've dropped it when I came in.

"Thank you," I whisper.

Before I even realize time has passed, the class fills with students, including Scar, who brings nothing but a pencil.

"Where's all your stuff?" I ask her as she taps said pencil repeatedly against the table.

Rubbing the back of her neck, she looks down, avoiding eye contact. "I may or may not have left it in a janitor's closet that is now locked."

"Um, Scar. Please tell me why you were in the janitor's closet." As soon as the words leave my mouth, it hits me. I hold a hand up, stopping her. "Wait. Don't tell me."

She nods, biting back a smile. "Yeah. You already know."

"Which of your fuck boys was it this time?"

She snickers. "Jagger."

Jagger enters class, looking satisfied, with a wide grin. Lucky bastard. He kisses Scar's cheek and takes the seat beside her.

"Sheds, closets. What's next? And why am I so jealous?"

"Hmm. Let's see. Maybe because you're a nineteen-year-old virgin."

"Scar!" I slap a hand over her mouth, shutting her up while

I look around to make sure no one heard what she said. Of course, they did. She didn't exactly whisper.

Jagger laughs into his hands and I reach around Scar to sock him in the shoulder. "Shut up. It's not funny."

Stealing a glance over my shoulder, I see Ridge. His eyes are down, locked on an open textbook, but there's a glint of a smile on his face.

The tips of my ears feel like they've caught fire. I pull my hair out from behind them to hide my humiliation.

He most definitely heard.

His eyes lift to mine, and his smile widens, showing two parallel dimples on the sides of his cheeks.

Didn't realize he was capable of a smile that's not laced with malice. It's sorta sexy.

With my eyes downcast, I turn back in my seat, and sink down for the rest of class.

The second we're dismissed, I gather up my things and haul ass out of the room to avoid any interaction with Ridge—or any student who may have heard for that matter.

I'm standing outside the room, my back pressed against the wall, waiting for Scar, when two hands plant on either side of me. Resting my head back, I get a look at my captor. A tall, blond guy from the class I just left, who I'm pretty sure is also on the football team.

"Excuse you." I slap one of his arms down, but he immediately puts it back up.

His mouth arches smugly, eyes vampish. "Ya know, if you're looking to lose your V-card before you're a twenty-year-old virgin, I'm happy to offer my..." He glances down at his cock before his gaze travels back up to mine. "...services."

"Ugh," I grumble, ducking under one of his arms. "Fuck off." Scar comes out of the room and I immediately say, "Let's go."

"If you change your mind, hit me up," the asshole hollers down the hall.

"What was that all about?" Scar asks.

"I cannot believe you did that!"

"What?"

"Practically announced to the entire class that I'm a virgin. Now they all think I'm a total prude. Which I am not! I've done stuff. Lots of stuff. I just haven't...ya know. Done *it*."

"Relax, babe. No one cares, and if they do, they'll forget by tomorrow. Besides, I wasn't *that* loud."

We make a turn, and this is where we have to part ways, so we both stop walking. "Well, it was enough for me to get an offer from some random dude who wants to help me lose my V-card before I'm twenty."

Scar bursts out laughing.

"It's not funny, dammit!"

I find myself laughing, too. My streak of bad luck has to be laughed at, otherwise I might cry.

"It sort of is." Her expression shifts abruptly to one of sympathy. "But for what it's worth, I am sorry."

"Mmhmm," I hum. My way of saying, 'I don't accept, but I'm not mad at you anymore.'

"I'll make it up to you. Promise."

"And how do you plan to do that? Lend me one of your boyfriends for a night to ease the pain of this humiliating moment?"

"No," she quips. "But I will buy you lunch. Meet me in the student center after class and we'll go out."

"Fine."

"I gotta go. Professor Dickens is a real dick to anyone who's late. Student center. Don't forget." She heads down the hall while I allow myself a moment of tranquility before I head to my next class. "Oh, and, Ry," she hollers over her shoulder, "Ridge says hi."

My neck draws back. "He what? Wait. Scar," I yell back... but she's gone.

Ridge says hi? But Ridge doesn't talk. At least, not to me. So why did he talk to Scar? And why the hell would the first word he have relayed to me be 'hi'?

Ridge is an enigma and the less I know about him, the more I want to know it all.

CHAPTER 9

MADDOX

"WHO'S THE BRUNETTE? Hannah, is it?" Ridge asks as he passes behind me. His legs swing around as he drops down, straddling the bench of the picnic table in the courtyard—his paper bag lunch landing with a thud. "She's pretty cute. Might give you the time of day."

"Already has. And I'm not watching her. I'm watching him." I nod toward Cade who's got his head down while Melody and Hannah parade around him. "You really fucked him up."

Ridge pulls out a can of Coke and a homemade sandwich. "Should've beat his ass harder. Would have, if you hadn't interrupted me."

Shifting gears, I opt for a conversation that's a bit lighter. I know he's still pissed about that. "You know they have food here you can buy."

He bites into his sandwich, eating half of it at once. "And you know I'm only here because I'm a poor-ass fucker who can't afford college elsewhere." He holds up his sandwich before stuffing the rest in his mouth. "Hence the homemade meal."

"Gross, dude. Chew with your mouth closed."

All The Blue Bloods have the opportunity to attend BCU

86

free of charge. It's encouraged, since it's where the second phase of our initiation takes place, bringing us one step closer to being Elders. Ridge is protected by The Society, but none of us reap the financial benefits until we pass the initiation. His parents never made it this far, and Ridge wasn't raised with the luxuries some of us have. Since his dad bailed, and his mom passed away, neither of them being Elders, he has to earn the money and power that's available to us on his own.

The money doesn't matter to him. He's only here for the power. Well, that was the case—until Riley showed up.

It's always been our goal to rule The Blue Bloods one day, so he can make certain Elders—that will one day sit beneath us —pay for their sins. They've never personally brought harm to me, but Ridge and Lev have endured hellish lives because of one—or more—of *them*. Each day brings us one step closer to where we want to be.

Lev joins us, his hands empty. He rarely eats at school, and if he does, it's a candy bar or a bag of chips. "What up, fuckers?" he asks, slapping his hands to the table on the bench across from us.

"Our boy Ridge here beat your cousin's ass last night. Did he tell ya that?"

Oh yeah. Cade and Lev are first cousins. Their dads are brothers, and Cade's parents actually raised Lev for a couple years after his parents passed away. That was, before she kicked him out and sent him to the care of an abusive prick because she couldn't deal with his mood swings. Now their whole family makes a spectacle of Lev and uses his behavior as a way of telling Cade what not to be like.

In short, none of us like Cade.

Lev looks past my shoulder at Cade, who still manages to hold the attention of the ladies with a wrapped nose. "Well, he's still walking, so apparently Ridge did a terrible fucking job."

I'm warranted a sour-ass look from Ridge, while he crunches his can with one hand. Thankfully, his attention is pulled when he spots Riley with her friend, Scar. They're walking away from campus toward the parking lot.

Ridge bolts without a word, heading in their direction. As he approaches them, his steps slow, until he's just casually creeping behind them.

"Who are they?" Lev asks, oblivious to the whole situation. And, once again, color me lucky, because my phone pings with a text, vibrating against the table. Lev leans forward, forgetting the question he just asked. "Your old man's texting. What's he want?"

"No clue," I lie, swinging my leg over the bench and getting to my feet, so I can have some privacy without Lev peering over my shoulder. "Be right back."

There's only one reason my dad would text me. It's normal for my mom to check in from time to time because she's that kind of mother, but my dad rarely reaches out.

Yesterday, he called to let me know a couple of men, who worked for the late governor, went missing in this vicinity and told me to keep an eye out for anything suspicious around campus. My first thought was Ridge, since he's working an assignment on the governor's death. I'm still not certain he had nothing to do with it, but the information I gather will aid me in finding out the truth.

> Dad: Bodies found. Foul play suspected. Any word around campus?

I immediately text him back.

Me: Damn. That sucks. Haven't heard anything. I'll do a little digging of my own. Do they have any connection to The Blue Bloods?

Dad: No connection to The Society, aside from being employed by Sebastian Saint. There's something suspicious about this case and we need to figure it out before law enforcement digs too deep into it.

He's right. If a member of The Society had anything to do with this, we need to know who, and why. I don't condone murder and don't agree that members should get off scot-free, but I know when something like this happens, and it involves one of our members, there is almost always a reason. Even if it isn't a justifiable one.

Me: Keep me updated.

Dad: Be safe, son.

My dad, who is an Elder in The Society, and also the superior of The Guardians, is adamant that I take over his role one day. I've always been highly intuitive with a keen sense of justice. However, my idea of justice is not the same as everyone else's. Karma always spins the wheel. Just because someone doesn't get caught, doesn't mean they won't pay. And sometimes, that's even worse.

I stick my phone in the pocket of my jacket and head back over to Lev. But he's gone. My eyes skim the courtyard in search of him, but he's nowhere to be seen.

Being the decent human being that I am, I gather up all the trash on the table and toss it in the bin beside the door before going back into the main building.

I've only got two more classes left today, and it just so

happens that my next one is with Riley. It wasn't until Ridge told me she, too, is a Guardian that I really took an interest in the girl and switched to this class three weeks into the semester. It's not that I'm into her...much. But I do think it's a good idea to keep her under my thumb when Ridge is thinking with his dick instead of his brain. We've got a lot to lose if he fucks this assignment up, and I'd also hate to see him expose the girl and ruin her life, too.

In some ways, Riley and I are alike. We're both weaving our way through a new position, while trying not to disappoint The Guardians above us. Chances are, she doesn't know I'm one of them, too. I shouldn't even know she is. But now that I do, I constantly find my eyes wandering to hers.

Maybe it's because my dad instilled it in my brain that I have to marry a Guardian one day. He's adamant that our family maintains the bloodlines. All of my paternal ancestors are Guardians. It's not a rule by any means; my dad is just stuck in the ways of the past.

Sometimes I wish I'd seen her first or had the option to take the assignment Ridge was given. Other times, I'm reminded of what she did. My father would never approve if he knew she was behind the governor's death. I'm also not sure I'd have been as generous as Ridge. Guardians have duties to uphold and unless I fall head over heels for Riley, the way Ridge has, I'm not sure I'd risk it all to protect her.

Nah. Riley's not the girl for me, though. She's on Ridge's radar. Although, she is hot as fuck.

I shake away the thoughts as I enter my psychology class. I'm surprised when I don't see Riley front and center. She's usually here before I am. Wonder if she and her friend ditched the rest of their classes today. That would mean Ridge did, too. It's not often Riley goes anywhere without Ridge following.

I know Ridge is fucked up. Everyone who knows him

knows he's fucked up. Hell, so is Lev. I'm surrounded by emotionally fucked-up friends. Yet, I keep myself surrounded by them because they're the truest friends anyone could ask for. We'd do damn near anything for each other. We *have* done pretty much everything for each other.

But when Riley walks in through the door just before Professor Atkins closes it, her blonde hair flowing behind her, cheeks cherry red like she ran just to get here in time, I question how loyal I really am—to my father, to The Society, and to my friends.

CHAPTER 10
LEV

Everyone who knows me will tell you I feel nothing. That I'm an empty shell of a human who just exists in their world. What they don't know is that I feel everything. I feel it all at once.

Swimming in an ocean of endless emotions. Slowly drowning, or at least hoping I will because the emotions inside me are doused in black, pulling me under into the darkest depths.

I don't know what I feel, but it's something. As I try to sort through the sensations surfacing in my body like molten lava, anger is the one I always fall back on. It's the only emotion I recognize. An old friend that's always there.

I no longer cry. Rarely laugh. But I know how to be angry—how to hate. I'm an enemy to love. Whatever love is. I'll never know because I will never understand the feeling, even if it existed *inside me. My heartstrings snapped and they're beyond repair.*

I CLOSE the notebook and toss it into the middle of the room.

"Very good, Lev. That wasn't so bad, was it?"

"It was fucking torture."

"And how did it make you feel?"

I scowl at Dr. Edmonds. A heavy scowl that shows him exactly how I feel.

"Are you angry, Lev?"

"I told you I didn't wanna do that shit. You know I hate writing."

"Part of overcoming an obstacle is facing it head-on. And that's what you did. You hate writing because it forces you to think. In order for your words to go onto the paper, they must first come to mind, am I right?"

"I guess. So what about it? It didn't help me. Just pissed me off more."

"It's okay to be angry, Lev. It means you're feeling something, even if what you're feeling really isn't anger at all. It's just the emotion you know how to express right now."

I lean forward on the couch in the space I rented for Dr. Edmonds. We only use this space for us, and only when he comes for my appointments. There's no one else I'd do this shit with but him. So, I pay him to come here. And I pay for this space. And sometimes, I occupy it when I want to be alone. This room I've set up sits inside an old run-down building. Options were limited if I wanted to be close to campus, but this seems to work well for us.

I just met with Dr. Edmonds yesterday, and already called him back for an emergency meeting after lunch today. Just up and left while Maddox was on the phone with his dad.

I haven't been well. Something is brewing inside me and if I don't get to the bottom of it soon, something bad could happen. Something very bad.

Elbows pressed to my knees, I rest my head in my hands.

"What are you thinking?" he asks, and I just shake my head back and forth, not bothering to look at him.

"That this was a waste of time."

"Let's try again."

I lift my head abruptly as Dr. Edmonds picks up my notebook from the center of the room. When he offers it to me, I slap it out of his hand, sending it to the floor. "Fuck no. I'm not writing anymore."

"Then will you talk?"

A heavy sigh escapes me, and I roll my neck, stretching my tense muscles. "Fine. You talk. I'll listen."

"How about, I ask questions and you answer?"

My hands go in the air before I slap them to my knees. I sink back into the couch, knowing this is going to take a while.

"At what point did you feel like something shifted inside you?"

My eyes snap wide open.

"No. No, Lev. Not that. I'm talking about recently. What was it that unsettled you?"

I relax again, glad he's not taking me back to *that* day.

Those meetings are the worst. Those are the ones that bring me into the depthless parts of the ocean and make me want to never come up for air.

"It's Maddox and Ridge. They've been preoccupied with school and other shit and I'm feeling..." My words trail off, unsure how to finish. What am I feeling? Why can't I understand what I'm feeling?

"Go on," Dr. Edmonds presses. "You're feeling?"

My shoulders rise, holding their position, but when I say, "Lost," they relax.

"You feel lost?"

"Dammit!" I snap. "Quit repeating what I say. You know damn well what I just said."

Dr. Edmonds raises both his hands, slowly lowering them in an attempt to calm me, but it does just the opposite. "Why do you feel lost, Lev?"

I flee from the couch. My heart fucking pounding. Sweat blanketing my forehead. My hands. My balls. Everywhere. Everything is sweaty. Everything hurts. I tear open the office door and slam it shut then slowly slide down to the floor.

Then I scream at the top of my lungs. The sound echoes off the surrounding walls, hitting my ears again and again and again.

I reach into the left pocket of my coat and pull out a bottle of pills. I always keep these on me because they're the ones I need the most.

With two in my hand, I pop them in my mouth.

Dr. Edmonds doesn't know it, but I've been trying to wean myself off all my medication. All of them. They make me so damn tired all the time. I live each day like a fucking zombie. Unless that's what I want my whole life to be like, something needs to change. For years, I've done what Dr. Edmonds says. I've taken the pills he prescribed. I do the work. I do it all. Nothing is working. Nothing is helping. It's been six years since I started treatment. When does the medication stop and my life begin?

I spit the pills into my palm then stuff them into my coat pocket.

I'm not sure what's going to happen next, but these pills in my pocket instead of inside me tell me we're all in for a hell of a ride.

CHAPTER 11
RILEY

IT'S BEEN three days since Scar made it public knowledge that I'm a virgin. I've got not one, not two, but three offers to fix that 'problem.'

Walking into my creative writing class today, I'm hopeful it's all blown over. No weird looks. No whispers. I find myself smiling internally. If that's even a thing. Either way, I feel relieved.

"Hey, Riley," Zeke calls out from the back of the room. He's the same jackass that cornered me three days ago. I didn't learn his name until yesterday, when I overheard some guys down the hall calling him.

All hope diminishes when Zeke pats his knee, smirking. "Come sit on my lap and let's see what pops up."

Ugh.

I flash him a smug look. "Zeke, if I sit on your lap, the only thing that will pop up is my fist to your face." I set my bag on the table, standing behind my chair, and mutter under my breath, "Asshole."

"I'm sorry. I'm sorry. I'm sorry," Scar repeats for the dozenth time since she outed me.

"I hate you."

She knows I don't. But I'm still so angry and embarrassed... and annoyed with myself. There have been so many opportunities for me to lose my virginity, but for some reason, I never did. I'm not a prude or anything. I have no morals that I'm sticking to. Honestly, I want to fuck. I want to fuck hard and a lot.

And I'm going to, dammit.

The sound of someone thrashing against the back wall has my eyes bolting behind me. Everyone's attention darts to the back of the room, including mine.

"Oh my god!" I gasp, hand covering my mouth.

Zeke is pinned against the wall with Ridge's hand around his throat.

Professor Atkins shoves past students, making his way to them while shouting, "Ridge Foster! Put him down, immediately."

The class stands by, silently watching, while trying to hear what Ridge is saying.

Soon, everyone is whispering and looking at me.

My body itches at the unwanted attention.

"What did I do?" I whisper to Scar, who shrugs because she's none the wiser.

"Hey," she says to a girl who moved from the back row to the middle where we are. "What happened?"

"He threatened Zeke if he ever talks to Riley again."

My eyes widen in horror. "Me?" I clap my hands to my chest. "Why me?"

"No clue. Are you two...like a thing?"

"God no," I blurt out. "I barely know the guy."

It's true. I don't know Ridge. Not in the way I should if he's threatening guys or coming to my defense. It's more than obvious he likes me. But this is too much. He's gone too far this time. Not only is it equally as humiliating as Scar announcing I'm a virgin, it's psychotic. Which is totally in line with Ridge's behavior. Watching me. Entering my room. Now this.

And...the cuts on his hand from the other day. It all makes sense now. He must have seen me talking with Cade, and he broke his nose.

"Ridge!" I shout, garnering the attention of the entire class. But it's his I want, and it's his I get. "Put him down, now!"

Slowly, Ridge lowers Zeke to the floor. When he drops his hand from his throat, Zeke curls over, gasping for air.

"In the hall, now!" I point a stern finger at the door, feeling like I'm his fucking mom. Either way, it works.

Ridge's eyebrows pinch together tightly and it's not a pleasant look he's shooting back at me, but I'm not too pleased with him at the moment either.

"What are you doing?" Scar asks, her voice low.

"Dealing with this shit."

Before Ridge even moves his feet, I slide down the row between the tables, certain he'll follow.

I tear open the door, leaving it open behind me, then I pace in front of the classroom, waiting for him to show his face.

Not even a minute later, he comes out, closing the door behind him.

Standing in front of the wall, he rests one foot on it behind him, appearing bored.

Now that he's here, I'm not sure what I want to say. Why does he have the ability to make my mind go blank and my body tingle in places it shouldn't?

It's like he's some sort of supernatural force put on this earth to hypnotize me.

With his chin to his chest, his eyes lift to mine in a heated glare, hands snug in the front pockets of his ripped black jeans.

My chest tightens, unwilling to inflate. I feel nervous. I shouldn't, though. Ridge is the one who should be nervous.

He's the one making an ass out of himself, and me in the process. "Why'd you do that to Zeke?"

He doesn't say anything. Of course.

His silence makes the thoughts in my head so loud and intolerable. "Jesus, Ridge. Just fucking say something!"

I watch intently as his chest rises and falls rapidly. There's the unease I was waiting for. "You're not going to say anything?" I step closer to him, and he doesn't move an inch. Just stands firmly and lets me invade his personal space.

"Why'd you threaten Zeke?" I ask again, now so close I could touch him. "Why'd you tell my best friend to tell me hi instead of saying it yourself? Why do you do anything you do?"

His breath hitches and his mouth opens. "Say something," I beg him. "Anything."

Yet, he remains silent.

"Ugh!" I stomp my foot in annoyance. "You're so infuriating!"

He will speak to me before this one-sided conversation ends. I will do whatever it takes. I will hear his voice.

One more step forward and my chest is flush with his. I can feel his warm breath travel down the dipped V of my shirt and my nipples pucker on impact.

"Do I make you nervous, Ridge?"

My hand extends, fingers spread, and I rest it on his cheek. "Well...do I?"

When he still doesn't speak, standing there completely unaffected by me, I rest my other hand on his other cheek, then before he can do anything about it, I pull his mouth to mine.

I'm surprised when his hands lift to my head, gripping the sides, clenching my hair so tightly, my hair follicles feel like they're on fire.

He kisses me hard and he holds me so tightly that I'm not

sure he'll ever let go. He'd die in this kiss if it meant he died with his mouth on mine.

I'm desperate for a word. Just one simple word. Anything he'll give me that proves he's not completely dead inside when I'm around. But this kiss...this consuming kiss proves that Ridge is more alive than any other guy I've kissed before.

Our lips connect magnetically, never parting or shying away. My heart thuds in my chest and I hold my breath while time stands still.

It's actually...nice. In a screwed-up sort of way.

He smells fucking amazing and seeing Ridge from afar, with his grunge appeal, you wouldn't guess he'd smell this good. A stranger might assume he reeks of cigarettes and beer, and while there is a tinge of smoke on his breath, there's a minty taste that overpowers it.

My hands slide down to his jacket, gripping the outer edges, and I tug him closer, wanting more, but unsure of what it is I want more of.

I didn't expect to like this. It was supposed to be a tactic to get him to react, and holy shit is he reacting. When I open my eyes, I see that his are wide open, watching me.

Always watching me.

When I take a step back, he pulls me right back in, unwilling to let this end just yet, or ever.

I peer up at him, searching for any glint of adoration. Any sentiment. Any...*thing.*

"Please," I whisper against his lips, but before he can even attempt to speak, the classroom door swings open and Zeke comes on, fuming.

"You wanna fucking go?" He pats his hands to his chest, challenging Ridge. "Let's fucking go."

Professor Atkins comes to the doorway, spewing words at Zeke to get him back in class, but before he can tell us to do the same, I grab Ridge by his jacket and haul ass with him in tow down the hall. "Come on. Let's get outta here."

He obeys, not putting up an ounce of resistance. "Zeke is pissed and I've got no doubt he'll skip class to come for you."

I'm not sure why I'm protecting him after what he did. It was embarrassing to say the least, but also, sort of humbling, knowing Ridge came to my defense once again.

CHAPTER 12
RIDGE

NO. Fuck no. That's not how our first kiss was supposed to be. It should have been longer, more passionate. More...everything.

Forget Zeke. And fuck him for interrupting such a pivotal moment for me and Riley. I don't care about that bastard. In fact, he's the last person on my mind. Right now, all I can focus on is Riley and kissing her again.

I've dreamt of that moment for weeks and that's not at all what I envisioned.

We're walking steadfast, Riley holding my jacket tightly, practically dragging me down the hall. After a few turns, we end up down an empty hallway. Riley loosens her hold on me but doesn't let go, and when she steals a glance over her shoulder, I take my shot.

Catching her off guard, I grab her by the waist, spin her around, and push her back to the wall. She yelps on impact, but doesn't fend me off, which doesn't surprise me, considering she's the one who initiated our first kiss.

Yeah. She fucking wants me. Knew it all along.

With her spine pinned to the wall, I pinch her waist tightly, my fingers delving so deep into her flesh, it wouldn't surprise me if I bruise her delicate skin.

Then, I kiss her. Really fucking hard. There is nothing sweet and gentle about it and it's something she needs to get used to because sweet and gentle is not my style.

Her head tilts slightly to the right, while mine angles to the left. Our noses brush and I exhale all of my venomous breath into her mouth, while filling her lungs with my own oxygen.

God, she tastes better than I ever could have imagined. The taste of lemon still lingers on her tongue from the lemonade she drank this morning. I know because I watched her drink it.

Our mouths part, teeth clanking as my tongue overpowers hers. Every now and then, Riley likes to show me she has all the control. In the bathroom at the party last weekend, she pushed me into the shower and yelled at me. Minutes ago, she forced me out of class and into the hall.

Feeding into her demands is a power move on my part, and it's working.

Riley's hand slides up to my cheek, cupping it in her soft palm. Her other hand moves to the back of my head and her fingers fist around my hair.

A subtle moan slips through her lips, vibrating against my mouth, and I growl in response.

I did that. I forced that pleasurable sound out of her.

I lift her leg, bringing her knee to my waist as I grind myself against her, seeking pressure.

Riley Cross is my own personal drug, and I want to overdose on her. If I could choose my way of death, I'd choose her. I'd rip my heart out of my chest if it meant hers would beat a second longer.

My hand slides abrasively down her side and I stop mid-thigh. Every cell in my body is alerted. My cock throbbing with a vast amount of pressure.

With one hand holding her leg against me, I put the other on the small of her back and thrust her forward. My cock strains against my jeans, fucking starving for her. I move faster, knowing that I just need a minute. That's all it takes when she's around.

Riley pulls out of the kiss, a look of disgust on her face as if she just had some sort of realization. "What...what are you doing?"

I'm dumbstruck. What the fuck does she mean, what am I doing?

I move my mouth back to hers, attempting to pry her lips apart with my tongue.

Her head turns, but I put it back in place. *We're not finished yet.*

"What the hell, Ridge! Let me go!" Her malevolent words spill into my mouth, but she doesn't mean them.

I try again, but she puts up a fight, turning her head and spewing nonsense.

Say something, you fucking idiot. *Anything.* Yell at her. Tell her she started this and you have every intention of finishing it.

Still, I say nothing because my voice fails me. Time and time again, it fucking fails me and I wanna tear out my vocal cords because what good are they if I can't even talk to her?

"Dammit, Ridge! What the hell do you want from me?" Her voice rises to a near shout as she shoves me back a few steps. "Now is the time to say something, and if you don't, I'm walking away and you'll never hear my voice again."

The fuck I won't.

I close the space between us in two big steps, grabbing her again. My thoughts elude me as I grip her tightly.

We just need to get back to that kiss. She fucking loved it. She'll love it again.

I crush her mouth with mine, but she pinches her lips closed tightly. She's resisting me. She's actually fucking resisting me. My hand moves to the back of her neck and I forcefully coerce her lips to stay pressed to mine, not giving her a choice.

She squirms and fights, but I don't stop because I need her to feel what I feel. I know she felt it earlier and I know she can feel it again.

Voices come from down the hall, drawing closer and closer before they hush. Then a familiar voice comes from behind me.

I'm completely caught off guard when Riley's hand flies across my face, slapping me hard.

She really just fucking hit me.

And why the hell am I so turned on?

I'm pulled from my thoughts when Maddox puts a hand on my shoulder, inching me back. "What the fuck, man? Let her go."

The guys he was walking with continue on their way, while Maddox inserts himself into my business, once again.

"Don't you ever come near me again!" Riley slithers from the space between me and the wall, before stalking down the hall.

I spin around, face to face with my best friend, who is about to become my worst enemy. "Mind your fucking business," I snap. "She wanted it."

"The imprint of her hand on your cheek says differently."

I rub my cheek, still feeling the sting of her slap. "It was a misunderstanding. I need to talk to her." I attempt to follow Riley, but Maddox grabs me by the collar of my jacket.

"You need to give her some time to cool off. If you go after her now, you're just gonna make things worse."

"Fuck!" I shout, the sound echoing down the empty hall.

"Let me talk to her for you. See where her head is at."

"No," I say abruptly. "Stay away from her."

The words fly out of my mouth with no thought process behind them, but when I clear my head, it starts to make sense. "Okay," I say, correcting myself, "find out how pissed she is. And keep an eye on her for me. I have some shit to take care of."

His response is just a nod, so I leave him there, walking as fast as I can to get away from this space. A space that will always be a constant reminder of what just happened.

Riley thinks she can be a little tease, huh? She wants to play? Well, I'm fucking ready to play.

CHAPTER 13
RILEY

I STILL CAN'T GET over how aggressive Ridge was yesterday. A kiss is one thing, but the look in his eyes and the tight hold he had on me... It's as if he wanted to prove he could do whatever he wanted with my body. Every time I pushed him away, he pulled me right back in, like I was the crazy one.

I haven't told Scar, or anyone for that matter. No one will understand why I even let him get as close to me as I do. I don't even understand it. It's over, though. I meant it when I told him to stay away from me.

You're darkness and doom.

You shy away from sanity.

My heart jumped and skipped for you.

But only momentarily.

I saw your true colors.

Dark gray and black.

Now you can take your obsession.

And shove it up your ass.

So emo, but so true. I can't believe there was ever a part of me that thought I could be attracted to a guy like Ridge.

"Everything okay?" I jolt at the voice over my shoulder. Not just any voice, it's Maddox.

"Yeah," I tell him, closing my notebook and sliding the pen down the coil binding, reminding me to keep looking for the matching pen that disappeared.

Maddox pulls out the chair beside me in the student center, gives it a turn, and sits down on it with the back of the chair between his legs. "You sure about that?"

"Look," I tell him, "if this is about yesterday with Ridge, I told you when you chased me down that I don't want to talk about it."

"Nah. This is about you, and right now, you seem stressed."

"I am stressed. Your friend is a damn lunatic. What makes him think it's okay to stalk me like this?" I look past Maddox at Ridge, who's literally watching me at this very moment. "It's getting creepy as hell." I gather up my stuff in frustration then stuff it in my bag. My leg flings over the stool I was on and I get up. "You're welcome to come with me if you want, but I have to get the hell away from him."

Maddox steals a glance at Ridge before standing up. "Coffee shop by Delta Chi?"

"Yesss," I gush. "Coffee sounds amazing right about now."

I don't even give Ridge the satisfaction of another look as I head to the door with Maddox. But when a loud crash has me grabbing Maddox's arm, I'm certain Ridge is watching me walk away. The sound of footsteps scattering has me sweeping the area where Ridge was sitting, and sure enough, he's on his feet with his chair tipped over beside him.

I jerk my head back, eyes in front of me. "Why is he like that?"

Maddox plays it off with a shrug and I assume it's because he doesn't want to throw his best friend under the bus, but come on now, someone has to. The guy is a maniac. He's already attacked two men who made passes at me. Maddox might be his friend, but if Ridge's as obsessed with me as I think he is, it won't matter how close they are.

"Hey," I say to Maddox as we're walking out the front doors of the student center. "How close are you and Ridge anyway?"

"Very." His tongue clicks on the roof of his mouth and he pauses for a beat before continuing, "I've known him for as long as I can remember. We're in the same chapter of The Society, from the same small town. Then when he was eleven years old, he moved in with me."

My wide eyes show my surprise. "He did? Why? What happened to his parents?"

I'm being nosey, but I feel like I need these answers. Maybe they'll help me understand Ridge a little better.

We turn onto the sidewalk, walking leisurely in the direction of Delta Chi. The one and only coffee shop on campus sits in front of the property that is the girls' sorority house—lucky for them.

Maddox grips the straps of his backpack. "We were neighbors, best friends, practically family. His dad left when he was young. Just disappeared one night, never to be heard from again."

"That's so sad. And what about his mom?"

Maddox glances over at me and I can tell he's unsure if he should be telling me any of this. His fingers stretch and close around his straps and he bites his lip. "I think you need to ask Ridge all this. It's not really my place to tell."

"I can respect that," I tell him. "But can you answer one question?"

"Depends on the question."

"Has he always been like this? Mysterious and neurotic?"

"Eh." His head seesaws from side to side. "Yes and no. Ridge wears his heart on his sleeve and I'll be the first to tell you, his heart is fucking huge. If you're in his good graces, you're golden. But anyone who's not better watch out because he's a wrecking ball."

All of what he's saying is fairly obvious from Ridge's actions. He's beat the shit out of two guys in the last five days. A fight with Cade hasn't been confirmed, but I'd bet money on it.

"Do you think I'm on his bad side now?"

Maddox looks up at the sky and chuckles before bringing his head back down. "Not even a little bit."

"Wow." I'm not sure what else to say. "I guess...I don't know if that's a good thing or a bad thing."

When he doesn't say anything, I nudge my shoulder against his, an unsettling feeling consuming my stomach. "Well? You're practically his brother. Tell me."

"I really shouldn't..."

Out of nowhere, something hits Maddox's shoulder, and when it drops to the ground, I realize it's a piece of a broken stick. We both skim the area, looking for where it might have come from, but we aren't even under any trees.

How weird.

Before Maddox can even acknowledge what just happened, he reaches into the front pocket of his jeans and pulls out his phone. One glance at it and he stops walking.

I'm two feet ahead of him when I turn around. His wide eyes stay locked on his phone before they slowly slide up to mine. His mouth falls open and he draws his fingers to his lips.

"Is everything okay? You look concerned."

"Uh. Yeah," he stutters. "It's my dad. Go ahead and I'll catch up."

"Okay." I nod. "I've got an hour before my next class so take your time."

I leave him behind me, walking slowly, in hopes he won't

take long. Just that five-minute conversation gave me so much insight into Ridge's behavior. Something had to have happened to his mom for him to move in with Maddox's family at such a young age. I was fortunate enough to have two parents raise me and love me in a warm and happy home. I can't imagine growing up without them. If I had, I probably wouldn't be completely sane either. Then again, lately, I'm not even sure I *am* sane.

It's been getting better, though. And I'm surprised to find how much I like being in Maddox's company. It's a sticky situation with Ridge, but I have no loyalty to him. Maddox does, but that's his choice to make. Doesn't matter, though. We're just friends—if we're even that.

Who knows, maybe after today, we will be.

Pulling open the door to the small coffee shop, the bell jingles overhead. You'd think I had a horn sticking out of my forehead with the way everyone looks at me. I don't come here often since the student center also has coffee, but I'm no stranger to the place.

The majority of the girls here are Delta Chi girls. Thankfully, Melody isn't one of them. This might be a good opportunity to talk to Carly, the president of the sorority, about joining the decorating committee. While she's intimidating with her seniority at BCU, paired with her gorgeous looks—I'm talking drop-dead gorgeous, sleek blonde hair that rests in the middle of her back, saucer blue eyes, and legs for days—she's always been super kind, so I'm only slightly nervous.

"Hey, Carly." I lift my hand in an awkward wave. The other two girls at her table lift their heads, giving me the impression they're not thrilled with me interrupting them. Carly smiles widely, showing her paper-white teeth.

"Oh, hi," she says, her southern accent thick. "Y'all, this is... Ryder. We met during the freshman welcome party."

"Actually, it's Riley. But yes, we did meet. I'm surprised you remember."

"Of course I remember. How can I forget that stunning streak of purple in your hair?"

For some reason, my fingers find the streak and I twirl it around my finger like a jittery schoolgirl. "Thanks. I was gonna do pink. Then blue. And somehow settled on purple. Anyways," my tone shifts to a higher note, "enough about me. I actually wanted to know if you need help with any of the decorating around campus for Halloween? I was always super involved in my previous schools and I'd love to give a helping hand." I draw in a deep breath, refilling my lungs. Oh my god, how am I still standing after that? I don't think I took a single breath.

Carly shares a look with her friends, who force fake smiles and shrug their shoulders.

"Um. Yeah," she chirps. "We don't usually get offers like this, but sure. We'll take all the help we can get." Her hand shields her mouth as she whisper-laughs. "Some of the new girls are a little lazy, if you know what I mean."

"Oh, I'm sure. There's always a few bad eggs in the bunch." A really weird, awkward sound that I think is a laugh climbs up my throat. Why am I making this more tortuous than it needs to be?

"Great. Sunday we'll be getting together in the meeting room at the football stadium. Three o'clock."

"I'll be there." I shoot her a thumbs-up and literally want to bite the stupid digit off. I stick it back down quickly, then turn around and head straight for the counter.

Nice one, Riley. I'm sure they're thrilled to have you help, you awkward idiot.

After ordering a mocha latte, I take one of the stools at the counter at the end, leaving an empty seat for Maddox.

Five minutes in, and I've already downed the entire thing.

I spin around on the stool, looking at the door as if I expect him to suddenly walk in. When he doesn't, I tip my cup back, hoping for one more drop. Now I feel like a dumbass, just sitting here alone with nothing to drink. So, I flag the student barista down. "Could I get another mocha latte, please?"

"Sure thing. For here or to-go?"

"Here, please." I slide her my student card to pay for my second cup. She leaves it sitting there until she returns with my coffee.

I bring the cup to my mouth, sucking in some of the whipped cream, when someone pulls out the stool beside me. At first I assume it's Maddox. But before I even get a look, his scent hits me.

I set my mug down on the counter and swivel in my stool to face him. "Why are you here? Where's Maddox?"

An audible growl escapes him and his hands fold together, landing on the countertop with a thud. Neck twisted, he glowers at me, as if I'm the one who's done something wrong.

"Well? Cat got your tongue?"

It's cruel, but for the love of all that is mighty, this guy is fucking creeping me out.

I grab my card off the table and stuff it back into my bag, not bothering to search for my wallet. I just need to keep my hands busy, so I don't slap him in front of all these people.

"You know what?" My legs fling over the opposite side, and I stand up. "Fuck you," I deadpan, eyes on the barista who's coming my way. I hold up my half-empty coffee mug. "Can I get this in a to-go cup, please?"

In two seconds flat, Ridge is at my side all crazy-eyed and weird. His hand reaches toward my face, but I swat it down. "Don't touch me. I told you to stay away from me."

His fingers tangle around my wrist, squeezing hard, and

humiliation flushes my entire body with heat when I see the Delta Chi girls watching.

Their eyes are full of panic as they whisper. Probably something like, 'Is that her boyfriend? Should we help her?'

I try to pull away, gritting my teeth while remaining calm as not to pull more attention from those around us. "Let me go."

He doesn't. Instead, he uses his other hand to sweep his finger across my nose. When he holds it up, there's a dollop of whipped cream on the tip of his index finger. I cringe when he slides it into his mouth and sucks it off.

"You're..." I can't even think. I'm too stunned. "What the hell is the matter with you?"

He grins devilishly, not a care in the world about the unwanted attention pinned to us.

The barista returns with my coffee and I jerk my hand away quickly before snatching it off the counter.

I have to get out of here.

My body can barely keep up with my feet as I hurry to the door. Once I'm out, I don't stop until I'm far enough away from him.

It's apparent Maddox isn't coming back. *Ugh!* Do I have 'stank pussy' tattooed on my forehead or something? Why the hell am I so resistible to normal guys?

Earlier this week, Scar mentioned a party at the hot springs. Didn't plan on going. But my plans just changed. I need to find myself a guy, so *this one* leaves me the hell alone.

CHAPTER 14
MADDOX

SITTING on the wall in front of the main campus building, I'm staring out at the high-top mountains in the distance. A few peaks are already snow-covered, but down here, it's all green. Some might argue that it's not really snow but clouds over the top of them. Goes to show that not everything is as it seems, but there is always an answer. There is always a right one and a wrong one. Right? Or am I wrong?

Forget about the fucking mountains.

Think, Maddox!

An hour ago, I was walking with Riley and everything was great. I was enjoying her company. Even felt a little rush of giddiness inside that I wasn't planning to explore because of Ridge. The next minute, everything changed. Then I stood her up because I can't face her until I know what the fuck I plan to do.

I grab my phone beside me and re-read the messages from my dad for the third time, just to make sure I didn't miss something that proves it can't be true.

Dad: Foul play on the victims was confirmed. Evidence was found at the second site and handed over to us by our detective on the inside. We're certain it's a member. Maybe even more than one.

Me: Damn. So those guys were murdered? Who are the suspects?

Dad: Based on the evidence handed over? Samson Cross's daughter. Riley Cross. She's a student there. I need you to keep a close eye on her, Maddox. Report to me with any wrongdoings or anything suspicious. She's also one of the students being investigated by The Sleuths in the governor's death. Her friends might be involved, too.

Me: No way! Where the hell are you getting this information? I'm gonna call you. This doesn't make any sense.

Dad: I'm on a job right now. Can't talk. The evidence is damning. They found a stainless-steel pen in the ash and rubble with her name engraved on it.

Me: Okay. Well, someone might've borrowed it or set her up.

Dad: Too much of a coincidence with The Society's ongoing investigation into the governor's death. My gut tells me she's involved. These are things you need to learn as a Guardian, Maddox. Trust your instincts. Things aren't always what they seem, but there is always an answer. That pen didn't get placed there after the fact. It landed while the fire was still hot.

Me: You're sure about this? You really think it's her?

Dad: I'd bet my life on it.

> Me: Tell me everything you know about her. Everything!

> Dad: You know I can't tell you everything, son.

> Me: Then tell me everything you can.

> Dad: She's a Guardian, Maddox. That's why it's imperative this doesn't get out. If Samson Cross caught wind of any of this, he'd raise hell. We can't risk him trying to cover it up too fast.

I've known Riley was a Guardian, but my father telling me so proves just how serious this is to him. He'd never let such valuable information slip.

> Me: So it will be covered up, regardless?

> Dad: From law enforcement? Yes. From the other Elders? Not likely. I'll be working this case day and night. I expect you to do the same from your side of things. I'll be in touch.

I can argue that Riley's not capable of murder, but I know the truth—Riley killed the governor.

But this? No way.

Fuck. I slam my phone against the concrete wall. A crack spreads on the back of the case, but that's the least of my concerns right now.

What the hell am I supposed to do with this information? What's right and what's wrong?

Do I tell Ridge? We tell each other everything.

He'll want to help her. I warned him this was a possibility. No matter what I said, he was blinded by his obsession for her. And still, no matter what I do, it's all he'll see.

But I see it, too. Riley isn't the type of storm you run from, she's the storm you chase. And fuck if we're not both headed right into the eye.

———

"Come with us tonight," I tell Lev, snatching the bag of potato chips from his lap. I stuff my hand in and get a fistful before tossing it back to him.

There's a party at the hot springs tonight. No significant planning went into the party, but there'll be a couple kegs and a bonfire. Boulder Cove is well-known for their hot spring pools. There are about seven of them spread out through the small town. The one here is off-campus, but it's on private property owned by The Blue Bloods. Technically, the area is off-limits to students, but we've been frequenting them for years and have yet to get penalized.

"Not really my thing," Lev quips, confident in his decision.

Lev doesn't go out much, or at all for that matter, but the last couple days he's been a little livelier, so it's worth a shot.

"Might be a good chance to work toward those new goals you made for yourself."

Lev snarls, crumpling the chip bag in both his hands. "Fucking knew I shouldn't have told you about those. Now you're gonna hang 'em over my head, aren't you?"

"Not hanging anything over your head. Just trying to help a friend."

Part of Lev's therapy involves making a list of goals he wants to accomplish over a course of a couple months. In confidence, he told me his number one goal was to get out more. His second goal: find out if he's capable of loving another human.

Lev tosses the empty bag on the table in front of the couch, wipes his greasy hands on his sweatpants, and stands.

"Then I guess I better put on my best party clothes."

"Fuck yeah!" I beam, hands in the air. This is monumental. Lev hasn't attended a party at all since the start of summer, and even then, he only stayed for no more than twenty minutes. Social anxiety mixed with his temper don't pair well. He needs this, though. These are days he won't get back, and as his friend, I don't want him to regret missing out on so much.

Lev grabs some clothes from his drawer in the corner of the room, then heads for the door. "Gotta take a quick shower then I'll be ready."

As he goes out, the door flies back open, and Ridge comes in, his frustration apparent when he slams the door so hard, the mini fridge against the wall rattles.

"Your girl making you cry again?" I tease, knowing I'm just fueling the fire.

"Fuck off and tell me what she said?"

I raise an eyebrow, unsure what he's talking about. "What she said?"

"You're supposed to talk to her for me. See where her head is at. Last night you said you had nothing, so I assume that's why you were with her today."

Shit. I forgot all about that. "Oh, right. Haven't really had a chance, but I'll talk to her tonight."

"Really?" He lifts his chin, fostering a look of indignation. "Because I saw you two leaving the student center earlier and you seemed to be conversing just fine."

"It was a short-lived walk. Don't get your panties in a bunch."

I knew he saw. Heard the chair slam and saw his face. It was no surprise—Ridge always has his eyes on Riley. But she still has a life and she's allowed to have friends.

"A walk in silence, I presume?"

"Chill out, man. It slipped my mind. But I'll talk to her tonight."

"Don't bother. It's time I talk to her myself."

I tsk. "Yeah. Okay."

"Is that funny to you?" His voice rises a few octaves. "You think it's funny that I haven't talked to her yet? That I *can't* talk to her?"

"Chill the fuck out. Never said it was funny. Just find it hard to believe after all this time you're suddenly going to talk to her."

The door comes open and Lev steps inside, his damp hair proof that he just got out of the shower. With his hand held to the frame, he observes the tense situation. "You two at it again?"

"No," I lie. "You ready?"

Ridge does a double take between Lev and me before stomping his feet to the mini fridge. Crouched down, he takes out his flask and sticks it in the inside pocket of his jacket. "Ready for what?"

"The party. I'm going with you guys," Lev tells him, his lack of enthusiasm apparent.

The shift in Ridge's mood is immediate. The scowl on his face is replaced with a wide grin. "Hell yes!"

Ridge, Lev, and I have a lot of differences, but one thing we have in common is our determination to be there for one another. No matter what happens, or who comes into our lives, or even who leaves—we've always got each other's backs.

Which is exactly why I need to do everything I can to protect my boy. Even if it means hurting him a little in the process.

CHAPTER 15
RILEY

AFTER GETTING STOOD up by Maddox earlier, my mind is on one track—get fucked up tonight.

It's so hard always being the odd one out. Scar with Crew, Jagger, and Neo. Hell, even Cade has Melody and Hannah. I'm not asking for a relationship. A girl just needs a little attention every now and then from someone who is not a deranged stalker or a rapist.

Speaking of... "Still back there?" I ask Scar, as we walk down the beaten trail to the hot springs. It's a short distance from campus. Not nearly as far as the hot springs were from The Academy we attended last year.

Scar retorts with, "Yup."

"How many of them?"

She makes no attempt to be inconspicuous as she turns around, now walking backward. "Three. The crazy one. The cute one. And the weird one."

It's funny that I know exactly who she's talking about and in which order—Ridge, Maddox, and Lev. Although, they're all cute, in their own way.

"Who's the cute one?" Jagger asks, walking with us on the other side of Scar.

"Maddox," she tells him. "But don't worry, babe. You're much cuter."

Jagger grabs Scar by the waist and spins her around. A humorous yelp escapes her as she crashes into his side. "You want me to take care of them?" Jagger asks. "I've got no problem putting those fuckers in their place."

"No," I blurt out. "The last thing I want is for any of you guys to get in trouble because of me. It's fine. Ridge doesn't bother me...much." The last word came out in a whisper, meant only for me, but Scar heard it. I'm warranted with a look of disappointment because, up until now, I've made it known that I don't view Ridge as a threat to me. Now, I'm not sure what to think of him.

"You and Scar are always together," Jagger says, a seriousness to his tone. "Not to mention you live together. Not so sure I like these freaks hanging around. If anything happens to my girl—"

"Nothing's gonna happen," Scar cuts in. "Not to me and not to Riley," Scar assures him. "Right, Ry?"

My girl. Is it terrible of me to want someone to refer to me as their girl?

For the love of God. I need to get out of my own head. If I'm not a downer in the dark over the past, then I'm a whiny ass who's over feeling unloved. But is it so bad to just want someone to love me? Does Ridge love me? Sometimes I think maybe he does, but that guy is so damn intense. I can't imagine him ever being the type of guy I want. I want someone who will get excited for the holidays with me. Watch movies in bed. Laugh at my stupid jokes. And hold me when I feel like I'm going to fall apart.

Scar snaps her fingers directly in front of my face, causing me to go cross-eyed. "Earth to Riley."

My eyebrows shoot up. "Huh?"

"I was telling Jagger nothing is going to happen to me, or you."

"Oh. Right. We're fine. I barely even know them, but they're harmless. No need to worry. Let's just relax and have some fun tonight. Forget they even exist."

"If you barely know them, then how do you know they're harmless?" Jagger asks the question, and I'm not sure how to answer it.

"Intuition, I guess. Now, can we drop it?"

The smell of cedar embers fills my senses, telling me we're close. With each step, the music grows louder, as does the voices of students trying to be heard over the music.

A minute later, we arrive. A rush of excitement swirls through me and it's the first time in a while I've felt like myself. I used to live for this scene—bonfires, crowds, and fun. I was the life of the party and people literally flocked around me because of my magnetic energy.

Crew and Neo spot us from the other side of the fire and make their way in our direction. Scar takes my hand in hers and we meet them halfway.

A loud boom coming from the fire has my body jolting, feet practically leaving the ground. I grab Scar's arm, holding it like my life depends on it.

Scar rubs my sleeved arm, calming me down. "It was just a firework some idiot threw in the fire. You're all right, babe."

She's right. I am all right. Nothing happened. I'm still standing. Still alive.

"What's up, Ry?" Crew asks as he and Neo join us by the fire. "You doing all right? Is this too much for you?"

"Actually, I'm doing great. I'm glad Scar talked me into coming."

Crew, Jagger, and sometimes Neo, all treat me like I'm Scar's little sister. It's sweet how they, too, look after me. But as with Scar, I need to show them I am stronger than what I appear to be.

"You all go ahead and do your thing. Drink. Orgy. Whatever the night brings."

"All of the above, please." Jagger smirks, grabbing Scar by the waist and pulling her close. Neo stands by quietly, sipping on his beer. He's not much of a talker and not very friendly. Actually, he's the least friendly person I know, but he's come a long way since he's joined Scar's harem.

"Where are you going?" Scar asks. "You really shouldn't be wandering around alone with those creeps lurking."

Neo finally speaks. "What creeps?"

"There's this guy who's been watching Riley. Like all the damn time."

Crew's eyebrows cave in, a look of concern on his face. "What guy?"

"You guys. It's nothing. Just let it go." I turn my attention to Scar, who I know is going to make this a thing with the guys. "Please," I drag out the word. "Do not make this a big deal. The last thing I want at this school is negative attention."

"Then you better promise me you'll tell me if Ridge does anything to make you feel uncomfortable."

"I promise. Now, I'm going to get a drink."

Scar steps out from Jagger's hold on her waist. "I'll go with you."

"No. I'll be okay. We have to loosen this leash, Scar."

She fakes a pout and it's cute how much she cares. Scar is not one for being soft, but lately, she has been with me. "You sure?"

"Absolutely. It's a party. Go have fun with your guys. I'll catch up with you later."

She grabs my hand, squeezing it. "Scream if you need me."

"Like...help?"

"Sure." She laughs. "Help works."

The second I turn away from the fire, my eyes land on Ridge. Only, he's not looking at me. He's talking to a girl.

Something stirs inside me. A feeling I don't like. It's a mixture of butterflies and bee stings.

His arms are stiff with his hands in the front pocket of his jeans, and he looks past her while she talks, but whatever she's talking about brings a smile to his face. And when she rubs her hand down his arm, I wanna chop it off and toss it in the fire.

Then it happens. His mouth moves.

Rage consumes me and I can't stop myself as I walk steadfastly toward them. I'm dodging people left and right when they walk away...together.

My eyes stay locked to Ridge's leather jacket, but when someone steps in front of me, blocking my view, I lose it.

"Move, please." I look around him, but he hinders my view once again. I step to the left, and he does the same. "Listen, asshole..." I look up and swallow hard. "Hey, Maddox."

"Where ya headed?" he asks, a seriousness to his tone.

"I was just going to get a drink," I lie.

Dammit. Ridge is gone. How dare he talk to another girl when he can't even say a single word to me. And where are they going? Is he leaving with *her*? She wasn't even cute. Or maybe that's my jealousy talking. Oh my god. Am I jealous? *I am!*

"Me, too. I'll join you."

Ignoring Maddox, I find myself still searching for Ridge. But it's pointless. There are over a hundred people gathered at this small parcel of land.

"I'm sorry, what?"

"I said I'll join you. Make peace, if possible. What will it be? Beer?" He reaches into his pocket and pulls out a bottle of liquor. "Or vodka?"

With Ridge still in the back of my mind, I focus on the here and now. I'm still upset with Maddox for standing me up, but it seems he's trying to make up for it.

I snare the vodka from his hand and crack a smile as I twist off the top. "Clear liquor, huh? Where's the whiskey?"

"It just so happens that dark liquor makes a girl I like sick, so I left it behind."

My chest flutters. Did he just admit that he likes me?

"Ahh. A girl you like?" I bring the bottle to my mouth and take a sip while watching him. It goes down smooth and the burn in my chest ignites my adrenaline. After a good shot's worth, I hand it back to him with the top on. "If you like this girl, then why'd you stand her up earlier?"

"I didn't stand her up. Are we talking about the same girl?"

He wasn't talking about me. I'm beyond mortified. Nervously, I fidget with the sleeve of my sweatshirt. "Guess not."

Maddox laughs, mouth curled upward, and he nudges my arm with the bottle. "I'm fucking with you, Riley."

I exhale an audible breath. "You asshole," I tease. "Seriously, though. Why'd you ditch me earlier?"

Maddox takes a drink of the vodka, averting his gaze, then he puts the top on and sticks it back in his jacket. "Got a text from my dad. He's sort of a hard-ass and left me feeling a little defeated. Didn't wanna drag you down with my sour attitude. Do you forgive me?"

The puppy pout on his face makes it hard not to forgive him.

"Sure. I guess I can forgive you. Even if Ridge showed up there instead of you. I'm not kidding, Maddox. I think you need to have a talk with your friend about proper etiquette when approaching someone."

"Oh yeah?" He purses his lips. "If he's so improper, then why were you just trying to chase him down?"

"You saw that?"

He nods. "Mmhm. Maybe this mysterious side to Ridge intrigues you more than you care to admit."

My cheeks fill with air, like balloons on each side, and I blow it out all at once. "Fine. I'll admit, I'm slightly intrigued. I just don't get it. Why won't he talk to me?"

Maddox nods his head to the right and starts walking slowly, talking as we leave the crowded space by the fire. "I shouldn't tell you this, but it's really not his fault. Ridge doesn't speak under immense pressure or when he's nervous. It all started when he was a kid. Believe me, he has a lot he wants to say to you."

I stop walking, and Maddox does the same. "But why would Ridge be nervous around me?"

"Because he likes you. A lot."

I know that to be true. There's no other reason Ridge would watch me the way he does. But the whole nervousness thing seems very childish. "He was talking to that other girl just fine."

"Because she wasn't you." Maddox starts moving again, heading toward a fallen tree that's lying on the ground. "I shouldn't be sharing this with you because it's Ridge's business, and because..."

His words trail off, so I finish them for him. "Because...you like me, too?" Talk about putting myself out there. Wow. I wanna crawl in a hole and die.

Teeth grazing his bottom lip, he smirks. "I did say that, didn't I?"

"You did." I roll my lips together, blushing. Thankfully it's dark, and the only light is the glow of the fire behind me.

Maddox takes a seat on the fallen log and retrieves the

vodka from his pocket. After taking a swig, he passes it to me. "I shouldn't have. Not with everything going on."

With the bottle in hand, I sit beside him, curling one leg under the other, while turning in his direction. "What's going on? Did something happen?"

He's silent for a minute, staring off as he thinks. It's something I notice he does often. Like there are so many thoughts circulating his mind at once that he needs to take a second to sort through them.

"No," he finally says, "not anything you need to worry about." Changing the subject, he nods toward the bottle. "You gonna drink that or just hold it all night."

I bite back a smile as I bring the bottle to my mouth, Maddox watching intently. I tip it back, keeping my eyes on his as the liquid courage slithers down my throat.

As I pull the bottle away, Maddox immediately replaces it with his lips.

The vodka on our tongues collides with tenacity, igniting something inside me that I've never felt before. It's different from my kiss with Ridge, which was both satisfying and intense. This kiss with Maddox appears soft and gentle on the outside while a war wages inside our mouths. Our tongues go head-to-head. A fight for dominance. Before I even realize what's happening, the bottle slips out of my hand, landing next to my feet. Now that my hand is free, I bring it to Maddox's shoulder, curling his jacket between my fingers. One of his hands lands on my hip, while the other cradles my cheek, pulling me closer.

Then as fast as it started, it stops. I shake my head. "Don't stop," I feel the need to beg. This is what I want. That feeling inside me that tells me I'm worthy. That I'm not a third, fourth, or fifth wheel. That I'm the wanted one.

Maddox doesn't let go of me. His nose rests on mine, and he whispers, "This is wrong."

"No. No, it's not."

"But it is. Ridge is my best friend."

My heart is pounding in my chest and the vibration of his jacket proves his is doing the same thing.

"He'll get over it."

"No," he shakes his head, our noses brushing, "he'd kill me. Quite literally, actually." He chuckles and I do the same.

I didn't realize until now how much I really like Maddox. The urge to see where this could go has heightened to an extreme and I wanna throat punch Ridge for being so damn obsessive. He's in the way. He's hindering my chances of getting to know a great guy.

"What the fuck are you two doing?" The voice comes from behind me, and Maddox lifts his head abruptly, letting go of my cheek.

"Lev. What's up, man? I don't think you two have met. This is Riley."

I can only assume from the death glare I'm getting, he's heard of me, but also has zero interest in *getting* to know me.

"Hi," I say, extending my hand to him politely, "I've heard so much about you." It's a lie, but an icebreaker, nonetheless.

Lev narrows his gaze to my hand, and he scoffs. "You talking shit about me to this girl, Maddox?"

"What? No," I intercept the conversation. "Nothing bad. I swear."

Maddox places his hand on my lower back, leading me a few feet away from Lev. "Ignore him. He's not very social. Sucks with words. Don't take it personally."

Ah. Another Neo. Well, if I can handle Neo Saint, then I can handle Lev just fine.

"Maddox is the one you should ignore." Lev raises his voice.

"Take it personally, Riley. Take it very personally." His tone is uncompromising and a bit unnerving. This guy doesn't even know me, but that felt like a threat of sorts.

My eyebrows rise and I tsk. "Well then. I guess we won't all be getting together for Monopoly anytime soon."

Maddox chuckles, taking my arms in both his hands. "Seriously. He doesn't know better."

"Doesn't know better?" I huff. "He's what? Twenty? Twenty-one? He should know better." I look over Maddox's shoulder at Lev, who looks like he wants to squish me in his hands and eat me for dinner. He's cute, but in a punky sort of way. Messy, almost spikey blond hair, and the prettiest blue eyes I've ever seen. All his fingers have rings on them and he, too, has tattoos on his hands, though I can't see what they are from here. Curiosity has me wondering, though.

"Twenty-one. Buys all our booze. He's good for something, I swear." A smile parts Maddox's lips and I'm reminded of how good they felt against mine.

"Well, at least he's got that going for him."

My phone vibrates in the front pocket of my hoodie and I reach my hand inside and pull it out. When I see the sender, my eyes widen, and I stuff it right back in.

"What's wrong?" Maddox asks, while Lev lingers behind him like a bad case of herpes.

Instead of telling him who's texting me, I force a smile on my face and say, "Nothing's wrong. Go ahead and catch up with Lev. He obviously wants something. I'll find you in a bit." I go to walk away but stop mid-turn. "Oh, and sorry about the vodka. It slipped out of my hand."

"It's cool. Plenty more where that came from. You sure you're okay?"

I nod. "Fine. Thanks."

Once there's enough space between me and Maddox, I take my phone back out and read the message from Ridge.

> Ridge: I see you're getting to know my friends. Beware of the blond. He bites.

My gaze sails from face to face in search of Ridge, but he's nowhere in sight.

> Me: Where are you?

His response is immediate.

> Ridge: Around. You look beautiful tonight, by the way.

> Me: Why now? Why are you texting me now, yet you ignored the message I sent you days ago?

> Ridge: I never know what to say. You once asked if you make me nervous. You do.

There's a tingling in my chest and I'm not sure what to think of it. I'm still pissed at Ridge, but after hearing what Maddox said about him not speaking under pressure, it's all starting to make sense.

I walk backward a few steps as I type out another message.

> Me: Why do I make you so nervous?

Unable to take my eyes off the phone, I sit down, almost missing the resting log.

> Ridge: Why don't I make you nervous?

> Me: Maybe you do. But you didn't answer my question.

> Ridge: You've moved me, Angel. You've woken something inside my soul and now it will never rest again. I can't risk fucking it up.

> Me: And what if you already have? I did slap you. Have you forgotten?

> Ridge: I'll never forget. I'd happily let you do whatever you want to me, as long as your hands are on my body. In fact, I want to tattoo your handprint on my cheek as a constant reminder of the first day we kissed.

My breath hitches in my throat. No one has ever said words like this to me before. No one has ever made me feel so seen. They may be words on a phone, but they're coming from Ridge. From deep in his heart, where he's made a home for me.

> Me: Where are you? I want to see you.

> Ridge: Come find me.

I stand up and start walking slowly toward the fire, unsure where to look, but it's a start.

> Me: I'm by the fire now.

> Ridge: I know.

I see Scar holding a drink in the air, waving at me. I'm not sure if she's calling me over, but I wave back and keep on my path of finding Ridge.

Then suddenly, two hands plant on my waist from behind me. I spin around, coming face to face with Maddox.

"There you are." He hands me another bottle of vodka, this one's only three quarters full.

"Where do you hide all these?" I pat his jacket, jokingly. "Do you have an endless supply in there or something?"

"I have my ways."

My phone pings and I steal a glance at it.

> Ridge: Walk away from him.

I gulp. Unsure what to do. Maddox is being so sweet and I want more than anything to continue what we started earlier. But, Ridge is having an actual conversation with me for the first time. There's a desperation inside me that wants to find him and finally talk with him face to face—if he's able to do so.

Maddox bends his knees, getting eye level with me as I'm scouring the crowd. "You seem distracted."

"Sorry," I tell him. "I'm just looking for a friend of mine."

"Riley," Scar hollers over the music from the other side of the fire. "Come here, girl." She's holding up a drink and I use this as my out.

"And I've found her."

"Oh, right. Scar, is it? Isn't she your roommate?"

"Roommate and best friend."

"Sweet. I'll go with you. I don't think I've met her or her boyfriend yet. Which one is it?"

"Boyfriends," I correct him, "Crew, Jagger, and Neo."

Maddox's mouth draws back, and he nods. "Okay then. That's pretty...cool."

My phone pings again and I slide it halfway out of my pocket to read the message.

> Ridge: Walk away from him now, Angel. Don't test me.

My heart races, thoughts swirling. *What do I do?*

"Actually. Would you mind getting me a beer from the keg? I should probably take it easy tonight."

"Yeah. Of course. I'll meet you over with your friends."

"Thanks, Maddox."

Once he leaves, I breathe out a sigh of relief as I take my phone out.

As my finger taps hastily onto my phone, I can't type fast enough.

> Me: Are you threatening me? I don't take kindly to threats.

> Ridge: I don't make threats. I make promises. You're really trying me today, Angel. First the walk out of the student center with Maddox and now this. Why are you letting him get close to you?

Anger ripples through me, heating the blood in my veins. I almost thought we were making progress but then he pulls something like this.

> Me: Why do you care?

> Ridge: Because he's not the one for you. I am.

Ridge is unhinged—unpredictable—and totally freaks me out. But temptation is strong and it's as if he's got a rope around my waist, slowly weeding me toward him. Only, I don't know where he's pulling me from.

> Me: If I'm the one for you, then tell me how to find you.

I've gone in circles, scouring every bit of the area, even

stepped into the woods a few times. Now I'm back at the fire and still don't know where he is.

Minutes have passed since I sent the last message with no response. So I send another...

> Me: Can you give me a hint?

Ignoring everyone around me, I keep searching, but I'm halted when my body collides with another. I look up and I'm face to face with Lev.

"You lost, Trouble?" he asks, tone flat.

My eyebrows pinch together tightly. "Trouble?"

"That's what you are, right? Out there trying to stir up trouble. Playing both sides with two of my friends?"

An airy laugh rushes out of me. "Playing both sides?"

"You always answer questions with questions or are you just fucking dumb?"

I'm rendered speechless. When I met Neo Saint, Scar's boyfriend, I thought I'd seen the worst a guy could get. I was dead wrong. Lev is quite literally the spawn of the devil. I've known him for one hour and have no intentions of knowing him any longer.

"Wow!" My neck stiffens. "You are something else and I don't have time for this. Enjoy your night, *Lev.*" I go to walk around him, but stop myself, unsatisfied with letting him think he can talk to me that way. I spin back around, now at his side. "What kind of name is Lev anyways. It's fucking dumb. That's what it is."

"It means lion, smartass. And you know what lions like to eat?" He leans close, almost too close for comfort. His hot breath fans my face as I watch his lips move with each word they speak, slightly curved upward in a malicious smirk. "Little whores who like to play games," he growls, closing in on me. "And I'm hungry, Trouble. In fact, I'm fucking starving." The next thing I know, his teeth are on my cheek and I'm certain he's going to bite me. When he pulls back, I draw in a deep breath of relief, wiping his saliva from my face.

I expect some sort of malicious laugh, but he's desensitized. Completely void of any emotion, though his words tell me otherwise.

A lump lodges in my throat, but I swallow it down in one gulp. My mind is too stunned to react, so I hold my breath and quickly walk away, feeling like I've been kicked in the gut.

Once I'm out of Lev's reach, I exhale audibly. Tears well in my eyes. No one has ever talked down to me that way. No one. Ever.

Was he threatening me, again?

Lev doesn't know a thing about me. Earlier, he asked Maddox who I was, as if he'd never seen me before in his life. Something tells me he knows exactly who I am, and that thought terrifies me.

CHAPTER 16

RILEY

"NEXT THING I KNOW, Neo is dragging him down the trail by the feet and we're all laughing our asses off while his head ricochets off branches and rocks." Crew takes another sip of his beer, then continues with his story. "So we got him here," he points over to the hot springs where people are parading around in swimwear like it's a hot summer's day, "dumped his ass in, and left him."

I cringe at the mental image in my head. "You guys are downright evil."

"He fucking deserved it," Neo chimes in, one arm wrapped around Scar's waist and the other gripping a plastic cup of beer. "No one grabs our girl's ass and gets away with it."

Scar shakes her head, but the cracked smile on her face tells me she loves the protection she gets from her guys.

It's cute, and I'm slightly jealous.

Everyone continues to engage in conversation while I'm nursing my own beer, eyes feverishly searching for any sign of Ridge or Maddox. I can only ascertain they left the party. Ridge left me hanging with that last message: *Because he's not the one for you. I am.* And Maddox just up and disappeared. I blame myself for brushing him off during our last encounter. I was so eager to find Ridge. I wouldn't blame Maddox if he felt rejected. Though that wasn't my intention at all.

I never fail to complicate things for myself.

Scar plops down on the log beside me in front of the fire. Her arm swings around my shoulder and she pulls me close. "Having fun, babe?"

"Ah. You've escaped the clutches of Neo Saint. Lucky you."

Neo and I have a love/hate relationship. He gives me shit and I give it right back, in my own kind and respectful sort of way. Regardless, he's good to Scar, and I love that for her.

"Quit it." She giggles, bumping her hip to mine. "What's wrong? You look down."

I drop my cup to the ground then I take the open bottle of booze Scar hands me. "No. This is nice. Coming tonight was a great idea." I down a good two shots' worth of the liquor, hoping to make it an even better night.

"Easy, killer." Scar snatches the bottle back and holds it up, studying it. "This is potent shit. Like, eighty proof or something like that."

"Even better." I waggle my brows, while attempting to grab the bottle, but she laughs and takes a drink for herself before handing it back to me.

"This is better than just *nice*, right? No stress over school. No idiot guys around. Just us. Having a good ole time."

I point to my mouth that's rimmed with the bottle. I tip it back and the liquid slides down, warming my stomach. My mouth draws back after that drink, cringing at the grotesque taste. "That is definitely potent. And you're right. This is fun. It's not raging party fun, but it's relaxed, and I'm having a decent time."

Those words were nothing but truth. I'm actually enjoying the ease of the night, even if my head is swimming with thoughts of Ridge and Maddox, and even Lev. The party has dwindled down, and while there are some plastered idiots raising hell in the distance, those of us circling the fire are enjoying the night.

Scar and I pass the bottle back and forth a few more times, reminiscing about where we were this time last year. So yeah. This night isn't half bad compared to the fucked-up fiasco we were involved in during our time at Boulder Cove Academy.

"I gotta pee," Scar announces as she gets to her feet. Or attempts to, at least. We both bust out in laughter when she stumbles onto my lap, taking us both to the ground.

My arms wrap around her, holding her like she's a warm blanket while giggles escape us both. "Don't take her from me," I sing, while Crew lifts her up.

I hold her tighter, feeling like I'm going to piss my pants from how hard we're both laughing.

"All right. I think it's time to get you two tucked in for the night."

"Whaaaa," Scar cries. "I wanna stay here until the fire burns out and the sun comes up."

She rolls off me and I lie there, flat in the ash-covered dirt, with my arms spread out. "Let's make ash angels."

Scar plops down beside me. "I wanna make an ash angel."

"Oh no, you don't." Neo tucks his arms under her pits and lifts her up, putting a damper on our fun. "I'll bring Scar back to our place," he tells Crew and Jagger. "One of you take that one back to her dorm."

"That one?" I scoff. "Is that who I am? *That one?*"

Scar blows me a kiss as she's being hauled away. "You're much more than that, babe. I'll come home in the morning. You okay without me tonight?"

"I survive every other night you stay with the guys. I'll survive tonight, too." I blow her a kiss back. "Love you."

Next thing I know, Crew is lifting me to my feet. "Such a gentleman, you are." I look up at him, smiling. "Like a big brother who's screwing my best friend." My body sways back and forth, and no matter how hard I try to steady myself, I fail.

"And you're not gonna make this easy on me, are ya?"

"I'm difficult. A downright pain in the ass."

"That you are, Ry."

I'm not sure how or when we make it back to my dorm, but it feels like I blinked and I'm in my bed. I must've passed out somewhere between the party and here.

It's so cozy. So warm. I feel so content. And so fucking thirsty.

Hand stretched out, I slap around on my nightstand until I find an old bottle of water. I down the entire thing, then toss the bottle away from me. It lands somewhere on the floor. Then, I slap my hand around again, searching for my phone, but it's not there.

Dammit. Really don't wanna get up and look for it. I'm beyond wasted and my head is spinning. I'm not even sure I could walk to turn on the closet light I usually keep on.

It's strange that it's off because it's been on since mine and Scar's first night here.

My dry lips smack together and I curl up in a ball with my comforter wrapped snugly around me.

Then I close my eyes, willing myself to go to sleep.

The second they close, they shoot back open when something falls. I'm not sure what, or where, but something definitely fell. "Hello," I whisper, staying as still as a board.

It's so dark. Eerily so. A strange feeling washes over me. And when the mattress at the end of the bed shifts, I realize I'm not alone.

"It's you," I choke out through strained vocal cords. "You're here."

140

"I'm here. I came for you."

I'm stunned. Rendered speechless. He spoke. My God, he has a beautiful voice. Raspy, thick, and masculine.

I feel his presence beside me. He could reach out and touch me. I turn to my side, facing his direction, while freeing my arms from the comforter. I scoot up, hoping to get a glimpse of his face, but it's pointless.

"I wanna see you when you talk. Turn on the light."

He doesn't respond, or do as I ask. He sits down, slumping into the mattress.

"You're drunk, baby girl. You need water." He brings a glass to my mouth and I sip the contents. He doesn't stop until I've guzzled the whole glass of water.

"Thank you," I tell him.

I reach out, touching his bare arm. His skin is ice cold and I'm wondering if he walked here like that. But when I trail my hand farther, I realize he's not only sleeveless, but completely shirtless. My fingers graze over the fluff on his chest, trailing down the cut of his abs. I'm heavily intoxicated and unable to make responsible choices, so when he takes my hand and drags it downward, I don't even second-guess the action. Cupping my hand, he curls my fingers and rests them on his erection that's poking through a pair of sweatpants.

"See what you do to me, Riley?"

His voice again. It sends chills down my spine, but in a good way.

The blanket lifts from my body and he lies down beside me. He's so cold, yet the heat he's radiating makes up for the loss of warmth from the blanket.

"I never found you," I tell him. "You left me hanging."

"I'm here now."

"I'm really angry with you. I shouldn't allow you to lay here with me like nothing ever happened."

His fingers trail up my leg, not stopping until he's rimming the hem of my jeans. In a swift motion, he pops the button, and while I should stop him, I don't. I'm not sure if it's the alcohol swimming through my bloodstream, or the curiosity of how far he'll go—how far I'll *let* him go.

"What are you doing?" I ask, but he keeps his lips tight and doesn't speak.

When he lifts up and tugs my pants and panties down, my heart gallops. He doesn't seek approval, or let me aid in the removal. He just tugs them off in one quick jerk, until I'm lying there naked from the waist down.

Ridge maneuvers his body until he's blanketing mine. I wince as my back sinks into the mattress from the full weight of him lying on top of me.

Biting hard on my bottom lip, I battle the thoughts in my head:

I should stop him.

But I want this.

It's been so long.

I barely know the guy.

I'm drunk as shit.

And hungry.

A burger sounds so fucking good.

I wonder if the student center is still open.

With no tenderness behind his action, he shoves two fingers deep inside me. I whimper as my body shoots upward, my skull crashing into the headboard.

My mouth gapes and he leans down, breathing audibly between my lips without touching them. "Where's your sweet spot, baby girl?"

He doesn't smell nearly as good as he usually does. The scent of stale beer rolls off his tongue, so I turn my head.

Is this really happening? It feels like a drunken dream. I don't know what's real and what isn't.

His fingers flex, spreading me apart. There's a bite of pain and I'm certain this is no dream.

Tingles shoot through my body, a feeling I'm not foreign to. I've been fingered before. I've done everything but have actual sex. My heart beats faster at the realization that tonight might be the night. Will I allow it? Will he give me a choice?

Fingers curled, he digs deeper, and I yelp.

"Ah. There it is," he croons into my ear. My ass lifts off the bed, seeking friction. Hands on his back, fingernails delving into his skin. "You like when my fingers fuck you, baby girl?"

My only response is a whimper because I'm not sure if I do. He's so aggressive. So rough. My chest rises and falls rapidly as I battle my internal thoughts. I should stop him. *Why am I not stopping him?*

With one hand to his chest, I subtly push him. "I'm really drunk. Maybe we should—"

I'm silenced by a hand over my mouth and flags are raised. "Shhh. I'll take care of you, baby girl."

My thoughts are swirling, and the faster his fingers move, the quicker my head spins.

He doesn't stop. Instead, he rests his forehead against mine.

Another finger slides in, making that three inside of me. I enter a breathless state, squeezing his shoulder blades while lifting my head against his.

It's okay. This is okay. Just relax. Enjoy it.

Everything is so foggy. My eyes feel heavy and I can barely keep them open.

For a moment, I'm certain I fell asleep, but my heart pounds as my eyes shoot back open.

My hips roll, trying to get into it, and after a minute or two,

I do. Electricity ripples through me, hitting every nerve in my body.

I can't enjoy this. I won't do it. Not like this.

But my body is not my own when I hold my breath and my pussy clenches around his fingers.

I attempt to mask the sounds of my pleasure, but it's pointless. One by one, moans slip between my lips and I cry out in ecstasy.

My eyes close and I fight like hell to open them, but they're too heavy.

Slowly, I fade into a deep, dark sleep.

CHAPTER 17

RIDGE

"YOU LOOK LIKE SHIT." Maddox states the obvious as he strolls into our dorm room with a beverage holder and three coffees.

"I feel like shit. Wish I could say it was the booze, but unfortunately, that's not the case."

I haven't looked in the mirror, and don't really care to. I know as soon as I do, I'll have an even greater urge to murder Zeke with my own bare hands.

The fucker jumped me last night. Completely caught off guard, I had no chance to defend myself.

I'm not sure who his accomplice was, because he ran off, but I will find out.

"Don't worry, man. Lev and I have already talked and that son of a bitch is gonna pay with every fucking bone in his body."

It's odd hearing Maddox talk like this. He's usually the mediator. Always trying to keep the peace, but lately, he's been making waves. I'm not even sure who this guy standing in front of me is. Sure as fuck isn't my loyal best friend.

I scoff at his remark. "You mean, the same way you should

145

pay for the shit you pulled last night? And the day before? Oh, and how about the day before that?"

He sighs, handing me a cup of coffee. "This shit again?"

I turn my nose up at his offering, my pride front and center. "Yes. Again and a-fucking-gain until you admit you've got a thing for her. This little show of telling me I should give up on her was all just part of your game, wasn't it?"

His silence is telling. I don't need to hear the words. I know he's caught feelings for my girl. Honestly, I don't blame him. Riley's perfect. The only flaw I've found is her ability to tease the fuck out of me. It could be the magnitude of my love for her making her appear that much more exquisite, but I doubt it. I'm sure every guy in this school has a boner for her. The thought alone makes the vein in my neck throb.

"Don't have feelings for her, Ridge. In fact, it's not like that at all. I'm a Guardian and it's my job to protect the students here. Maybe that's exactly what I'm doing."

"Fuck off," I snap. "Protect the students? From Riley?" An unamusing laugh bursts out of me. "You've lost your damn mind."

He shrugs, taking back the coffee he got me and setting it on the table. "I'm not saying that's the case. But she's got a past and needs an extra eye on her. Just so happens, I've got both of them on her. If I remember right, you told me to do just that."

My voice rises to a shout. "I told you to keep your eyes on her. Not your fucking hands and mouth, dumbass. And it was only that one day. One fucking day, and now you're everywhere she is."

"I beg to differ. I'm here and she's currently at the coffee house with Scar." He takes a sly sip of his coffee, peering at me over the cup with a smirk.

Something awakens inside me. "You saw her?"

He nods and it's such a cocky fucking nod that I wanna tip

his cup and splash his face with hot coffee. "Did you talk to her?"

Pausing for a beat, he sets his cup down and licks his lips. "No."

"Good. Ya know, if you were any other guy, I'd be serving Lev your dick on a platter for breakfast. The sick fuck would probably eat it, too."

"I didn't talk to her because she looked stressed. She and Scar were deep in conversation and I didn't wanna interrupt."

My heart pangs with agony. "She was stressed?"

"Something was definitely wrong."

In a knee-jerk reaction, I flip the hood on my sweatshirt and grab my wallet and keys off the table.

"Because that's the kind of guy I am, Ridge." His voice rises as I pull open the door, and I know it's intentional. "I don't interrupt important—"

I slam the door closed, shutting out the rest of his sentence. He can play the part of the almighty good guy, but Maddox is no better than me. When he falls in love one day, he'll understand the lengths I'm willing to go to for this girl. And when he does, I won't judge him. Hell, I'll even help him bury the bodies.

———

The looks I'm getting on my walk to the coffee shop confirm that my face is royally fucked. When I stop at the glass window, peering in at a teary-eyed Riley, I catch my reflection.

Fucking Zeke. A busted lip and two black eyes that match Cade's. At least my nose isn't broken. But the pain at the base of my skull is proof that he got me good. I rub the top of my head, feeling a goop of dried blood.

The asshole came out of nowhere. I was standing by a tree,

texting Riley, and bam! He sucker punched me right in the back of my head. I went straight down, too stunned to react, then the blows just kept coming. He had on a mask, but I was able to pull it down enough to see who it was.

Ready or not, shithead. I'm coming for ya.

I walk into the coffee shop, wearing a pair of bloodstained gray joggers and a solid black hoodie. For once, it's my own blood—my damn head wouldn't quit bleeding last night. I can imagine I look like hell, but it doesn't matter. I needed to see for myself if Riley was hurting. Sure enough, she is.

Pulling open the door, a bell jingles overtop, grabbing the attention of everyone inside, but most importantly, it grabs Riley's attention. If looks could kill, I'd be stone-cold dead right now. She pins with me a scathing glare, tears pinching out of each eye. Then she lifts her hand slowly, giving me her middle finger.

At the same time, Scar rises from her seat at the corner booth, ready to come at me, but Riley waves her back down.

What the fuck did I do this time?

I take the first open booth and sit down, still able to see my angel if I lean out enough.

Didn't drink much last night. In fact, I only had one beer. My messages to her were cordial. I was polite and kind. I don't get it. Why's she so damn pissed?

Screw this. I slide out of the booth, bumping into a barista carrying a tray of coffee. At least, she was. Now the mugs are shattered glass and spilled coffee at my feet.

Stepping over the mess, I walk toward Riley, who's taking in my battered face, along with Scar. Riley raises a hand. "Don't come near me," she sputters and chokes, and it's obvious she's been crying.

I stop walking, a bit taken aback by her behavior, but also loving the challenge. I take another step, then another. Each one has her eyebrows lifting higher and higher on her flawless forehead. "Ridge," she warns, feet now outside of the booth while she remains sitting.

Scar stands up, shoulders drawn back, and she grits out, "Walk the fuck away, asshole, or I'll fuck your face up even more than it already is."

Everyone heard her. Everyone is watching. But I don't pay them, or Scar, any attention. I crouch down beside Riley. My mouth opens, ready to talk. Finally ready.

But...

I don't.

I don't say anything. Nothing. Not a word.

My chest is rattling, pulse rapid-firing against my wrists. I wanna slice open those scars beneath the hammering vein and try again. That's how painful this is. That's how bad I want to talk to my angel.

Scar steps out from the booth, fuming, but Riley softens her tone and says, "It's okay, Scar. I'll deal with this asshole and meet you back at the dorm."

"Uh-uh." She shakes her head. "Not a chance in hell am I leaving you with him."

"I'm fine. I promise."

Scar's shoulders slump in defeat before she snatches her phone off the table then points it at me. "You hurt her again and I will claw your fucking eyeballs out."

I roll said eyeballs, knowing she doesn't stand a chance. Then again, that girl is feisty as fuck. She could teach Riley a thing or two. Might aid her in fending off all the guys who are pining for her.

I watch Scar walk away and once she's out the door, I return my attention to Riley. Still kneeling, I attempt to grab her hand, but she snatches it away—playing hard to get again. This is all a game to her, isn't it? I chase; she runs.

"You're unbelievable. Wouldn't surprise me if you beat your own ass just so I'd feel pity for you. That's how psychotic you are." Riley spins her legs back under the table, her hands folding on top of it as she stares out the window, not even giving me the satisfaction of eye contact. "First, you waste an hour of my time at the party, playing hide-and-seek. Then, you come into my room when I'm shit-faced..."

What?

"...you undress me and..." Her voice drops a few octaves as she tries to get the words out. "...you put your fingers inside me."

Is she fucking joking right now?

"...and you drugged me."

Her room? Drugged? What the hell is she talking about? I didn't go to her room last night.

"Oh." She finally looks at me. "Now you can't talk again? You talked last night. What's the problem, Ridge? Did the guilt eat your vocal cords?"

Talked to her last night? No. I didn't. Fuck. I'm light-headed. I grab the sides of my head, feeling like all the blood has drained from my face. Someone went into her room? Someone...touched her?

No. God no!

"Well, asshole!" she stammers, "What is it? Why are you here? What did you forget to say last night that you need to say now? Did you come to finish me off? You didn't steal my virginity last night when I passed out so you want it now? Well, Ridge? Out with it!"

When I say nothing, she catapults from the booth, knocking me out of her way. My first instinct is to give her space, but space isn't something I allow between her and me.

I'm in her shadow as she tears open the door in a fit of rage. That damn bell jingles, stirring everyone in their seats, and I reach up, ripping the damn thing off the frame before tossing it in the snow. Stupid fucking thing.

A barista hollers something at me, but I ignore her and trail right behind Riley, who's picking up her pace.

"Leave me alone!"

I don't. I can't. Instead, I take three large steps and grab her by the back of her arm.

"I said leave me alone!" She jerks her arm, but I grip her tighter.

"I didn't come in your fucking room," I blurt out, barely recognizing my own voice. It was my voice, wasn't it? I said the words? "I...I didn't come into your room, Angel. It wasn't me."

Fucking finally! A rush of relief washes over me.

She turns around, her eyes widening in horror, and I'm not sure if it's because of the sound of my voice or my remark about it not being me that went into her room.

"Say something again, Ridge. Anything."

"If I came into your room and undressed you, I'd certainly put more than my fingers inside you, Angel. And I'd *never* drug you."

I don't even see it coming when her hand flies across my face. I'm also not the least bit surprised if she sincerely thought it was me. I can guarantee her that if I touched her pussy, she'd know exactly who it was.

I'm cupping my cheek, babying that slap more than the marks from fists being thrown at my face last night. This one stung a little more. This one felt like the first time she slapped me. Only, it's not a painful sting, it's an eye-opening one. One I deserved because I was not there to protect her last night.

"You like hitting me, Angel." I tap my cheek. "Hit me again. I deserve it. Give me all you've got."

And she does. She slaps me again, this time even harder.

Nodding my head, I bite down on my grin, waiting for the next blow.

But we're both interrupted when Scar joins us again. She's out of breath, panic-stricken.

"You have to come with me."

Scar grabs Riley's arm, but I grab the other, playing tug-of-war. "You're not going anywhere," I tell Riley. "We're not finished here."

Scar pays me no attention as she looks Riley dead in the eye and says, "Someone was pushed from a window at the Willamette House. *Our* window."

CHAPTER 18

MADDOX

Dad: Get to the Willamette House dorms now.
I'll meet you there.

WHAT THE HELL is he talking about, he'll meet me there?

Me: Are you on campus?

Minutes pass with no response and I'm walking as fast as I can to the Willamette House, thanks to the shuttles being overbooked.

Riley stays at the Willamette House. I can only conclude this has something to do with her and the suspicion in my father that Riley has been on a killing spree. Which is fucking ridiculous.

Regardless, if something else has happened, I need to know about it fast before word spreads. My mission in The Society might be to protect the students, but Riley is a student, too, and something tells me she needs protection more than any of us.

The flashing lights are the first thing I see and panic takes over until I'm full-on running toward the gathered crowd.

My dad comes walking briskly toward me, clad in his typical suit and tie.

Hands in the air, I ask, "What the hell happened?"

"Zeke Martin committed suicide. He jumped from a second-story window with a shard of glass in his throat."

"Fuck!" I run my fingers through my hair before lifting my eyes to my dad's. "Zeke's dead?" I quirk a brow, not buying this suicide story. "Glass doesn't just end up in someone's throat. What really happened, Dad?"

"That's what we're going to find out. It was Riley Cross and Scarlett Sunder's window he came out of. I told you that girl was up to no good. Outside law enforcement has deemed his fall intentional, but I know better. The Elders know better. And they're not going to—"

"No. Hell no," I cut him off. "Riley didn't do this. She's not who you think she is, Dad. She's a good girl. She's a Guardian, for Christ's sake."

Dad reaches into his pocket and pulls out a plastic Ziploc baggie holding what appears to be a phone.

I tip my head at it. "What's that?"

"Riley Cross's phone. Our officer on the inside handed it over to me. It was found on the victim."

"Fuuuuck." My head drops back and I blow out a heavy gust of air. "You're kidding me?"

I snatch the phone from his hand, pacing the sidewalk in front of the dormitory, sorting through all the possible scenarios in my head. Zeke jumped Ridge last night. He was pissed off about some bullshit that happened in class and he beat the fuck out of him.

Could Ridge have...

No. Don't go there, Maddox. Not only would Ridge go to the ends of the earth to protect Riley, Ridge isn't a killer—just like Riley isn't. This is too coincidental. Even if they've both taken a life in the past, it doesn't mean either of them are truly capable of murder. Ridge was defending his mom when he killed that rat bastard years ago. And Riley, she was protecting herself and her friends from a dirty politician. We don't live normal lives like those outside of The Society, but it doesn't mean we're all crooked.

"So what the hell do you want me to do? Ask her if it was her? Give her the phone back?"

"No!" He huffs. "I don't want you to take your eyes off that girl. Watch her and look through that damn phone." He takes the phone from my hand and sticks it right into the pocket of my jeans, patting it for safe keep. "This is part of your training, son. This is what you need to do to be a successful Guardian."

"None of this makes sense, Dad. You've gotta believe me when I say I'm positive someone is framing Riley."

"You could be right. But we can't take any chances." He gives the area a lazy sweep before stepping closer and lowering his voice. "I came here with a couple other Elders who are adamant on getting to the bottom of this. I don't know what the fuck you've got going on with that girl, but if you believe her, you better prove her innocence fast before a Sleuth is brought in because once they start digging, no one can protect her from what comes next."

He means abolishment from The Society. Life as she knows it will be over. For her and her family.

"Okay," I tell him, "keep this under wraps a little longer and I'll do what I can from the inside. I've got a foot in the door with Riley. She trusts me."

Dad pats me on the shoulder proudly and I feel a sense of approval from him. It doesn't happen often, but when it does, I'm on a high for weeks. All I ever wanted was to make my dad proud. To be as good at what I do as he is.

The downfall? It's another secret I'm forced to keep from

Ridge and Lev. I don't believe Riley is guilty of murdering these guys, but I have to look at things from every angle. Sometimes believing someone and trusting them are completely different ideas.

CHAPTER 19
RILEY

SCAR and I are walking so fast, our feet can barely keep up. In fact, everyone who overheard us outside the coffee shop is hauling ass to the Willamette House.

I rest my hand over my heart, willing it to slow down, but I know it won't until I know what's going on. "Where did they find him?"

"Beneath a busted-out window. Our fucking window, Riley!"

"How is that possible? I was just in our room."

It's possible she didn't get her facts straight. There are many windows on that side of the house. There are also three stories so he could've fallen from the floor above us.

"Was the curtain closed by any chance?"

Now that I think about it, it was closed. As soon as I woke up, I changed quickly and went to the guys' dorm to get Scar, so we could have coffee.

"And they haven't said who it is?" I ask her, anxious to know who died but also completely terrified that it might be someone we know.

"I...I don't know. A couple names were tossed around while I was weaving through the crowd around the body. Staff was holding everyone back. One person said Archer Redwig. Another said Zeke Martin. Could be anyone."

"And you've talked with Crew, Jagger, and Neo?"

She nods. "Yeah. They're fine. Jagger told me to stay put and that he was on his way to find me. I would have called, but I knew you lost your phone. I take it you haven't found it yet?"

"No."

She takes my hand in hers, squeezing it tightly. "Once things calm down, we'll bring the guys and go look for it."

A quick glance behind me proves that Ridge is still hot on my trail. I turn back around and draw in a deep breath. "He said it wasn't him."

"Who said what?"

"Ridge. He said he didn't come into my room last night."

"And you believe him?"

"He called me baby girl. The guy from last night, I mean. He called me baby girl. Ridge always calls me Angel."

"So the lunatic has many nicknames for you. You don't seriously think he'd tell you the truth, do you?" She mocks him in a masculine voice, "No, Angel. I didn't sneak into your room and drug you just so I could finger you."

"It's just so out of character for Ridge. He might be crazy, but this isn't his style."

Scar will always only see the worst in Ridge because it's the only thing I've given her to go on.

I look over my shoulder again, catching his stare.

But I see beyond that deranged look in his eye. I see someone who would truly go to the ends of the earth for me.

"There he is," Scar says, nodding toward the stretcher with a black blanket draped over the body.

I cover my mouth with my hand and pinch my eyes shut, unable to look. It's all too familiar. Memories of the night the governor died flood my mind. Seeing him like that. Dead.

Jagger and Crew come rushing toward us and Scar meets them halfway. Then, two arms wrap around me from behind, pulling me close. I don't even have to look up to see that it's Ridge. I know it's him.

I push him away, not willing to get close to this guy. I don't trust him and I'm not sure I ever will.

Two of the public safety officers from campus approach Scar, and I step away from Ridge. Though, he never leaves my side.

Scar, Jagger, and Crew all look at me, along with the officers. There's a brief moment where everyone is mute. No one says anything. Then, they all move toward me.

"Riley Cross?" one of the officers asks, and I nod. "We're gonna need to have a few words with you."

My heart drops into my stomach and my legs go weak. I look at Scar, who's just as shocked as I am.

"What is this all about?"

"Both of you," he points from me to Scar, "come with me."

Given no choice, Scar and I follow.

Ridge grabs my arm, jerking me back. "Don't fucking listen to him. You're not going anywhere."

"Let go of me!" It's still surreal hearing him talk, but I can't focus on that right now. Ridge needs to back off before he makes matters worse.

"Sir. You need to step back," the officer says to Ridge. "This is not your concern."

"Like hell it's not," Ridge snaps back. He levels his body with mine, hands on my shoulders. "You don't have to do this."

I lick my lips, thoughts running rampant as I jerk from his touch. "I have nothing to hide. Can you say the same?"

The officer opens the back door of his car as Scar and I approach it. The flashing lights all around make my head spin faster than it did last night. "You're welcome to have a seat inside, or you can stand."

I hesitate, looking at Scar, then Ridge. "Do...do we need a lawyer for this?" Tears pool in my eyes and I can't help but wonder if they think one of us had something to do with this.

"No," Crew says. "I'll call my dad. Don't answer anything this guy asks you."

"But we didn't do anything wrong."

"Doesn't matter," Neo cuts in. "There's always someone who will try and twist your narrative to make you appear guilty."

"Guilty?" I sob. Full of tears and panic. "I'm not guilty of anything."

"We're not accusing you girls of anything. We're talking to all the girls with windows on the east side of the hall." He looks at the guys, as if they're all overreacting. "No need to call anyone's parents. They're not in any trouble."

Relief washes over me and I release all the pent-up air I've been holding in. This is just routine. We're not in any trouble. It's my own guilty conscience getting the better of me. After being questioned by police for the death of the governor, even the lights alone send me into a full-blown panic.

"Listen, Ry," Scar pulls me away and whispers, "things are different here. We don't exist in the laws of the real world. Whatever happened, is not what these officers will be led to believe. Always remember, The Elders have people on the inside who are bigger than any situation we might encounter."

She's right. For once, I'm grateful for the protection we have from The Society. I don't know what happened to the guy who died, but regardless, if foul play was involved, The Elders would never let the Blue Blood name be tarnished by convicting one of our own. They'd kill them first.

The thought sends chills down my spine.

Scar slides in the back seat of the patrol car and I join her. With the door ajar, and Ridge and Scar's guys lingering outside, I whisper, "What if the guy who fell is the one who came into my room last night?"

Scar shakes her head. "It was Ridge, babe. He's playing you. Don't let him get in your head like this."

Something in my gut tells me Scar is wrong. I don't think it was Ridge. And now, I have this dreadful feeling it may have been the guy who potentially flew out of our window.

"Holy fuck," Maddox mutters, appearing out of nowhere. "Zeke fucking Martin committed suicide."

My hand flies to my mouth, eyes wide on Scar. "It's Zeke? Zeke who made a pass at me. Zeke who Ridge threatened in class."

"Calm down, Ry. It could all just be a coincidence." I look at Ridge dumbfoundedly. Completely fucking shook. Scar follows my line of sight. "Unless you think…"

"No. He wouldn't."

Her shoulders rise then fall abruptly. "You said it yourself that you barely know him and his friends."

"Murder, Scar. Really?" I shake my head. "This isn't true crime. There's no way. Besides, you heard Maddox. They said it was a suicide."

"They? Or The Elders? There's a big difference."

I watch keenly as Ridge jerks Maddox by the collar of his shirt, lugging him off to the side. I can't hear what they're saying, but every couple seconds, one or both of them glances in my direction.

The same officer who brought us over here approaches Maddox and Ridge. With a pen, he points to the marks on Ridge's face then begins writing something down.

A few minutes later, the officer comes over to us, crouched down by the door with a notepad in his hand and a pen pressed to it. "Which floor and room do you girls stay in?"

"Umm. Second floor," I tell him. "Room 213."

"And have either of you had any encounters with Zeke Martin over the last twenty-four hours?"

"No," Scar blurts out, honestly, while I shake my head no. Even if it's very possible I did have an encounter with him last night. Now, I might never know.

"How close are you with Ridge Foster?"

My neck draws back in confusion. "What does Ridge have to do with this?"

"Did either of you witness the fight between the two of them last night?"

"Fight?" I gasp. "What fight?"

Officer Dangle—which is the name on his badge—quirks a brow. "I'm going to assume that's a no?"

"No," I say, "I didn't even know Ridge had a fight with Zeke. I mean, I saw the bruises, but, to be honest, I hardly know Ridge, so I didn't press him on it."

The officer writes a few more things down then waves his hand in the air, allowing us to get out. "We'll be in touch if we have any further questions."

My thoughts elude me. I feel like I'm living in some sort of fucked-up nightmare.

Who came into my room last night? Who did I allow in my bed? Was it Zeke? Did Ridge find out and track Zeke down, only to get his ass beat by him—before he killed Zeke?

CHAPTER 20
RIDGE

"WHAT THE FUCK DID YOU DO?" Maddox charges at me the second I walk in the door to our dorm room. When he knocks me into the couch, I simply sink down, getting comfortable.

I've got no idea what he's pissed about when I'm the one who should be livid.

"It was you, wasn't it? You saw that bastard in her room and pushed him out the window."

"Are you kidding me right now? Shut the fuck up." I jump to my feet. "I didn't lay a hand on Zeke." I point to the twin black eyes on my face. "As you can see, he's the one who attacked me."

"And you retaliated. Didn't you?"

"I came home last night and passed the fuck out. Didn't even go to Riley's room."

"How'd you do it, Ridge? Did you push him then jab his throat with glass or was it the other way around?"

Springing to my own defense, I shove Maddox until he crashes into the round table, tipping it over. "How about you tell me where you were last night? Was it you that crept into Riley's room and had your way with her?"

I know damn well it wasn't Maddox. He isn't capable of such a heinous act, but the fact that he's questioning me pisses me off. He doesn't know what I've done, or plan to do, to protect Riley, so he should have no reason to assume I'd go to those kinds of lengths.

Maddox shifts upward, his elbows pressed to the table with his legs dangling off the side. "Someone went into Riley's room last night?"

I can't even fathom the idea of what happened in that room last night. Can't even get the words out to tell Maddox that someone...drugged her, touched her, used her body.

Offering him a hand, I pull him off the table. "Yeah. Someone fucking did. She thought it was me, but as I mentioned, I came home and passed out with ice packs on my face."

He lifts a brow. "Wasn't me. You think it was Zeke?"

I make my way back over to the couch, calmer than I was a second ago. Fighting over this will get us nowhere. "It looks that way, and if the guy were still alive, I'd fucking kill him."

"I wouldn't repeat that if I were you. The last thing you need is your name connected to that guy. You're already gonna be on their radar from the fight."

"Doesn't matter. They ruled it a suicide. Just like they did with the governor."

"But we know better. And so do The Elders." He side-eyes me, and I know I'm not gonna like his next words. "You don't think Riley..."

"No!" I blurt. "Not a chance. This is Riley we're talking about. The girl is a fucking angel."

Thoughts skate through my mind that I try to shut down, but they keep creeping back in like a sex fiend at a whore house. If this guy drugged Riley, that means she wasn't in her right mind.

No. She wouldn't. She couldn't.

"All right then." Maddox continues, "So, Zeke must've gone to her room after he jumped you. Then, somehow, he managed to throw himself out the window out of guilt, crashing through tempered glass, stabbing his own jugular. Or, someone pushed him and finished him off while he was already on the ground. Something tells me this was no accident." His tone is stern. "Someone killed him."

I have to ask the question weighing heavily on my mind. I need to know what he thinks. "And you think it was her?"

"Not at all. I think someone is setting her up."

Maddox reaches his hand into the front pocket of his jeans. "There's something I need to..." He's cut off when the door opens.

Lev steps in, flips his hood down, and goes to drop his keys on the table. "What the hell happened to that?"

Maddox raises his empty hand from his pocket. "I tripped."

"Can't even stand on your own two feet. Typical." He drops his keys anyway and they slide down the tipped table. "Did you guys see all the cops on campus? Rumor has it someone committed suicide. Any idea who it was?"

I kick my feet up on the coffee table and rest my head back. "Zeke Martin." I don't elaborate on the details because, once again, the less Lev knows, the better. "Where have you been?"

"Meeting." He returns to the matter of Zeke. "So it's the same fucker who jumped you last night?"

I nod.

"Damn. And here I thought we were gonna have some fun with that shithead."

Maddox and Lev keep talking, but all I can think about is Riley. I can't imagine how she's feeling right now, knowing some creep came into her room and fucking touched her.

Every damn time I think about it, my blood boils and I wanna break shit.

"I gotta get outta here." I drop my feet from the table and stand up. Still wearing the same bloodstained joggers I've had on since last night, I grab my jacket off the hook and leave without another word.

———

Tapping my knuckles to the door, I hope for the best because, if it comes down to it, I'll use the key I have to her room.

"Go away," Riley hollers from the other side.

I turn the handle to no avail, then knock again. "I just wanna talk."

"Oh, now you wanna talk? Maybe you should have tried that days ago before you pushed an innocent guy out my window."

"Zeke was far from innocent."

"So you admit it? You pushed him?"

"No, I didn't push him."

"I don't believe you."

I knock harder and louder, hoping she'll get annoyed enough to let me in. Or, at the very least, the other girls in this dormitory will get pissed and demand she let me in. Either way, I'm going inside.

"Let me in the fucking room, Angel. This won't end the way you want it to."

"Are you gonna push me out a window, too?"

My cheek presses to the door and I trail my fingers on it in the shape of a heart. "I'd never hurt you. I'd allow myself to bleed out before letting any pain come to you."

"Liar! I felt pain last night and where were you?"

"Practically bleeding out. Should be getting stitches in my head right now, but instead, I'm here begging to talk to you."

There's a long beat of silence and I press my ear closer to the door, listening. A couple girls come out of the communal bathroom, wearing robes with towels on their heads, and when they see me, they run to their room giggling.

"Angel." I knock again. "Open up."

When she still doesn't, I reach into my pocket and pull out my key. "I'm coming in," I warn her. Then I stick the key in and turn it, allowing myself entry.

The door opens and Riley springs from her bed, a sheet pulled up over her chest. "Get out of my room!" She points a stern finger at the open door.

"I can't do that." I step inside, closing the door behind me. I rest my head against the door, looking at her beautiful form. Damp hair piled in a bun. Bare shoulders that leave me wondering if she's wearing anything beneath the sheet.

"Ridge! You better leave my room right now or I will call campus security."

Stepping away from the door, I trek toward her slowly. "No, you won't."

She scoots up on the bed until her back is flush with the headboard. Her bottom lip quivers and I wanna suck it between my teeth to stop it from shaking. "Don't come any closer to me."

"Tell me what he did to you. In detail. I need to know everything." It pains me to know someone else touched her delicate skin. "Did you try and fight him off or did you lie there and take it?"

Her face is pallid, shoulders tight. "Please just leave me alone." There's a crack in her voice and tears pool in the corners of her eyes.

With my hands pressed firmly to the mattress, I lean forward and kiss her damp cheek. "Everything I do is for you, Angel." Quivering in fear, she turns away, not willing to look at me. "You think I'm a monster, don't you?"

Her head turns slowly, eyes squinted in anger. "You *are* a monster."

Those words are like a knife straight to my chest. I grab her hands quickly, lifting them over her head and pinning them to the headboard.

"Help!" she shouts. "Someone help me."

"If I'm a monster, it's because you made me one. Everything I do is for you. Every damn breath I take is for you. Don't you see it, Angel? I love you, and I will no longer love you from afar. It's too painful being apart. We're destined to be together, you and me."

She wriggles and fights to try and free her wrists, but I can't let her go. Not until she understands. I can finally tell her how I truly feel and there's no fucking way I am giving up this fast. Not when she's right in front of me. Not when I'm so damn close to getting everything I want.

Tears drop one by one from her eyes, landing on her mouth. With my tongue, I lick each one off, tasting the saltiness of her pain.

"You're scaring me, Ridge."

"You never have to be afraid of me, Angel. I'll leave once you tell me everything that guy did to you last night. I can't go on another minute not knowing which parts of your body he touched."

Her shallow breaths and sniffling nose are the only sounds heard.

"Tell me. Tell me everything."

I quickly take both her wrists in one hand then trail my

fingers down the soft cotton sheet, cupping her crotch. "Did he touch you here?"

She swallows hard, then nods.

I move slowly to her breast, cupping it in my palm while grazing my thumb against her pebbled nipple. "Did he touch you here?"

Trembling, she nods.

My soul crushes again. I pinch my eyes closed, steadying my breaths before they all rush out. I drop her hand and straighten my back.

"Son of a bitch," I roar, sweeping my hand across her nightstand and knocking down everything that sat on it.

Riley uses this opportunity to flee from the bed. Her feet move quickly, but as she approaches the door, I throw my arm out, taking her by the waist. With her back flush against my chest, I bury my nose in her damp hair. "He can't hurt you anymore. He's dead, Angel. Zeke Martin is dead."

Her chest rises and falls rapidly as she croaks, "You killed him, didn't you?"

"No, Angel. I didn't kill him. But I think we both know who did."

After Riley accused me of coming into her room last night, I was stunned. Couldn't figure out what she was talking about. It wasn't me. Then Scar announced someone fell from their window. The same window that's behind me and boarded up. That's when I knew. Riley had to have pushed him to protect herself. Maybe she thought it was me, maybe she didn't. Either way, she's lying.

Lifting her legs off the ground, she flails and kicks, trying to break free from my hold, but I hug her tighter. "Are you accusing me? I didn't push him! I didn't even know who it was."

She's sobbing now, so I hold her, showing her that I'm here and that she'll always have me. "Let me go!" she cries, but it's her hurt lashing out. Her guilt and her pain. She doesn't mean it. She doesn't really want me to leave.

Instead of letting go, I bury my ear into the nape of her neck and listen to the thumping of her pulse.

A few moments pass and her tired body surrenders as her walls slowly come down.

I slacken my hold a bit, putting a small amount of space between us. "Can we sit now?"

She nods slowly, so I lead her to the bed. We sit down simultaneously and I take her hand in mine. "I don't blame you for pushing him, Angel. I'm just sorry you had to go through that. I should have been here to protect you. I should have been the one with his blood on my hands."

Eyes straight ahead, with a look of shock on her face, she says, "I didn't push him."

"You were drugged. You don't remember. No one needs to know but us. The Society will protect—"

"I didn't push him!" she shouts at the top of her lungs. "Stop trying to make me question myself! Stop planting seeds in my head that won't grow!"

"Fine." I stand up. "Then there's only one thing we can do. We need to find out what he put in your system, so we know what to look for."

"No," she snaps back. "I'm not going anywhere with you and I'm not telling anyone about this! Do you have any idea how it would look if it was Zeke who came in here? They'll think I killed him. I'll be banished. My life will be over."

I take her hand, holding it tightly as I trail the lines of her palm with my fingers. "Then you need to tell me everything."

"It...it wasn't something real potent. I don't think it was any sort of date-rape drug. The effects took a little bit, but after a few minutes, my head started to feel funny. My eyes were heavy."

"Did you want him to touch you?"

Fuck. I can't help myself. I need to know. I just can't imagine Riley allowing someone to do this shit to her.

"At first," she says, tone soft, "because I thought it was you."

I'm not sure what words will appease me more, those ones, or when I hear her tell me she loves me for the first time. Either way, my heart fucking doubles in size.

"Do you believe it wasn't me?"

"Don't want to because it leaves so many unanswered questions. But, yes, I don't think it was you who came in here first—"

"Good. Because it wasn't."

"I'm not finished. I don't think you came here first. But I think you came after I passed out and you found Zeke, then you threw him out my window."

"That's exactly what I would have done had I walked in and seen him in your bed, taking advantage of you. But I didn't."

Tears fall recklessly down her face and her voice shrills. "Then someone else did."

I sweep her tears away with the pad of my thumb, and while she tugs her head back, she doesn't fully retreat. It's progress. Riley doesn't trust me, but she will.

"Where is your roommate?"

"She's having lunch with Crew. She'll be home later."

I'm given no choice here, but I can't be in two places at once. Riley needs someone with her, and I need to find out who did this. Maddox is too good to take matters into his own hands, and Lev is too careless and sloppy. If Riley did do this when she was out of her mind, I need to cover her tracks. If she didn't, then I need to find out who the fuck did.

I reach into my pocket and pull out my phone.

Me: I need you to come to Riley's dorm and stay with her for a bit.

Maddox: On my way.

CHAPTER 21

RILEY

"YOU KEEP your hands to your fucking self." I hear Ridge say to Maddox in a gritted whisper. "You're here for her. Not for your own benefit. I'm trusting you, man."

"Chill out, Ridge. I'm not gonna throw myself at Riley. You know me better than that."

"Thought I did. Until I saw you kiss her last night."

"Maybe if you stopped watching her so closely, you wouldn't see every damn thing she does."

"All right," I cut in loud and clear. I grab Ridge by the arm and steer him toward the door. "You go do...whatever it is you need to do. Maddox and I will be fine."

Ridge hesitates a moment, shooting Maddox a look of warning before finally exiting the room. Once the door closes, I click the lock. Little good it does, though, since it seems everyone has a key to this damn room. I make a mental note to contact campus security to have the locks changed when they replace the window.

"Well," I wave my hand around the room, "this is my place. It's small and there isn't much to do except watch TV."

Maddox kicks off his shoes like he's at home and makes his

way over to the bed and then drops down. "What do you like to watch?"

I chuckle behind the palm of my hand. "Ya know. Scar will chop your head off if she walks in and sees you in her bed."

I've never seen someone jump up so fast. My lips twitch with humor. "Are you scared of my roommate?"

"No," he quips, "she's just a chick. A chick who looks like she carries around a switchblade to chop off the dicks of any guy who pisses her off."

"And you'd be correct." I take a seat on my bed, and he joins me. "Do you know Melody Higgins?"

"Why? What have you heard from her? Whatever it is, it's a lie. It might be smaller than an eggplant, but it's definitely bigger than a banana."

As if a banana is small? Wow! Now my wheels are turning. Annnnd...there's a visual. My cheeks tinge pink and I'm thankful no one can hear the thoughts in my head.

"Whoa," I chuckle, hand in the air, "not at all where I was going with this."

Maddox snatches a textbook off my nightstand, places it in his lap, and begins nervously flipping through the pages. "Okay then."

I slam the cover of the book closed. "Are you embarrassed, Maddox?"

"It really is bigger than a banana."

It's been so long since laughter has come so easily. "I believe you."

In those brief moments, I almost forgot about all the chaos surrounding me. One glance at my boarded window, though, and I'm instantly reminded.

"All right, so now that we've made it clear I do, in fact, know who Melody Higgins is..."

"Right. So, last year at The Academy, Melody did some

cruel shit. Scar took the bitch to the ground, and I'm not kidding you, she chopped her hair off."

"Damn. Honestly, I'm not a bit surprised. I can see that Scar has some fucking balls."

"Yeah," I mutter. "If only I could grow a pair."

Don't do it, Riley. Don't get down on yourself. You've been doing so well given the circumstances.

Pity sucks.

Pity burns.

Pity leaves.

Pity returns.

"What are you talking about?" Maddox asks as he slides closer. "You're tough, too. Look at you sitting tall after the shit you've been through."

Really should have kept my mouth shut. I don't want any more pity and I need to quit feeling it myself. My rumbling stomach reminds me I haven't eaten today, so I use that as an out. "Are you hungry? I'm starving."

"Sure. I could eat."

"Pizza at the student center?"

Maddox grabs my thigh and squeezes. "It's a date."

Giddiness replaces the hunger pangs inside me and my body flushes with heat. "I guess it is."

———

"So, at this point, Ridge is running through the house naked with his eyes closed. He runs smack-dab into the refrigerator and cuts himself on one of my mom's magnets."

My stomach literally aches from laughing so hard. "I guess that's what he gets for stripping down in your mom's bathroom."

"In his defense, he had no idea she was in bed with my dad. At least, that's what he claims."

"Wouldn't surprise me if he lied and was actually trying to get with your mom."

"Nah. I don't think he's ever had any interest in my mom; she was like a mom to him. Besides, he claimed his eyes burned for days after that."

I take another bite of my pizza, thoughts now on Ridge. The guy has been through so much and part of me thinks I should cut him some slack.

"You don't like him much, do you?"

"Ridge?" My eyebrows perk up. "I don't know him. The only version he's ever given me of himself is the obsessive, control-freak version."

"There's more to him than meets the eye. Ridge is the most loyal human being to grace this earth." Maddox lifts his glass of soda in the air. "I can promise you that."

"Yeah. Well, at what point do I get to see it? Because he's given me no inclination that inside him is an actual beating heart."

"Really? Because I'm certain all of his possessive ways are proof that he has one. If anything, it shows how big his heart really is. And it's full of love for you."

"Love?" I gag. "He doesn't love me."

"Ridge loves you the way Ridge knows how to love. It's messy and chaotic. A bit distorted and morbid. But I can guarantee you're the safest in his presence."

I take a sip of my lemonade, then set it back down while licking my sour lips. "And what about you? Am I safe in your presence?"

"Fuck yeah," he sings. "I'll keep you safe." Maddox reaches across the table and grabs my hand. "Things aren't always what they seem, Riley. There's a lot of shit us guys have to go through that we can't speak on. But believe me when I say, no one is working harder for you than Ridge and me."

I'm not sure what he means by that, but for some reason, I find comfort in it.

My eyes slide over Maddox's shoulder, when a dark, shadowy figure appears outside the main doors. They open up, and in steps Lev.

I'm immediately reminded of how awful he was to me at the party last night. "What about him?" I tip my chin and Maddox follows my gaze to where Lev is strutting toward us. "Should I feel safe in his presence?"

Maddox turns his head back around. "No. In fact, it's best if you just avoid that one. He's good to some, but not many."

Lev's stare never leaves me. Even when I look away for a second, I return to feel the heat of his glowering eyes. They burn into my skin like a branding iron. Leaving an imprint that won't soon fade.

Once he reaches us, he grabs the chair beside me and spins it around, inviting himself to our table. His hands lock together on top of it and he leans forward slightly, invading my personal space.

No words are spoken. No movements are made.

"Can we...help you?" I ask him, knowing damn well this one talks.

"No," he deadpans. His eyes slide over to Maddox. "Where the fuck is Ridge?"

Lev has a way of making me feel two inches tall. Not only because he's at least six-foot-four, but also because he exudes confidence along with a heavy dose of brashness. The thing is, I can tell this is one hundred percent Lev's personality. It's not some game to intimidate people.

Maddox drops the crust of his pizza on his paper plate. "He's out working his assignment."

I've heard of these assignments, but the girls here have no idea what they entail. Crew, Jagger, and Neo won't even speak about them to Scar, so that alone proves how confidential they are.

"Whereabouts?" Lev presses.

Maddox shrugs. "No clue. Call him."

"Tried. He's not picking up."

"Weird," Maddox says, reaching in his pocket and pulling out his phone. "That's not like him."

He taps into it, then sets it screen down on the table.

"Any word on that fucker that fell from this girl's window?" He's looking at me now, while asking Maddox the question. "Do they think she did it?"

My mouth opens, but Maddox speaks instead. "Riley didn't do shit."

"Riley didn't do shit, huh? Then why are you and Ridge following her around like lost puppies? She had to have done something to catch your eye. What is it, a pussy made of gold?"

I scoff. "Screw you, asshole."

Maddox's phone vibrates against the table and he grabs it quickly. "Shit. It's my dad." He looks at Lev. "Can you play nice for a second? I've gotta take this. You okay, Riley?"

I nod, cutting Lev a glare. "I can handle him."

Lev throws his hands up in surrender, but I can guarantee he's not surrendering to shit. The minute Maddox walks away, he's in my face.

"Screw me? Screw you, Trouble. If you think you're gonna drag my friends down your dirty hole of unruliness, you're sadly mistaken."

Feeling tough, because I am *Trouble*, after all, I lean into his space. "I can't drag someone who wants to follow, *Lion*."

"It'll do you good to remember that I am like a lion. Your goody-two-shoes attitude doesn't fool me one bit." Lev picks up the half-eaten pizza on my plate, chews off a bite, then tosses it back down before getting up.

Just when I think he's gone, he leans over my shoulder, the scent of pepperoni on his breath. "When I say jump, you better fucking ask me how high, because I know what you're capable of, and soon, everyone else will know it, too."

I gulp, feeling like my heart has fallen into my stomach.

If that wasn't a threat, I don't know what one is. Lev thinks I killed Zeke and now, it sounds like he plans to use it against me.

I'm already on my feet, pacing back and forth in front of the table, when Maddox returns. I'm just grateful he *did* return this time. Last call he took from his dad left me sitting at the coffee shop alone.

His eyes scan the student center. "Where's Lev?"

"He left," I say point-blankly.

Noticing how tense I am, Maddox stops my manic steps. "What did he say to you?"

I pinch my eyes closed, warding off the tears that threaten to fall, but it's useless, they spill without fail. "Everyone thinks I killed Zeke." I fall into Maddox's arms. "I wouldn't kill him, I swear."

"I know you didn't. And no one else thinks that either."

"Ridge assumed it was me. Lev thinks it was me. Now they both have me questioning myself. I was so out of it. I don't even remember anything after..."

"After you were drugged?"

I take a step back, remaining in his arms, and my eyes shoot to his. "Ridge told you?"

His features soften, and he nods.

"I can't believe he told you."

"We tell each other everything. Well, almost everything."

Maddox's phone vibrates again, only his phone is in his

hand and the sound is coming from the chair where Maddox's coat is hanging. When the vibrating stops, the phone chirps, a familiar sound—the sound of my phone when I get a voicemail.

Stepping away from him, I haul ass toward it, but he races me to it. "No," he barks as I grab the coat. "Why do you have two phones?" I dig my hand in the pocket, and at the same time, Maddox's face falls in his hands.

When I pull the phone out, my soul feels like it's been sliced in two. "It was you?" I hold it up, showing proof that I'm onto him. "You stole my phone. When was it? The party? Or are you the one who came into my room?"

"I can explain." He comes toward me, but I take a step back, away from him.

"You better explain fast or I'm calling The Elders right fucking now." My posture slumps, along with my heart. "I trusted you."

"You can trust me. I mean it, Riley. Let me explain."

When he tries to come closer again, I shout, "Stop. Stop right there and tell me why the hell you have my phone."

"It was on Zeke when his body was found. It was handed over to my dad, who handed it over to me."

"Zeke had my phone?"

He comes closer, both hands in the air. "There's no way of knowing if Zeke actually had it in his possession while he was alive. All I can conclude is that someone's either trying to frame you for his fall or they accidentally left it behind when they killed him."

Really don't want to talk about Zeke coming into my room last night, but it seems it's a conversation that needs to be had. "He must have stolen it after he..." My words trail off, unable to even finish the sentence.

Maddox nods toward a smaller room off to the right that's empty. "I think we should talk about this in private."

180

I probably shouldn't believe what he, or either of the other two, says but I don't have much of a choice. If given one, I'd trust Maddox over any of them. Still, I can't be sure.

"Fine." I walk toward the meeting room, while keeping my eyes on him. "But don't come close to me. I mean it, Maddox. I will call The Elders."

"You don't wanna do that, Riley."

"Just because you don't want me to, doesn't mean I won't."

We step into the room and Maddox closes the door. As I pace one side of the small space, he remains on the other side. "If you call The Elders, you risk incriminating yourself."

I pull out a chair at the oblong table and sit down, feeling faint. With my elbow pressed to the table, I rest my forehead on my balled right fist. Just when I think things can't get much worse, this shit gets sprung on me. Lifting my head, I roll my lips together and take a deep breath. On a clipped exhale, I ask, "Who gave it to your dad, and why?"

Maddox takes a seat at the opposite end of the table, making this 'talk' feel like an interrogation. "The first cop on the scene. He's employed by The Society. My dad met him there and collected the only piece of evidence found—your phone."

"It had to have been Zeke that came in last night. He must have stolen my phone and then someone pushed him out the window."

"Maybe. But, maybe not. We can't be too sure. I'm not even certain Zeke actually had it. My gut tells me someone planted it after he was already dead. Someone linked to your past at The Academy, perhaps."

"Who would do that, though?"

He's quiet for a minute, before asking, "How much do you trust Neo Saint?"

Why is he asking this?

181

"Why are you asking about Neo?"

Eyes wandering around the room, he avoids eye contact with me. My thoughts go crazy as I try to figure out what he's talking about. Is he hinting at the governor's death? Is he trying to get me to discuss it without being the first to bring it up? Where would he have gathered any information about that incident?

Unless...

"Are you a Guardian?" I spit out without thinking first. I, of all people, know he can't answer that, but this isn't your typical situation. Lives have been lost and mine is at stake. "That's why your dad came, isn't it? He's an Elder and a Guardian?"

He gives me a quizzical eye, hands now stretched out over the table. "Are you a Guardian, Riley?"

"Maybe."

"Well...maybe I am, too."

Relief washes over me. Guardians are good. Then again, we are only as good as we want to be. I'm a Guardian, and I've killed before. What's not to say Maddox isn't keeping secrets of his own.

"Okay. Now that we've established that, tell me what you know about my past at The Academy."

"I can't go into detail because it's not my place to say. Information was given to me in complete confidence. But I will say, The Elders have gathered a team who is looking into the governor's death."

"So, you know?"

"What you did? I know."

I'm mentally exhausted. Ready to throw in the towel and confess all my sins to anyone who will hear them. I'll take whatever punishment I'm given. Be it abolishment or a life of misery. I can't take it anymore.

My eyes close, lip quivering. "Do you also know that it was in self-defense? I never wanted to kill anyone."

"I believe you. But they won't. Which is why I asked, how well do you know Neo Saint? It was his dad, after all."

"No," I blurt. "Neo hated his dad. In fact, his dad shot him accidentally before he died. There's no way in hell Neo would try and frame me for Zeke's death."

"His sister?"

"Maddie? God, no. She's so sweet and she saw the worst of her dad's actions. Sebastian Saint had their mom killed, Maddox. They don't want to avenge his death. They're grateful he's out of their lives."

"I hope you're right. I wanna help you, Riley. But first I need to know I can trust you. If we're gonna do this, we have to work together. No one can know about this."

"Ridge?"

"He knows some, but not everything, and he can't know about all of this."

"Lev?"

"Fuck no. And I hate that we have to keep this from them, but Ridge and Lev both react on emotion, or lack thereof. We can't risk it."

There is a sense of relief that I can finally talk to someone about all of this, aside from Scar. "You can trust me, Maddox. I'm not a bad person. Question is, can I trust you?"

"I don't think you have much of a choice." He stands up and pushes his chair back in. "Let's go back to your room, where it's safe, and we'll make a plan."

CHAPTER 22
RIDGE

AFTER GOING to the morgue to take a look at Zeke's body, cussing him out a few times, I've concluded someone definitely stuck that tempered glass in his jugular. One doesn't just fall onto a shard of glass from that angle. So, whoever did it, knew exactly where to find that main artery that would end Zeke's life quickly.

I don't think Riley did it. At first, I toyed with the possibility, since she was under the influence of whatever drug Zeke slipped her. But there's no way in hell she overpowered him in that state and then not only threw him out a window, but also made it all the way downstairs to finish him off. There were no traces of blood in her room, so the fall had to have happened first.

Now, I just need to go and tell her. I need to apologize for even accusing her of such a thing. I'd understand if she never wants to speak to me again. But I won't allow that because I breathe just to hear her voice.

Pulling out the key from my pocket, I unlock her door. It's two o'clock in the morning, so I'm sure she's asleep, but I'll be waking her up for a good reason.

As I tiptoe quietly toward her bed, a strange feeling comes

over me. Maybe it's the way her body is laid out, which isn't her usual position.

But when I'm standing at the foot of her bed, looking down at her face resting against my best friend's chest, I lose it.

In one fell swoop, I grab Maddox's leg that's peeking out of the blanket and I tug hard. I pull him until his head flops over the footboard and his body crashes to the floor at my feet.

Riley flees from the bed, wearing nothing but an oversized tee shirt and—for the love of fucking God, she better have panties on.

A light comes on and my eyes pin to Maddox's, who's staring up at me wide-eyed. His mouth moves, but I don't hear the words that come out as I climb on top of him. My fingers tangle around his throat, and I scream in his face, "What the fuck have you done? I put my trust in you. I left you alone with her, and this is what I find."

"Ridge! Stop!" Riley shouts and pulls at me, but I fling my arm back, not realizing how hard. She crashes into a dresser and I gasp at what I've done.

Dropping my hold on Maddox, I crawl over to her as she pacifies the back of her head with her hand. "Shit. Shit. Shit. I'm so fucking sorry."

"Get the hell out of my room," she cries. And for the first time ever, I listen.

Pinning Maddox with a glare, I grit out, "If I have to leave, you're leaving, too."

"No," Riley sneers, "I want Maddox to stay."

"You don't mean that?"

"Actually, I do."

I get to my feet, remorse heavy on my heart, and I cross the room to the door. When I pull it open, I pause. "You are the only star in my sky, Angel. Guess I never realized you were also shining in someone else's."

Walking out of the Willamette House, I feel empty. Like I've left my heart behind. Maddox betrayed me in the worst way imaginable. He was holding her. She was curled up on his chest, sleeping peacefully in his arms. She was safe with him. He shouldn't be giving her that security. I should. Instead, I'm out fighting demons on her behalf, just so she can keep her wings.

And that's the thanks I get. I'd rather she spit in my face and tear my heart from my chest.

An hour, maybe two, later, I find myself inside the house of a stranger. My hands wrap around his throat and I revel in the way his eyes bulge from their sockets and his Adam's apple bobs beneath my palm.

His legs flail and he tries to fight, but when his air supply is depleted and he's unable to refill his lungs, he gives up the fight.

As he slowly slips away, all I can think about is her.

~~Dennis Mathers~~

~~Robby Nelson~~

~~Andy Porter~~

Eric Mathers

"I did this for her, Andy. Everything I do is for that girl, and this is the thanks I get from her? Can you believe it?" I chuckle. "Of course you can't."

With my prey dead in his bed, I strike a match and toss it at him. Then I watch him burn.

CHAPTER 23

RILEY

"YOU'RE SURE your dad will keep this under wraps from The Elders until we know who's behind everything?"

"I'm positive. Especially since he doesn't believe you were framed."

Maddox told me his dad thinks I killed the governor and Zeke. He's right about one, but he doesn't know the details of why I did it. Let's hope I never have to explain my reasoning to him, or anyone else.

"So what's next? You said they're looking for fingerprints on Zeke's body? Which we know mine will exist, considering he came into my room and drugged me."

"I'm sure yours will be there, but we're searching for other prints, too. One way or another, we'll get to the bottom of this."

Maddox has a way of making me feel better about all the terrible things happening in my life. I nudge his side, grinning. "Thanks for walking with me."

"Of course." His fingers run through my hair as we walk down the sidewalk to the stadium. "How's your head?"

"It's fine. Just a small bump. I still can't believe Ridge came into my room and did that. Everyone just needs to stop showing up in my room." I laugh, even if it's really not funny at all.

"I can believe it. I told you, Ridge loves you."

"You keep saying that, but I'm starting to wonder if Ridge even knows what love is. Because if his actions say anything about how he feels, I wouldn't call it love. It's more like obsessive fixation."

"Look, Riley." Maddox stops walking in front of the stadium entrance and scrapes his fingers through his hair, eyes downcast. "I know I said I'd help you, but after last night, I'm starting to think whatever is happening between us is a bad idea. Ridge is my best friend and when it comes down to it—"

"No, Maddox." I tip his chin up with my index finger. "Look at me. Ridge is unhinged. You're not doing anything wrong."

"You don't understand, and I don't expect you to. But I think it's best if we're just friends. I'll still help you with this Zeke bullshit, but nothing more can happen between us."

I take his hand in mine, my thumb sweeping over his knuckles. "I like you, Maddox. You make me laugh more than I have in months. I enjoy your company. And you're a really good kisser, too." He cracks a smile, so I keep going, putting my heart on the line. "I'm not asking you to choose. I'm just asking for a chance. And I don't mean a chance to clear my name. I mean, a chance for us."

Talk about vulnerability. I'm not even sure I took in any air during that confession. And now, as he stands here silent, I'm certain I'm going to pass out from humiliation.

"Please say something," I beg. "Anything. Tell me to eat rocks. Get lost. Just say something."

Biting his lip, he lifts his chin. "I like you, too, Riley. I enjoy your company and you're a damn good kisser, too. The thing is. Ridge, Lev, and I...we go way back. Before crushes and booze and stealing and sex. Not that I ever stole or did drugs.

Anyways, that's beside the point. The guys and I have a pact. My loyalty to them has to come first, and I guess...my heart gets second place."

"That's not fair to you."

"And going back on my pact wouldn't be fair to them either."

I swallow hard, nodding in agreement, even when I want to scream that he's making the wrong choice. "Okay. I guess when you satisfy your pact then maybe come find me." I push myself up on my tiptoes and kiss his cheek. "I'll be around."

———

"I was thinking," Carly beams, clasping her hands together. "We could decorate with a horror movie theme. Different villains displayed around campus. Then everyone can dress up as their favorite psycho for the party."

It's almost laughable that Ridge pops into my mind at the mention of the word psycho. I wonder how long he'll linger in my brain this time. Seems like the guy never leaves. He's sunk his claws into me, without me even knowing it.

I remember seeing him for the first time in that tree, and thinking, 'that guy is a gorgeous mess of trouble that I wanna get into.' Then the evil grin on his face spooked me and I took off, unsure if he was going to follow—but I was sort of hoping he would.

Now, I can't seem to get away from him. Can't stop thinking about him. He's wreaking havoc on my life in ways I'm not even aware of.

Except, he's not there anymore. I haven't seen him all day, and it feels...weird. Like something is missing. I guess I'm just so used to him being around.

After he left last night, I was lying on the floor with my head against my dresser and all I could think about were his last words. *You are the only star in my sky, Angel. Guess I didn't realize you were also shining in someone else's.*

Maybe Ridge does love me. No one does the insane shit he does for anything but love. I hate him for everything he's done. But there's also a part of me who basks in the idea of someone being that hopelessly devoted to me. *Me. Riley Cross.* I'm nobody to everybody, but everything to him.

I'm everything to him. My heart swells at the realization.

All this time I've been so down on myself, feeling so unwanted and unloved, and he's been right there. Watching. Waiting. Longing...for me.

"What do you think, Riley?"

My ears perk up and I drop my fist from my cheek. "I love that idea."

Carly chuckles. "Which one?"

Was there more than one?

"Umm. The first."

"I agree." She winks. "All in favor of a horror film theme, raise your hand."

I'm not sure how many hands go up, but I know mine does.

"And all in favor of a *The Nightmare Before Christmas* theme, raise your hand."

Shit. Scar would kill me if she knew that was an option and I didn't vote for it. She's obsessed with Jack and whoever that chick is. Once again, my hand goes up.

Melody sneers as she lowers my hand. "You can only vote once, Riley."

Sticking my hand back in the air, I scoff at Melody. "Well, I'll change my vote."

"No changes either." She lowers it again, and this girl is

really grating on my nerves. My chair slides back abruptly and I step up to her. "Do you have a problem, Melody?"

"Whoa, girls." Carly steps between us, arms spread wide, and she leads us both back a step. "This is a planning committee. If you want to duke it out, I suggest y'all visit the mud pit for that."

Melody crosses her arms over her chest, taking care to push up that sliver of cleavage she has. "I'm down."

"Well, then I'm down, too." I have no idea what mud pit Carly is referring to, but I'm in a mood right now, and I'd love nothing more than to take some aggression out on Melody.

"All right then," Carly singsongs in her southern accent. "Tomorrow. I guess we have our Monday night plans. Say, dusk?"

My forehead creases. "Like in the dark?"

"Oh, there'll be plenty of light, darling. Don't worry your pretty little face."

I've always liked Carly, but something tells me after tomorrow, I won't be her biggest fan. Then again, if it involves shoving Melody's face in a pit of mud, Carly might be my new favorite person.

"This was good, ladies. We've decided on a horror films theme and we'll start decorating campus next week. Meet back here Wednesday at six o'clock. Until then, I'll see y'all at the pit behind Delta Chi." Her brows waggle in my direction. "May the best girl win."

Fucking hell. This is some sorority shit. What in the world did I just agree to?

Everyone disperses and I'm dragging my feet toward the door when it comes back open. Carly slithers out, just as Ridge comes in.

I backstep, surprised to see him here.

I go to speak, not even sure what I was going to say, but he holds a hand up. "Me first."

Nodding, I allow him that courtesy, even if I'm not sure he deserves it.

He points at the meeting table. "Can we?"

Turning around, I pull out a chair and drop down on it. I knew I'd face him again eventually; I just hoped I'd have more time to sort through the array of emotions I'm feeling—hate, anger, disbelief, fear...curiosity, lust, attraction.

Ridge sits down right beside me, his body mirroring mine. "I suck at this shit, Angel. I've always worn my heart on my sleeve and assumed if someone could see it, they'd wanna keep it. I realized last night that's not the case with you. I got so tired of loving you from afar that I approached too soon. Probably should've kept my mouth shut, but I couldn't any longer."

"Do you love me, Ridge?" The words spill out of my mouth with no thought process behind them and now that they're out, I wish I could take them back. Once I know, I'll never forget.

"More than anything in this entire world. I remember the first time your heart called to me, unknowingly. It was like a song in the wind. I laid eyes on you and all hope for myself was lost because I knew I'd do anything in this fucked-up world to keep you safe, even if it meant slowly killing myself in the process."

"Why me?" My two-worded question comes out abrasive, but words mean nothing without actions to back them up.

He speaks like a poet,
but even poets lie.

"Three weeks before I saw you for the first time, at the end of the summer, I tried to end my life." He holds up his wrists, showing the marks I've seen before. "I failed miserably but told myself I'd try again. I was ready to leave this world. There was nothing left for me in it. Then you appeared, my angel. You revived my heart and breathed life back into me. I knew at that moment, I had to stay for you. Even if it was just to keep you safe for a little while."

No one has ever spoken such meaningful words to me, about me. I'm pretty sure my heart is now sitting somewhere in my shoe because I can't feel it. It's not rapid-firing; it's quite literally stunned, unable to beat.

"I...I don't know what to say."

"You don't have to say anything. That's not why I'm here. I came to tell you, I'm sorry."

"Your behavior is so unacceptable, Ridge. I'm not sure how I can ever move forward, even as your friend."

He smirks, a glint of defiance in the look. "I don't want your friendship, Angel. I'm not giving up on you. Just because *you've* closed the door on us, doesn't mean I won't keep trying to get through it. Take my apology if you will, and I hope you will, but I'm not going anywhere." He stands up and slides the seat beneath the table. "You've moved me more than any human can ever move another. That's not something I'm willing to let go of. Not in this lifetime, and not in the next."

As he goes to walk away, something awakens inside me. Call it foolishness, but I don't want him to leave. Even after he spewed another threat from his foul mouth.

"Wait." I grab his arm, which is odd, considering he's always the one stopping me while I'm trying to get away. Ridge spins around, peering down at me. I push myself up and grab his face, bringing his mouth to mine. I'm not sure why I do it. Maybe to see if that spark I felt the first time is still there. Regardless of my reasoning, it is. It's there. I feel it all. Deep in my core, between my legs, and even in my heart that's now found its place back in my chest. I feel every emotion in existence, and I hold on tight because the one that I feel the most is acceptance.

I felt something with Maddox, but he bailed. He made a choice, and he walked away when I was ready to drop to my knees and beg.

Ridge never leaves. He's *always* there. He doesn't judge me or put me in the back seat. He doesn't look down on me or treat me as if I'm beneath him. He doesn't pity me or back away, no matter how hard I push. For some fucked-up reason, this guy loves me, and maybe for just a minute, I'll let that be enough.

CHAPTER 24
RIDGE

STUNNED. Speechless. Completely fucking consumed by this girl. That's the only way to explain how it feels kissing her right now. The room could be filled with people and all I'd see is her. We could combust into flames and I'd only hold her tighter.

My hands slide down her long-sleeved tee shirt. I keep going until I'm holding either side of her waist beneath the fabric.

The nerves in my head erupt when her fingers weave through my hair. My head tilts slightly to the left, hers angled to the right. Our noses brush and I inhale a deep breath of the air she just exhaled. The overpowering scent of lemons floods my senses. Riley loves lemons, namely lemonade. It's fitting because my girl is as sweet as she is sour. Behind the lemon scent is a tinge of cotton candy and I'm certain it's her body spray. She must have replaced the bottle I stole from her room a couple weeks ago. I took it so I could smell her when I miss her the most.

Right now, though, I've got her. She's all mine. The way she pulls me closer and closer reaffirms that she's slowly falling. She can take her time. As I've told her, I'm not going anywhere.

Walking her back a few steps, I stop when her ass hits the table. She sits down, our mouths never parting. A whimper slips through her lips and the vibration against my mouth has my cock twitching. It feels like home between her legs, and I never want to leave.

"Ridge," she whispers, and on the off chance her mutter is a warning that we need to stop, I kiss her harder. She relents, pulling out of the kiss, no matter how hard I fight to keep her in it.

My soul shatters momentarily, but when she sucks in her bottom lip and smirks, the pieces come back together. Breathless, she says, "Not here."

"Not here," I repeat her words. "Okay." Taking her hand, I lead her quickly across the small meeting room. Through a door in the back, there's an auditorium that's used for plays by the drama club and concerts by the band. I take her through the door, moving quickly out of fear she'll change her mind.

Still holding her hand tightly, I push the drawn curtain on the stage back and lead her behind it.

It's fairly dark, but a dim light on the back wall shows me enough of her beautiful face.

Riley surprises me by grabbing my face in her hands and putting our mouths back together. I step into her, walking her backward until her back is mounted on the wall. Her legs wrap around my waist, caging me in while I hold her in place with an arm under her ass.

Trailing my mouth down her neck, I suck and kiss, feasting on her delicate flesh like it's my favorite dessert. Her skin tastes as good as her mouth, like salted caramel. A delicious fucking treat.

Self-control eludes me as I remove my hand that's keeping her pinned to the wall. Her feet catch her fall and I shove my hand down the front of her pants. There's no trailing of fingers leading up to it. Patience isn't my strong suit. I go straight for her cunt, cupping it with my palm. I'm a bit surprised to find that it's bare. It wasn't long ago I watched her shower, while getting herself off, and she had a mound of hair coating her pussy. I can only assume she did that for me.

She better have done it for me.

Wandering thoughts get the best of me, and now more than ever, I have an agonizing hunger to take what's mine.

With her head rested back against the wall, Riley keeps her eyes on mine. Peering up at her while I pepper kisses along her chin, I stick two fingers inside her wet pussy. Her legs open wider, inviting me in, and I accept the invitation. Curling my fingers, I plunge deeper, hitting her G-spot as she utters a yelp.

"You like that, Angel?"

Her chest rises and falls rapidly, her heart nearly beating out of her chest. Mouth agape, she drags her tongue across her top lip. I crush her mouth with mine, riding her up the wall with the fierce plunge of my digits inside her. "Your mouth tastes like a dream." I drag my tongue around her lips. "I wanna taste this, Angel." I pat her pussy with my palm. "Can I do that? Can I taste you?"

"Yes," she whimpers. "Please."

Her mannerisms turn me on. My cock's straining against my jeans, ready to break through the fabric just to climb inside her. I use her plea to my advantage. "Tell me you want my mouth on your cunt."

"I...I want you to."

"That's not what I said." I add another finger, shoving them so deep inside, her cries echo off the walls. "Tell me you want my mouth on your cunt."

"I want your mouth on my cunt," she sputters between breaths, her pussy soaked with desire.

In one swift motion, I pull my fingers out and drop to my

knees, taking her leggings and panties with me until they're settled around her ankles. Lifting one of her feet, I remove her tennis shoe, then the other. She steps out of her pants on her own, and when I look up, she's removing her shirt.

Fuck me. Her tits spring free as she unclasps her bra from the back. Wearing a smirk, she wraps it around my neck, holding on to each end.

Who the hell is this and where did my innocent girl go?

"You ever behave like this for anyone else and I'll lock you in a cage, Angel. You hear me?"

Biting her lip, she nods. She's so flirtatious tonight. So... provocative, and I'm not sure what to think about it.

"Spread your legs and let me get a look at your pretty cunt."

She steps one foot out, then the other, widening the space between her legs.

"Mmm," I purr, grabbing her ass with both hands, fingers sinking into her flesh. I pull her sex to my face, my nose writhing against her clit. With the muscle of my tongue stretched, I push it inside her. Her arousal coats my tongue as I open wide, sucking her in. She tastes better than I ever could have imagined.

Two fingers slide inside her and she lifts one leg, granting me more access. I take hold of it, bringing her foot to my shoulder.

"I want you to come on my face, Angel. And when you're done, I want you to come again around my cock."

While my fingers pump vigorously inside her, I give attention to her thigh, kissing my way down, hand trailing her smooth leg. Then I work my way back up.

Riley grabs a fistful of my hair and forces my mouth back on her. "Please," she begs, and God, do I love hearing her beg.

Flicking my tongue against her clit, I tease her a few times.

Stopping then starting again. She moans and cries, exhaling primitive sounds that drive my cock crazy.

I work harder and faster, desperate for her rapture, so she can clench my cock and milk every last drop while I come inside her. *And I will come inside her.* I have every intention of staking my claim on this girl, and while we're not ready for a baby yet, one day she will have my child.

Gripping my hair tighter, she rolls her hips, seeking friction against my face. My tongue slides up and down her sex while my fingers work inside her. When she explodes, I suck on her cunt, tasting every bit of what I just did to her.

Leg slowly dropping, her foot meets the floor and I stand up. In a fleet second, I spin her around and she squeals. I take one of her hands, plastering it to the wall, then the other.

With my chin on her shoulder, I fan her hair with my breath. "Can I fuck you, Angel? Let me be your first. Your last. Your only."

Her nod is subtle, but I accept it as a yes.

I take a step back, reveling in her beauty while ridding myself of my pants. Once I'm free from them, one of my hands slaps her ass, leaving an imprint I want to tattoo to her skin, so any man who catches a glimpse of this perfectly round flesh knows whose hand belongs here.

"Mine," I grumble before slapping the other cheek even harder. She winces, though her hands stay on the wall.

One hand trails up her inner thigh, fingers sweeping her swollen cunt, then I use the proof of her orgasm to lube my cock. I stroke once, twice, three times. "You ready?"

She nods again, but I'm not satisfied with her response. Gripping her hair from behind, I tug. "Tell me you want it."

"I want it," she wheezes.

"Yeah, you do."

I give her the shallow end of my cock with gentle care. "Tell me if I hurt you."

I'm not expecting to hear cries of pain because her pussy might be untouched by dick, but my fingers have already spread her wide.

Every cell in my body quivers in delight as her walls close around my cock. I feed it to her inch by inch, watching as her nails bed into the brick wall. Chin down, head hung low, she pants audibly.

I lean over her, my chest cloaking her back. The heat of her skin warms the cold blood in my veins. It's everything I thought it would be. So wet, so warm, so fucking tight.

My eyes roll into the back of my head as I enter her completely. She's all mine now. I bring one hand around to her front, cupping her breast. These tits, this ass, this pussy—all mine.

Her back arches, legs spread impossibly wide.

Choking on emotions, I feel like a goddamn king. As if I've just crowned my queen.

Rolling the bud of her nipple between my fingers, I pinch with enough force to elicit a whimper out of her. The sounds she makes have me fucking her faster and faster, desperate to hear more of her pleas. Her forehead presses to the wall, moving slightly with each thrust. She moans and cries and clenches around my cock.

I grab another fistful of her hair, lifting her head so she doesn't bruise her beautiful face on the wall because I have every intention of fucking her harder.

"Does that hurt, Angel."

When she doesn't say anything, I pull her head back farther until I can see her face to make sure she's free of pain. "Am I hurting you?"

"No," she mumbles. "Keep going."

Her words appease me. "That's what I wanted to hear." My lips brush her forehead and I whisper, "I wanna watch your face when I come inside you."

I'm on the brink of explosion but not ready for this to be over, so my movements freeze, her pussy full of my cock.

"Don't stop," she begs. "Please keep going."

Her words light a fire inside me. A flame that won't go out anytime soon.

"Fuck, Angel. I don't want this to end."

I tug her hair harder, watching her face while I resume fucking her. Crushing her ass with my pelvic bone, I give her every inch of my cock. I pant and groan and curse. Our souls connect on a new level as I plant the first of many seeds inside my angel.

Her mouth gapes. Cries ring out around us, echoing in my ears. Mixing with my own. This, right here, is why I exist. It's a sound that will forever be etched in my memory. One I will replay on the lonely nights while I stroke my cock, imagining it's her mouth sucking me off.

As I come down, I keep moving, wishing this wasn't the end. Fearful of what comes next. Will she be cursed with a mountain of regret? Or will she finally realize our futures don't exist without one another?

When Riley slackens her back, the tension falling from her shoulders, I let go of her hair. Her hands leave the wall and each simple movement is a reminder that this moment has passed and it's time to face whatever comes next.

I slide out of her, remnants of my orgasm dripping from my cock along with a tinge of blood—proof that I was her first. Riley turns around, covering her breasts with her hands. I peel one from her chest, then the other, holding them tightly. "Don't ever hide yourself from me. I want to see every flawless speck of your skin."

I'm trying to get a feel for her mood, but her expression is so stoic. So void of emotion. I drop her hand and then cradle her head in my palms. "Tell me what you're thinking."

She steps back, taking a sliver of my heart in the process. Another step, and it's as if she literally wants to tear my heart from my chest.

My eyes are wide with horror, proof of how much she's hurting me. "Say something, Angel."

"I...I don't know what to say."

I pull her face to mine, but she resists me. Tears sting the corners of my eyes, and I squeeze her face harder. I can literally feel the blood rushing to my head, clogging my emotions. "Don't you dare do this to us. We can be together now."

Her tongue drags across her dry lips, and she tries to cover herself again, legs crossed at the ankles. "I need my clothes."

"Why?" I shout so loudly she jerks. "Why do you want to hide your body from me after it just became mine?"

"I'm...I'm not yours, Ridge. I don't belong to anyone."

My head shakes in rapid movements. "No. You are mine. Always have been. Always will be. Don't talk like that."

"Can I please get my clothes?"

"You wanted this. You initiated it. You kissed me." Words spill from my mouth like running water, rising in pitch. "You wanted me to be your first! You wanted me to fuck you!"

"I did. And now...it's over."

"Oh, Angel." A devilish laugh vibrates in my throat. "It's not over. It's only just begun."

I bend down and grab her clothes, then shove them to her chest.

We dress in silence, and once we're decent, I take her hand and lead her back to the meeting room, where it all began.

She tries to pull her hand from mine, but I squeeze until all the blood drains from my knuckles. She looks down at our entwined fingers. "I have to go, Ridge."

"Your words really hurt me tonight. But I know you didn't mean them, and I forgive you."

I let her go, and she moves so fast toward the exit, you'd think a psycho was following her.

Which I am.

CHAPTER 25
RILEY

TEARS DON'T STOP FALLING as I walk as fast I can back to my dorm. He's six feet behind me, but he might as well be walking by my side.

I was caught up in the moment—let things go too far. I was vulnerable and desperate for someone's attention.

Ridge speaks such beautiful words and makes me feel emotions I've longed for, but he's not normal. There is something sickly wrong with his obsession for me and that was made clear when we finished. If he'd just kept his mouth shut afterward, then I wouldn't be panicking and stealing glances over my shoulder.

It's not too far-fetched. I wouldn't put it past him to grab me and drag me down to a dark dungeon, so he can perform satanic rituals with my body.

Everything was going seamlessly. We connected in a way I've never connected with another person. He complimented me and made me feel adored and loved. Every time we kiss, I feel a plethora of fireworks going off inside me. My body tingled with such deep desire that I felt I couldn't breathe any longer if he didn't touch me. Then I gave it all up to him. I have no time for regrets. My virginity was not something sacred I was holding on to, and honestly, I don't miss having it. The pain was barely noticeable, and I credit that to the foreplay in my past, and my many battery-operated boyfriends.

My only regret is that Ridge will forever be a part of my memory because of tonight. I will never forget him, and that thought hurts more than knowing him in the first place. I will always have a constant reminder of how close I was to finding the perfect man for me. One who cherishes the ground I walk on. Opens doors for me. Fights for me. Bleeds for me. Only, Ridge is so much more than that and I can't handle the other parts of him. The other parts of him terrify me.

Once I reach Willamette House, I pull open the door and glance over my shoulder one last time. Ridge is standing under a lamppost, hands in his pockets, hood lifted on his head.

"Good night, Angel," he says. "I'll see you soon."

I jerk open the door and quickly jog up the stairs. Not stopping until I reach my room. My trembling fingers toss the keys around as I try to find the right one, and once I've got it, I unlock the door and barrel into the room.

As soon as the door is closed and locked, my back hits the wall and I slide down, head between my knees, then I cry over everything I've lost in the last forty-eight hours.

My self-respect is gone. My dignity is crushed. The security of my room is lost, which I'm reminded of when I look at the boarded-up window. It's also proof that someone took advantage of my body in my drunken state. Zeke is dead. Someone is out to hurt me. And Maddox...

I cry harder at the reminder of losing him. I liked Maddox so much. His friendship, his company, his heart. I can only hope he will remain in my life. His loyalty is with Ridge, so a relationship is out of the question, but I hope I can still keep his friendship.

Everything feels so broken. I feel so lost.

"Babe," Scar springs from her bed, startling me. "What's wrong?"

I clutch my chest as I try to steady my rapid heartbeat. "Shit. I didn't know you were here."

"Of course I'm here. I'm not leaving you alone at night again. I only stayed away last night because Maddox was here."

I sniffle, sucking up the snot that's threatening to drip from my nose. "Why are you in bed already?"

She hides her face with a pillow. "Little sore. Let's just say, the guys took good care of me tonight."

I push myself off the floor, choking down my heartbreak. "Umm. Details, girl. Spill." I sit down beside her and rip the pillow from her face, holding it in my lap.

The second she sees my face, she bolts upright. "Why are you crying?"

"I'm not."

Her fingers sweep under my eyes and she holds them up, showing proof of my tears. "What the hell did Ridge do this time?"

Dropping my head into the pillow on my lap, I use it to mask my words. "I did something bad, Scar."

In a swift motion, she jerks the pillow from me, tossing it across the room. "What the fuck did you do?"

"Had sex with Ridge."

Her back hits the mattress and she stares wide-eyed at the ceiling. "Girrrrl. Are you fucking insane? You do realize you basically just invited that vampire into your life?"

"He's not a vampire." I tap my chin in thought. "Though, now that I think about it. I'm not sure I've ever seen him sleep."

"Is this a joke to you? You literally gave up your V-card to a psychopath."

"Yup. I'm a virgin no more." I sing the words, when internally, I am screaming. "It was bound to happen eventually."

"But, Ridge? He's so...scary."

"He is." My voice goes soft, and I'm given empathetic eyes from Scar, which was not my intention.

"He didn't force you, did he?"

"No. Actually, I'm the one who threw myself at him. He was being so sweet. Saying all the right words."

"He was grooming you, babe. That's what guys like Ridge do."

"It's not like that. In my heart, I truly believe Ridge cares about me. He's just terrible at expressing it and doesn't want anyone else to love me either."

"What happened with Maddox? It seemed like you two were getting closer."

"I thought so, too. Then out of nowhere, he told me nothing more could happen between us because of Ridge. I was really starting to like him, too. After our conversation, I was feeling unwanted and vulnerable, then Ridge said everything I needed to hear. And—"

"You fucked him."

"Yup."

While this conversation is great and needs to happen, I can't help but feel like I should fill Scar in on the situation with Zeke. I know she'll help me in any way she can. My only fear is that she'll help too much.

"We need to talk," I say, tone flat.

She sits up, back straight. "What is it?"

I swallow hard, hoping I can get through this without crying my eyes out.

Then, I tell her everything Maddox told me. My phone. Maddox being a Guardian and knowing about my involvement in the governor's death. I spill everything, including buckets worth of tears.

By the end of the conversation, Scar is speechless. Her first word out is, "Fuck."

"Fuck is right."

"I need to tell the guys," she says. "Neo can make the whole thing with his father go away. He's got pull with The Elders over that case that we don't have. He can demand they drop it and close the case on the inside, just like it's been done on the outside."

"That would definitely be helpful, but what about Zeke?"

"Zeke practically raped you, Ry. Even if in some off chance they did pin you with his death, or murder, or whatever the fuck happened to him, the guy drugged you and took advantage of your body."

"But no one can know that. I don't want that kind of attention, Scar."

"Babe. You need to speak the fuck up. Zeke can't hurt you again, but there are a million other Zekes out there. One voice can make waves."

Scar has a point, but I'm not as strong as she is. I can't handle the emotional repercussions.

"We'll see if it comes to that. Until then, you'll talk to Neo?"

She nods. "Of course. I will."

I fall into her arms and she holds me tight while the worries of the day slip away. Until one more comes to mind.

"Hey, Scar," I mutter into the sleeve of her hoodie. "There's one more thing."

I can feel the tension rise in her chest as her shoulders lift. "What the fuck, Ry. You're like a Sunday morning newspaper today. All depressing and shit."

"I may or may not have made plans for tomorrow night." I

sit up, lips tight, and the tendons in my neck exposed. "I agreed to wrestle Melody Higgins in a mud pit at Delta Chi."

Scar falls back on the bed, her body limp. "Riley Cross, what am I going to do with you?"

I lean over her with a cheesy grin. "Just love me like you always do."

CHAPTER 26

RILEY

LAST YEAR, if someone would have told me I'd be preparing to roll around in a mud pit with Melody, I'd keel over with laughter.

Why? Because I don't like getting dirty, that's why.

Oh, and how about the fact that hundreds of students are gathered around the pit. Drinks in hand. They're even passing money around and placing bets on who will win.

"Two hundred on the short one," one guy says as he passes a wad of cash to a guy with a manila envelope.

"Two. Hundred. Dollars?" I mutter to Scar. "On me?" My eyes are ready to pop out of their sockets. "This is fucking insane."

I tug down my black sports bra, trying to cover the skin still showing of my stomach. But that's not how sports bras work and there's nothing discreet in what I've got on. Matching black boy shorts and a bra. That's it. Nothing more and nothing less. No panties. No bra under the bra. And it's only fifty-five damn degrees out.

Yep. I've officially lost my mind.

"You've got this, Ry."

"Says the girl who wanted to slap me for agreeing to this."

"Well, now that you have, you can't back out. Melody will never let you live it down."

I find my corner near the pit. It's the size of a large pool filled with mud. If I had to guess, I'd say it's at least calf-deep. There's a wooden sign standing on a couple two-by-fours that says, *Delta Chi Mud Pit. Let's Get Dirty.*

My nerves are at an all-time high when I spot Melody on the other side. If I thought I was underdressed, I was wrong. She's wearing a two-piece bikini, white at that, and the bottoms are a thong. Her hair is down, which I may use to my advantage, if it's allowed. *Shit.* I don't even know the rules here. "What do I do?" I ask Scar. "I've never done this. Do I hit her?"

Scar laughs. "You do whatever the hell it takes. Melody is a pansy. You're badass. Keep that in mind. She might be taller than you, but you've got a good fifteen pounds on her. Just stay low and go for her waist."

I feel like one of those fighters getting a pep talk before a big match. Only, I don't get a mouthpiece and I have no prior training.

My eyes dance around the crowd from face to face. Tall flames dance in the distance, and I'm so jealous of the people surrounding the fire. I shiver, my nipples ready to slice through the cotton fabric of my bra. "There are so many people, Scar." She slaps my ass really fucking hard and I wince. "What the hell!"

"Just pumping you up. This is gonna be epic." The roar of her laugh is almost too evil.

"I hate you."

"You love me."

"Attention, everyone." Carly taps into the mic from where she's standing tall on a wooden stepladder. "We're so glad you could come to our last-minute event. We have two fierce competitors today. Give it up for one of our own, Delta Chi sister, Melody Higgins." The crowd erupts when Melody dances her way out to the center of the pit, mud sloshing around and already coating her cute white bikini. "And freshman hottie, Riley Cross."

My heart sinks into the mud beneath my feet as Scar shoves me out into the pit. I glance over my shoulder at her and mouth the words, "I do not love you."

She bursts out laughing, along with Crew and Jagger, who are now standing beside her. Neo stands off in the distance, but there's a smile playing on his lips, too. Of course, the only time the fucker would smile is when I'm about to become mud pie.

I'm drudging through the thick brown muck, heading to the center of the pit. It would be just my luck that I'd trip and fall over. Melody would probably pounce and drown me.

Once I'm in front of Melody, who is wearing the biggest, nastiest, shit-eating grin, Carly resumes her announcement. "The rules are simple, ladies. No hair pulling. And no face blows."

Chats and hollers surround us and my heart beats even faster.

And fuck my life, Melody's mischievous eyes say she's ready to go hog wild.

"Prepare yourself, bitch!"

"Teeth" by 5 Seconds of Summer comes on, blasting through the speakers on each side of the pit.

"Shoulders down for a three-count and the winner takes home...absolutely nothing, but a big ego and panties full of dirt." Carly beams. "Are y'all ready?"

No. No. No.

But I nod, and Melody throws her hands in the air and shouts, "Let's fucking go." The crowd goes insane. Singing, shouting, clapping. There are hoots and hollers and I know I have to at least try. Giving up is not an option.

Melody comes toward me and I hold my hands out like claws ready to grab, while keeping the distance between our bodies.

We do a little dance, slapping at each other's hands, but then I hear Scar shout, "Take her down, Ry!" And my adrenaline soars.

Springing at Melody, I'm able to catch her off guard. "Who's the bitch now, bitch." I grab her wrists, pulling and twisting, while mud splashes, coating both our bodies. I lean to the left, fighting like hell to toss her whole body in the mud, but my own leg is kicked out from underneath me and I'm the first to drop.

I hold on tight, my nails dragging down the surface of her arm, and she tumbles right beside me. Both on our sides, we snatch and seize and tug.

"You scratched me, whore!"

Her name-calling only fuels the fire inside me and I manage to get the upper hand by climbing on top of her. Legs straddling her waist, I knock away her hands that are coming right at my face. Somehow, I got a mouthful of dirt, the crunching an annoyance between my teeth. I turn my head to the right and spit.

Melody bucks her hips up hard and fast, sending me in the air a couple inches, but I drop right back down, thrusting a gasp out of her.

One of her hands lands on my shoulder and she drags her nails down as hard and as ferociously as she can. Ignoring the sting, I take that same hand and pin it over her head. My face is now hovering over hers. "Give up, Melody. You don't stand a chance."

"Oh yeah?" She smirks, using her other hand to scratch me

again, but this time, she gets a firm grip on my bra and pulls until one of the straps rips. She doesn't stop. She keeps pulling until it's resting around my stomach and my breasts are exposed.

"Fuck yeah. Nice tits. That's what I'm talking about." Those are a few of the things being said by the students surrounding the pit.

I lean forward, pressing my chest to hers in an attempt to hide myself, never once relenting on the hand that I have pinned. Squeezing her body as hard as I can with my legs that are caged around her, I peel off her other hand that's now pinching my bicep. I get a good grip on it and slam it into the mud, holding her down.

"One. Two," Carly counts, and I hold tighter, just needing that last number. "Three." Right as she says it, I'm wrapped up in a jacket—a black leather jacket—then I'm ripped off of Melody.

The next thing I know, I'm being tossed over someone's shoulder, dripping with mud.

It's not just someone. It's *him*.

"What the hell, Ridge?" I kick my legs and claw my mud-packed nails into the top of his head as I try to lift up. But he pushes his hand on my back, keeping me snug to his shoulder, while slogging through the mud. "Put me down. This is so fucking humiliating."

He climbs up the ledge and picks up his pace, hauling me away like a bag of trash. "Ridge Foster, I am going to *kill* you."

"Then you're gonna do it in private with your fucking shirt on." His voice is laced with malice and I'm certain his downright pissed.

"You have no right!"

"I have every right!" he shouts back even louder.

His hand moves from my back and he kicks open one of the French doors of the Delta Chi House.

"Let me go, asshole! We're not even supposed to be in here!"

He doesn't respond, nor does he set me down. Instead, he walks briskly down the narrow hall.

"Ridge!" I hear Scar shout as she enters the door we just came through. I lift up and look over my shoulder to see her and Crew coming toward us at full speed. Crew's clad with clenched fists and a smoldering glare. It's a look I've seen before, and not one I care to see right now.

"Put her down now!" Crew hollers.

Still, Ridge just keeps walking, as if no one is on our trail. His shoulders tighten and rise and he holds me closer, his arm snug around my muddy ass and his hand gripping my outer thigh.

I watch intently as Crew jogs to catch up, and once he does, he jumps in front of Ridge. "Put her the fuck down."

Ridge sweeps one hand out and shoves Crew hard into the wall. He bounces right off of it and lunges at Ridge, who is forced to loosen his hold on me. I slide down his back, feet catching on the floor before trying to position myself between them.

I slide my arms into the sleeves of Ridge's leather jacket and close it over my chest to hide my breasts. "Stop, you guys..."

My words trail off when Crew punches Ridge square in the eye. Like a complete psychopath, Ridge just stands there and takes it with a smirk on his face. Crew wraps his hands around Ridge's waist and brings him down to the floor. His back hits with a thud that has me wincing. Ridge doesn't even fight back. In fact, I'm sure I heard him laugh through the pain being inflicted on him.

"Stop!" I shout, while attempting to pull Crew off of Ridge.

"I'm okay," I tell him, hoping he ends this madness. I know he's doing this for me, and for Scar. I'm sure she told the guys to help me. But I don't need help.

Scar grabs a hold of me and pulls me back, wrapping her arms around my front and holding the jacket closed. "It's time Ridge gets what's coming to him, babe."

"No," I cry out. "He was just protecting me from prying eyes. I don't want him to get hurt."

"Ry! He carried you away like he owns you, even when you told him to stop. After everything he's done to you, he deserves this. He's a fucking sicko."

Crew lands two hard blows on Ridge's face and I beg and plead for him to stop—for someone to make him stop.

Then Ridge's tired eyes meet mine.

Suddenly, as if he just got a boost of adrenaline, Ridge grabs Crew and flips him over. Crew's back crashes against the floor and Ridge gains the upper hand.

With his fist cocked back, he looks at me again.

"No." I shake my head. "Please don't."

He drops his hand and leans down, whispering something in Crew's ear that has his eyes widening.

"Let go of me!" I squirm out of Scar's arms and drop to my knees beside Ridge, who's bleeding from his lip and his one eye is already swelling. Tears fall recklessly from my eyes and my heart pangs with such a deep agony.

Lifting my head slightly, I look at Scar. "He might be a sicko, but he's a sicko who would move heaven and earth for me."

Ridge has tormented me, instilled fear inside me, made me cry, and made me wanna hide, but he's the one person who is *always* there.

"I'm okay," Ridge chokes out, blood running down his face

as he tries to sit up. I push him back down gently, knowing it's too soon for him to try and stand.

Soon, we're surrounded by students, including angry girls who are pissed at the bloody mess made in the hallway.

Scar apologizes, and while I'm still so angry at her for siccing Crew on Ridge, I understand why she did it.

After a few minutes and a few towels to soak up the blood, Maddox appears. In all the commotion, I didn't realize he found us. He and I get Ridge to his feet, so we can get him home, but it's not an easy task.

"Shuttle's here," Maddox says.

With Ridge in the middle, he strings his arms around mine and Maddox's neck, and we walk out the front door to the campus shuttle waiting for us. It's a rarity to get space on one of these things, but I'm grateful we've got it tonight because Ridge's head seems to be in a fog.

The shuttle is packed full of students leaving Delta Chi and some who are coming and going elsewhere. My muddy state warrants me a glare from the driver, but I keep moving down the aisle. There's only one seat in the middle of the shuttle, so we get Ridge in it. Maddox slides in next to him and pats his lap. I hesitate, unsure how Ridge is going to react. It's more than apparent he doesn't play nice when it comes to me and other guys—or anyone for that matter.

But when his head rests against the window, blood dripping down the side of the seat, I'm sure he's not paying any attention.

"You're gonna get dirty," I warn Maddox, referencing the mud all over me.

"I don't mind."

"Suit yourself." I sit down, one foot in the aisle and the other snug against the seat in front of us. I keep my back straight. This whole situation is tense as hell. "You'll have to keep him awake for a while," I tell Maddox, hoping to ease some of the awkwardness.

"I'm fine," Ridge grumbles, lifting his wobbly head. It wavers back and forth as he tries to hold it upright, and now I'm starting to wonder if he's drunk.

"Has he been drinking tonight?"

"Yeah. He's shit-faced," Maddox tells me, and I sigh.

Ridge pats at his shirt before looking at the open leather jacket I'm wearing. Lustful eyes pin to my chest and I grasp it quickly, covering myself. "You got my booze." His hand extends and pushes one of the flaps of his jacket open, fingers grazing the skin of my breast. Goosebumps erupt over my body and my breath hitches as he pulls out a pocket-sized bottle of some clear liquor.

I gulp and toss a glance at Maddox, who's watching me with heavy concentration. It's apparent he saw my body react to Ridge's touch.

"What? Why are you looking at me like that?"

He turns his head away without a word. Maddox is so damn confusing and his behavior lately is giving me whiplash. He pushes me away, then pulls me back in. It's frustrating as hell. I liked him. I *really* liked him. But he made this choice for us, not me.

The shuttle stops in front of the main campus and a handful of students stand to get off. Maddox pats the side of my thigh, telling me this is where we exit.

I stand up...but he doesn't. "Are you coming?" I ask, gaze wandering from Maddox to Ridge, whose eyes are closed with an open bottle tilted in his hand.

"This is your stop. Not ours."

My heart drops. I'm not even sure why I assumed we were all going to the same place, but of course we're not.

I nod in response. "Take care of him, 'kay?"

Ignoring me, Maddox takes the bottle from Ridge before it spills and doesn't give me a second look.

"You getting off or what?" the driver calls out to me.

So I do, part of me wishing I'd never left Delta Chi with these guys in the first place.

CHAPTER 27
MADDOX

THREE YEARS AGO, my dad sat me down and explained to me what a Guardian is.

We're the good ones, son. We make good choices and we protect the good members by weeding out the bad ones.

Those were his words, among many others. In conclusion, I've been taught Guardians do no wrong. I've always believed it to be true. I walk alongside my friends, watching as they make wrong choice after wrong choice, never judging them in the process, but praying like hell they never get caught because I know what happens to those bad seeds. They never flourish. They're stomped in the dirt and left behind with no roots to grow.

Every choice I've made has been done with my dad in mind. All I've ever sought in life is his approval, and so far I've got it. He pats me on the back when I do good. He praises my achievements. And I walk away from him with my head held high and a smile on my face, knowing that I made him proud.

But what will he do when he finds out I've not only shared secrets with another member, but I'm also protecting her?

My dad wants so badly to believe that Riley is one of those bad seeds. He's working tirelessly to prove she not only killed the governor but is also involved in the death of these other men, Zeke included.

I also learned that my dad is the one who put out the assignment that was handed down to Ridge. For reasons unbeknown to me, my dad has a loyalty to the governor and wants the truth revealed and the members involved to pay.

Another life was taken. Another person connected to the governor, employed at a factory he owned. There was no evidence left behind, but naturally, my dad assumes it involves Riley. No matter how hard I try to convince him it's not her, it's all he believes.

I can't fathom why my dad is so hell-bent on proving the governor did not take his own life. What is his connection to Sebastian Saint? Where does this loyalty stem from? And why the hell does he have a vendetta against Riley?

Pieces of the puzzle are missing, but they exist. I just have to find them.

My phone beeps with a text, and I immediately know who it's from. Earlier today, I sent Riley a message just to thank her for helping with Ridge last night, and to let her know I still plan to help her. The choice I had to make wasn't an easy one, but it was the right one. Being around Riley so often is dangerous. I could already feel myself falling for her. Ridge is my best fucking friend and he doesn't deserve that sort of betrayal.

> Riley: Thank you.

That's it? Thank you. I asked her questions. Wanted to know how she was doing. And all I get is a 'thank you'?

> Me: You're pissed at me, aren't you?

I lean against the wall in front of the school, waiting for her response before my next class of the afternoon.

> Riley: Why would I be pissed at you? It's not like you told me you liked me, only to turn around and tell me nothing could come of it.

But I did do those things. And now I feel like a fucking asshole for it.

> Me: You should be pissed. I'm pretty mad at myself right now.

> Riley: Then don't let Ridge control your life.

> Me: Says the girl who fucked him...

I backspace and delete the message, knowing it'll just make things worse. *But dammit!* Why would she do that? I know I should be happy for my boy, but I'm not. It fucking kills me knowing that he got the girl I want.

> Me: It's not about control. It's about a twenty-year friendship.

> Riley: Then I guess I should be glad to have you as a friend, friend.

I don't respond because it'll be sent out of frustration and I'm likely to put my foot in my mouth. Or my hand. However that saying goes when it's a typed text message. Instead, I slide my phone in the front pocket of my jeans and head into class. Class with her.

She's wearing a scowl. Eyebrows caved and her bottom lip between her teeth. Her shoulders lift slightly when I pass behind her, but she doesn't even lift her head.

Yeah. She's pissed.

But you know what? So am I. I'm allowed to be pissed, too. I told her I liked her. We kissed a couple times. I risked a lot for those fucking moments, and the second I do the right thing, she falls right onto Ridge's cock.

He was grinning from ear to ear when he came home. Told me all about their rendezvous in the stadium theater room. It was fifteen minutes of pure fucking torture.

Forgoing my usual seat in the row behind Riley, I take it upon myself to drop my bag on the table right beside her. It lands with a thud, rattling the table.

We'll see if she can avoid looking at me after that.

Yet, her eyes stay fixed on her book.

She's a tough one, that's for sure.

Professor Atkins begins his lecture, so I pull out the chair and sit down. With my bag still on the table, I take out my shit for this class, making no attempt not to disrupt whatever she's got going on beside me. I glance over and it looks like she's reading last night's chapter on verbal and nonverbal cues.

"Ya know," I whisper, trying to steal her attention as I zip up my bag on the table. "One might say that nonverbal cues relay more information than verbal cues. And that look on your face right now, proves it to be true."

Her eyes roll toward me. "I'm not pissed, remember?"

"Oh, but I think you are."

She slams her textbook closed and turns to face me, while the rest of the class takes in Professor Atkins's lecture on last night's reading.

"I feel nothing toward you, Maddox. Therefore, I have no reason to be upset about anything you want or don't want from me."

I turn to face her, our knees resting against one another's, and I whisper, "And what is it you think I don't want from you, *Riley?*"

"I'm not playing these games with you. I have enough going on in my life already."

"You mean, like your mud wrestling tournament last night?" I swallow down the laugh bubbling in my throat and she swats my leg.

"Not funny."

"In that case, I'll try really hard not to laugh at the memory of Melody eating mud."

She tries hard not to smile, but it's not long before one grows on her lips. "How is Ridge doing?"

"He's fine. Skipping class today and nursing a hangover and a swollen face."

"Nothing's broken, right?"

"Nah. He'll be all right. Black eye on top of his other black eye, and a bruised cheek. Nothing Ridge hasn't had before."

"I'm glad to hear that. I didn't realize how drunk he was. I'm sure if Crew knew, he would have never gone at him like that."

"Fuck Crew. He wouldn't have cared either way. He'll get what's coming to him."

"No," she snaps, warranting a 'shh' from Professor Atkins. Her tone drops as she continues, "Please don't make more trouble. There's enough crazy stuff going on. The last thing any of us need is to make more enemies."

"No one said you have to. But Crew made three of them when he went at my boy. Sorry, Riley. It's nothing personal, and it's probably best if you stay out of it."

"It *is* personal, though. It puts me right in the middle."

"Of what? It's not like you have any loyalty to Ridge. He's just some obsessed psycho, right?"

My statement was more of a question to get a feel for where her head is at with Ridge. And she answers it as such. "Maybe I do feel some sort of loyalty to him. Ridge is protective of me, and I guess, in some weird way, I feel like I need to protect him, too."

"Look," I say, re-entering her personal space, "I don't want any hard feelings between us, Riley."

"I really don't either."

I put my hand out to her, hoping she'll return the gesture. "Friends?"

When she places her hand in mine, my gut wrenches. Was sort of hoping she'd give me shit for that. Really wanted her to show me that she wants more. It's best this way, though. Even if my heart is telling my brain to shut the fuck up.

"Friends," she says, sealing it with a handshake.

I did what I had to do. She's not my girl—she's his.

CHAPTER 28
RILEY

THERE ARE many times I question my actions, wondering how I could be such a complete idiot. This is one of those times.

I ball my fist, ready to knock, before dropping it back down and second-guessing myself. A sane person would turn and walk away. A sane person would have never come here in the first place. Maybe that's why Ridge is so drawn to me—because we're both fucking insane.

Swallowing hard, while hoping I'm not making the wrong choice, I knock on the door before I can change my mind again.

I've been so hurt over Maddox telling me we could only be friends, yet here I am pulling the same shit with Ridge. I shut him out, pretending he's not there, then I have sex with him, only to shoot him down again. Now I'm back, ready to do it all over again.

The door comes open and I immediately jump back when I'm face to face with someone unexpected.

"What the fuck do you want, Trouble?"

I'm not sure why Lev has the ability to make me feel like gum on the bottom of a shoe, but he does.

Standing tall, I keep my head held high, showing him I am not affected by his cruelty. "Hi, Lev. Is Ridge home?"

"Ridge? Why are you looking for Ridge? Didn't I just see you with Maddox the other night?"

There it is again. That two-inch-tall, gum-on-a-shoe feeling. "Yes, you did. But Ridge is my friend, too."

"Ridge doesn't have friends that aren't me and Maddox. So tell me what you really want with him."

There's no way Lev doesn't know how obsessed with me Ridge is. Unless he's really fucking blind. Or just plain oblivious. "Honestly, Lev. That's not any of your business. Is he home or not?"

Lev braces himself on the doorframe, a smug look on his face. "Yeah. Ridge is here. Wanna see him?"

I inhale a deep breath. "That *is* why I'm here."

He steps aside and waves me inside. The door closes with a bang, and I jump. When I hear the lock click, I spin around to see him standing with his back against the door, hands draped at his sides.

"Where is he?" I ask, seeing that all three beds are empty.

"Oh, right. Ridge." He takes a step toward me. Then another. "Yeah. He's not here."

"What the hell, Lev? Why'd you let me in then?"

"If you're fucking with my best friends, I think it's only fair I get to know you, too, Trouble."

"I'm not *fucking* with them. As I said, we're friends."

He comes closer, and each step has my pulse pounding. I can handle Ridge's crazy antics—he wouldn't hurt me. I can't say the same for Lev.

"And as I said," he sweeps my chin with his index finger, "Ridge doesn't have friends."

"Fine," I blurt out, passing by him to get to the door. "Tell Ridge I stopped by to check on him." I click the lock and turn the handle, but as I open it, it slams shut. I gasp when I see Lev's palm pressed to the door. "What are you doing?" I ask, staring straight ahead, avoiding eye contact—avoiding any sort of interaction with this guy at all.

"Thought we were gonna get to know each other."

I let go of the handle and lift my chin, still not looking at him. "The other night you threatened me. Why would I care to get to know you at all?"

"Oh, I didn't threaten you, Trouble. I made a promise. You fuck with my friends; you fuck with me. And you don't wanna do that." His hand finds the sheen of skin exposed from my cut-off sweatshirt, fingers teetering on my side. "Unless you do."

I slap his hand down, remembering when Zeke was in my room and how weak I was with him. Even if I thought it was Ridge, I was at his mercy. Never again will I be at another man's mercy. "Don't touch me," I grit out.

He leans close, breathing heavily into the small space between us. "Has Maddox touched you? How about Ridge?"

"I told you...we're just friends."

Lev tsks, clicking his tongue on the roof of his mouth. "You really gotta quit tossing that word around so lightly. How well do you even know my boys? Well enough to call them *friends?*"

"I know enough, and as I've said before, it's not your business. I have no interest in being your friend and I certainly don't have any interest in getting to know you." I look at his hand that's still cemented to the door. "Now if you don't mind, I'd like to leave."

He nods toward the door. "Go ahead. No one's stopping you."

Yet, his hand still remains pressed to it.

"Then move, *asshole!*"

"Make me, Trouble."

"Ugh!" I grumble, grabbing his hand and trying to pry it off the door. "You're so infuriating." In an instant, he grabs my hand, pinching my fingers together so tightly, I fear one will break. "Quit it. You're hurting me." I try to pull away to no avail because he only strengthens his hold.

"I'll let you go...for now. But when you come back, I'll have you begging on your knees for mercy."

I pull my hand again and tear open the door as fast as I can, not even bothering to close it behind me. My feet don't stop moving—down the hall, down the stairs, and out the main doors.

Once the cool, night air hits my face, I curl over and put my hands on my knees. A hand on my back has my soul jumping out of my skin.

When I stand up, I see Ridge. Breathing out a heavy sigh of relief, I grasp my chest. "Jesus, Ridge. You scared me."

"You never need to be afraid, Angel. I'm always keeping you safe."

I start walking down the sidewalk, knowing he'll follow. "You say that, and sometimes I think it's true, but do you realize how much bad shit has happened to me when you're *not* watching?"

"No. Tell me."

"How about the fact that you're emotionally fucked-up roommate just tried to keep me prisoner in your room. Or what about—"

"Lev did that?"

I nod, feet still moving. "Sure did."

Ridge puts a hand on my shoulder, stopping me. "Stay right here." Then he walks steadfastly back toward the hall.

"Ridge, no." I jog after him. When I catch up, I grab the back of his shirt. "Please, just let it go."

He spins around and I lose my hold on his shirt. "No one is

allowed to hurt you, Angel. Not physically, and not emotionally. I don't care who it is."

Why is he so good to me, yet so unruly at the same time?

Rain begins sprinkle down from the sky and I look up, noticing the dark clouds hovering. "I'm okay. I promise." I lick my lips, pausing for a beat before saying, "Can we go somewhere out of the rain and talk?"

"For once, I can say yes. Ya know, since I can talk now." His eyebrows rise and he cracks a smile. It's cute, especially the pronounced dimples on each cheek. I like when Ridge smiles. It's a reminder that he's human and not some robot. "I know just the spot." He takes my hand and walks with me in tow. His feet move so fast, I can barely keep up. "Hurry up," he says, urging me along like he's a child on his way to a toy store.

I try to keep up and I'm not sure when it happened, but suddenly, it's pouring out and then we're running through the rain, laughing our asses off.

We take a turn to the left, past the main campus, then a right. "Where are we going?" I roar over the downpour.

"Almost there."

It's really coming down hard and I've got no idea where Ridge is taking me, but we keep on running, entering a path in the woods. Before long, I spot the river. The rain pelts into the water, creating a mist of condensation overtop.

We're going too fast for me to even think that maybe this is a bad idea, and just when I decide to speak up, we stop. Right in front of us is a small shack—like a hunting shack of sorts. Ridge rips open the door and steps inside, waiting for me to follow.

When I enter, water dripping down my body, I see kayaks and paddles, life jackets, fishing rods, and hooks holding towels. "What is this place?"

"An old storage shed for river gear."

Bunching my hair to one side, I wring it out. "I'm soaked."

"You're beautiful. I think I love you even more in the rain."

I laugh, finding it odd. "Why's that?"

"Because I get to see the real you. No makeup. No hair spray. Just you. You're the most beautiful thing I've ever laid eyes on, Angel."

Wow. I didn't expect that. Also didn't anticipate the butterflies that are now fluttering in my stomach. I'm pretty sure my cheeks are blushing, but it's cloudy out, and there's not much daylight shining through the cracks, so Ridge can't see. Not that I'd care if he did. Ridge doesn't care if I blush. Or if I'm angry. Or sad. Or happy. Ridge doesn't care if I'm soaked with smeared mascara running down my face. In fact, he loves me even more when I'm me.

So why am I doing this? Why did I ask him to talk, just so I could break his heart?

"Talk to me," he says, sweeping a thumb under my eye, then the other, wiping away what I assume is smeared makeup. "What's on your mind, Angel?"

I don't know where to start. I don't even know what I plan to say, just that I need to finally tell him exactly what I think about him and the way he behaves. Only then can he finally move on and find someone who loves him the way I know he will fiercely love them.

"I don't know where you came from, Ridge. One day, you were just there and you never left. I'm pretty sure it was the end of the summer. I saw you sitting in a tree." He nods, confirming that was the first time. He takes my hands in his, and I know—I can tell by that look of adoration glistening in his eyes, he thinks I'm going to confess my undying love for him. But that's not at all what I'm doing. What I'm about to say is going to crush this guy—and that hurts. It hurts so damn bad.

I clear my throat and continue, "You took me by surprise.

Honestly didn't think I'd ever even stand face to face with you and have a conversation like this—"

"That's my fault, Angel. I should've been strong enough to speak to you in the first place. I tried. Lord knows I tried. You deserved so much more than what I gave you and I'm going to spend my life speaking and telling you just how perfect you are."

"Don't say that."

"It's true."

I remove my hands from his and sweep away the water under my eyes; only this time, it's not rainwater. "Don't say nice things to me like that, Ridge. I don't deserve it. Not from you."

"Angel," he spins me around, taking in my red eyes, "you deserve the world and more."

"But I don't. Your heart is so big, Ridge. But it's not mine for the taking, and mine is not yours."

"Stop that."

"Let me finish."

"No! I don't wanna hear it. Don't you dare talk like that." He grabs my shoulders, holding me with all his strength. My body shakes as words of pain and anger spill from his mouth. "We are destined to be together. Your heart is mine and mine is yours. Take it, break it, but please don't let it go."

"I...I can't." I swallow down the hard lump in my throat, feeling it settle at the bottom of my stomach. "I will never love you, Ridge. I want to be with Maddox and I want you to tell him it's okay to be with me."

Have you ever looked at someone and literally seen their heart break? Not just a sliver or a crack—a full-on break? I could have ripped it from his chest with my bare hands and he'd still have the same look of melancholy that he has right now.

Still holding me, I'm certain it's now because his legs have gone weak, he takes an uneven step to the left, then back to the center, and to the left again. His mouth opens, but no words come out.

"I'm so sorry, Ridge." Tears continue to slide down my cheeks and the second I see one fall from his eye, my own heart might as well have been torn from my chest.

A second of silence passes, then another, and another, and I'm desperate to hear his thoughts.

"Say something. Please."

His mouth opens and closes, only to open again, but there's no sound. No words. No screams. No whispers of the pain he's feeling inside.

It's just...silent.

With a trembling chin, he drops his hold on me and pushes open the door. I grab his arm as he steps off to the side, making room for me to exit. "Please..."

He knocks my arm down, forcing my hand off of him, then he shoves me out the door and slams it closed.

CHAPTER 29
RIDGE

MY WORDS FAILED ME AGAIN. At a time when I needed them most, they failed me. Will I ever be enough? Will this world ever accept me for my thorns, scars, and imperfections?

"My angel says she'll never love me and that's okay. I don't need her love. I only need her to accept mine. I long to shower her with sunshine and warmth. Pepper her body with kisses and see her smiling face when I wake, only to see it again before I sleep. There will never be another person for me. Even if there is someone else for her." I run my fingers down the bloody blade, wiping it clean. "What would you do, Eric?" He gurgles and chokes as blood spills from the corner of his mouth. But I know what he's thinking. "You're right. I have to fight harder."

I drag the clean blade across his throat, bloodying it again while smiling with gratitude. "Thanks for listening to me. Not many take the time to hear me out, but you did."

After cleaning the knife once more, I stick it in its black sheath and put it in the pocket of my coat. It's a different coat than the one I normally wear because Riley still has my favorite one. That's okay, though. She probably sleeps with it at night, a reminder of me—her first. No matter how hard she might try to replace me with Maddox, he can never take that moment from us. I will always be her first.

Lighting a match, I toss it on the body doused in lighter fluid, then I check him off my list.

~~Dennis Mathers~~
~~Robby Nelson~~
~~Andy Porter~~
~~Eric Mathers~~

Mission complete.

I did it all for her. Now there is no one left to trace her to the death of the governor. Aside from her friends. But they won't speak a word about it. I'll fabricate some sort of evidence that shows the governor wanted to take his own life, and The Elders will be pleased.

Riley's secret should be safe.

I'm sticking my notepad back in my pocket with the knife when leaves rustle from behind me. My eyes snap over my shoulder and the movements stop.

Pivoting around slowly, I keep my wits about me, watching for any sign of a lurker.

Then, a shadow bolts through the woods, hauling ass and making no attempt to quiet their steps.

I take off toward it. Running at full speed, I come up on the edge of the pines. Each row lined perfectly, my path a mix of brown, dead pine needles. "Come out, come out, wherever you are," I sing through the breeze that's making the branches sway above me.

Out of the corner of my eye, I see the lurker zip to the right. I head off the path in his direction, swerving and dodging trees.

Before long, I'm at the ledge of a small hill overlooking the river. Then I see the lurker bolt down the edge of the river, until he disappears from my eyesight.

Fuck!

Someone knows.

———

Feeling derailed and hopeless, I stumble through the door to my dorm. The second I see Maddox, my feelings of defeat are replaced with indignation. I reach into my pocket and pull out the sheath-covered knife, pointing at where he sits in his bed. His eyes lift from his laptop, wide and panic-stricken. "You think you can take her from me?"

"Whoa, Ridge." His hands go up in surrender. "Put the fucking knife down."

"It's covered, pussy. I'm not gonna stab you. But I should."

"I don't know why you're pissed, but if this is about Riley, I told her we could only be friends."

"Did you now?" I walk closer to him, still holding out the knife. "Well then, why did she come to me today and ask me to give my blessing for you two to be together?"

His eyebrows shoot to his forehead, and he drops his hands. "She did?"

I nod. "Yeah. She did. And I wanna know everything. Every single fucking detail of everything you two have ever talked about or done." I roll my neck, cracking it before narrowing my eyes at him again. "Did you fuck her, Maddox?"

"What? No! We kissed. You know that. That's it."

"What did you do to make her like you so much?"

"I swear, Ridge. I didn't do anything to try and pull her in. I was just myself."

Dammit. Had a feeling that was all. Everyone loves Maddox. Maddox is perfect. Maddox is good.

"I fucking hate you." I drop my hand, resting the knife at my side. "I really fucking hate your holier-than-thou bullshit. Your strikingly good looks. I hate the way you fucking smile,

Maddox. You know that? Everyone loves your smile. Not me. I hate it! You're like the Marcia fucking Brady of our bunch. Everyone loves Maddox."

He closes his laptop and swings his legs over the side of his bed. "I'm not gonna be with her. Not even gonna act on any feelings I've got."

My eyes shoot to his. "You have feelings for her?"

His shoulders rise, holding tight around his neck. "Well, yeah. I like her a lot, but you're my best friend. I'd never do that to you."

"See," I grumble, shaking the knife in my hand that's now pointed at the floor, "a fucking saint, you are."

"Hey," he says, now on his feet. "What's our motto?"

"Don't start with me right now. I don't need this sappy blast from the past pact bullshit."

"Say it, Ridge."

Dragging my words lazily, I say, "We will reign."

"Damn straight, we will, and no one, I mean no one, is going to get in our way. No one comes between us. We're brothers—me, you, and Lev."

"She did, though. She came between us. She's right in the center." I wave the knife toward the center of our room. "A big fucking elephant sitting right there."

"She's nothing to me."

"She's everything. She's everything, Maddox. She's the sun and the rain, and the stars and the moon. She's classic novels and horror movies. Song lyrics and music notes." I drop down on the couch, letting the knife fall to the floor. "She's fucking everything."

"Don't give up so soon, Ridge. She'll come around eventually. Just give her some space."

My eyes shoot to his. "Oh, I'm not giving up. And even as I tell you to go get her, I'm still not giving up. Her happiness is what's important and if you can make her happy while she waits for me, then I can deal. When I say we will reign, I mean it for all of us. Riley included. So go get her, but keep in mind, I'm going after her, too."

Maddox blows out an airy chuckle. "I'm not going after her. I already told you—"

"Yes, you are. Now get the fuck out of here." I reach down and pick the knife back up, then point it at the door. "I won't be the reason for your misery or hers. You can try, but I can't promise you'll win."

Maddox steps forward, then back. Forward then back like a damn toddler learning to walk. "Are you fucking with me?"

"I'm gonna fuck you up if you don't get out of here right now. Don't make me regret this, Maddox. And if you hurt her," I pull the sheath off the knife, exposing the blade, "I will choose her."

That's enough for him to snatch his jacket off the hook and leave.

I've always known I feel things too deeply and love too hard. But it's not just Riley. I love my boys, too. A life alone is not a life worth living, and I can't imagine doing it without her, or them. My happiness is in the back seat, and they're all riding shotgun.

CHAPTER 30

RILEY

"I NEEDED THIS," I tell Scar, who's standing behind me at her vanity, French-braiding my hair. "Everything has been so chaotic lately, so a night with my bestie is perfect."

Her hips sway to Taylor Swift's "Anti-Hero" as she weaves the braid. "Agreed. It's been great staying with the guys and my bed is going to be cold tonight, but I've missed this. We need to do it more often."

"I just still feel so bad for Ridge—"

"Ah," she cuts me off with a hard glare in the mirror, "we're not talking about him, remember?"

"Maddox?"

"Nope."

"The guy who fell to his death from our window?"

"Not a chance."

A knock at the door has us looking at each other in the mirror. "Who could that be?" I ask her.

"No clue. My guys are at the gym, so it must be one of yours."

My eyes roll. "I don't have any guys, Scar."

"Yeah." She snaps the small rubber band at the end of my hair. "You do. Whether you want to admit it or not."

She walks to the door, shaking her ass to the beat of the music, and I bark out a laugh.

When she pulls open the door and Maddox is standing there, the cheerful expression drops suddenly from my face.

Scar holds the door, waving me toward him. "Seems I was right."

Getting off the vanity stool, I cross the room. "What are you doing here?"

"Can we talk?"

I look at Scar, seeking approval, since this was supposed to be a *bestie night* for just us. She sighs heavily, then nods. "Go ahead."

In a pair of gray sweatpants and a tee shirt, with bare feet, I go into the hall and close the door behind me.

"Everything okay?"

"Yeah." Maddox scratches the back of head before retracting his one-word statement. "Actually...no." He grabs my face and pulls my mouth to his in an unexpected yet searing kiss.

Completely caught off guard, I'm not sure how to react. Pull away? Kiss him back?

I go for the latter and I have no regrets. My hands find his waist and I hold him tight while our mouths part, and my tongue slides in, tangling with his.

His warm lips open and close around mine, tingles of desire rippling through me. In an instant, Maddox pushes me against the wall, his heated body flush with mine.

I have no idea where this is coming from, but I hope it's not a fluke. Maddox said we could only be friends, so what the hell is going on?

Our mouths close, and he steps back, breaking the kiss but still holding my face in his palms. Before he can say anything, I blurt out, "What was that for?"

His mouth tugs up in a grin. "Just wanted to see if you were still a good kisser."

"And?" I grin back, warmth assaulting my belly.

"Even better than last time."

He pecks my mouth again, then runs his hands down my arms, watching his movements. "I fucked up, Riley. I can't be your friend. Not when I desperately want to be so much more."

"But...Ridge?"

"Told me to come here. He's fucking insane, but his heart is gold."

I'm speechless. I can't believe Ridge would encourage Maddox to pursue something with me.

"So he's moving on?"

"No," Maddox shakes his head, "not even a little bit. But he's not standing in our way. At least, not for now."

I'm not sure what that means, but I'll take it...for now. I'll take all I can get from Maddox.

Dropping his hands, he nods to the floor before sitting down. His knees bend with his wrists draped over them. "There's also something else."

"Oh boy." I sit down beside him. "What now?"

"Got a call from my dad. No prints were found on Zeke or the glass he was stabbed with. Not a single one."

My eyes widen. "What's that mean?"

"It means he either fell, or someone wiped him clean."

"And what do you think?"

"Someone killed Zeke. I've got a strong feeling about it and I just know I'm right. If Zeke was in your bed, kissed you, touched you, you had to have touched him, too. But your prints were nowhere on his body. Whoever did this was skilled. They knew exactly how to get away with murder."

"Then they planted my phone to make me look guilty?"

"That, or maybe he really did take it while he was there."

"I just can't understand why he'd do that. I referred to him as Ridge while he was there and he never corrected me. If he didn't want his identity to be found out, why would he incriminate himself by stealing my phone?"

"That's why I don't think it was him." His lips roll together, head resting against the wall. "There's more, Riley. If we're gonna give this thing between us a shot, I don't want any secrets, aside from the ones we're forced to keep. I probably shouldn't tell you this—"

"Tell me." I turn to face him, straightening my back with my hands folded in my lap.

He draws in a deep breath, while some of the color drains from his face. "I haven't been completely honest with you."

"Dammit, Maddox. You're scaring me. Just tell me."

Reaching over, he grabs my hand. "Zeke wasn't the first body found."

"What?" I gasp. "What do you mean he wasn't the first body?"

"There've been other murders around town. Not students. But men connected to the governor."

Now I'm certain the color has drained from my face. I let go of his hand and get to my feet, unable to sit still. "Who did it?"

Maddox gets up and stops me from pacing. "We don't know. But..."

"But what?" I huff. "Just tell me. Tell me everything."

"My dad is certain these men are connected to the death of the governor and could potentially have damning evidence that would incriminate you and your friends."

"That's not possible. No one was there but us."

"You're sure?"

"Pretty sure. At least, we didn't see anyone else."

"There's more."

I fill my lungs, preparing for a potential blackout because I'm not sure how much more bad news I can take.

"The bodies of these men were set on fire after they were murdered. Evidence was found in the rubble of ash at one of the sites."

"Okay." I nod. "That's good. So there's a lead?"

"Yeah. And it leads right to you."

Me? No way. My knees go weak, my brain congested. I can't even think enough to wrap my head around what he just said. I sit back down, now unable to stand because I'm certain I really am going to pass out.

"There was a pen with your name on it."

My eyes shoot wide open. "I lost a pen."

"Thought you might have."

"Dammit." I drop my face in my hands. "Every time you kiss me, you follow it up with some horrible news. I'm not sure I wanna kiss you anymore."

"Fuck that," Maddox crouches down in front of me and puts his hands on my knees, "I'm gonna kiss you any chance I get, so you better prepare yourself."

"The kiss I can handle. What comes after? Not so much."

"Listen. I'm working tirelessly with my dad on this. Well, working against him, technically. But as long as he assumes I'm helping on his side, he'll keep me in the loop on all the evidence and suspects. We're gonna clear your name."

"I'm not so sure you can when it comes to the governor. Although, Scar mentioned Neo could help. Since it's his dad and all." My hands rest on his. "I just don't wanna get you in any trouble, Maddox."

He turns my hands over, entwining our fingers. "We're in this together."

"I'm grateful for that. But we're still left with one big question: who is trying to frame me and why?"

"I'm not sure. But we will find out. And when we do, I'll make damn sure the fucker pays."

CHAPTER 31
RILEY

IT FEELS surreal holding Maddox's hand in public like this. There are whispers and weird looks from some, but also smiles from the people who seem to be genuinely happy for us. I mean, who wouldn't be? We're a cute fucking couple. Not that we have a title yet, but we really don't need one.

Then there's Ridge...

I see him in the woods, perched on a branch like he was the first time I saw him. He's watching from afar. Always watching.

It's definitely uncomfortable, but not in the way it used to be.

I drop Maddox's hand, warranting a look of confusion. When I nod toward Ridge and he follows my gaze, I'm sure he understands. Neither of us wants to shove what we have going down Ridge's throat.

"I've gotta get to my last class," Maddox says. "Can I walk you home after school?"

"My last class is an hour after yours. You don't have to do that."

He presses a chaste kiss to my cheek and whispers, "I want to."

"Okay then. If you insist."

I can't help the smile that grows on my face, but the minute I look back at Ridge, my heart sinks. Eyes pinned on me, he drops down, hanging from the branch with one hand. Then he lets go and his feet hit the ground.

Maddox leaves and I wait a second to see if Ridge is going to come in my direction. Wave me over. Talk to me. Anything. But when he doesn't, my stomach hardens.

I hate that I've hurt him—that *we've* hurt him.

I'm being selfish. I know this to be true. And Maddox is, too. I'm so happy when I'm not thinking about Ridge. Being with Maddox is everything I've ever wanted. But the minute I see Ridge, or he enters my thoughts, a little piece of my heart chips away. How long before it's completely broken?

I've got forty minutes before my next class and my stomach is growling, so I decide to go into the student center to get a snack. Every few seconds, I glance over my shoulder to see if Ridge is coming, but he's not there. My posture slumps and I pull open the doors. Just as I go to step inside, Cade comes out, bumping into me. I backstep, making room for him to exit, while avoiding a confrontation with him.

"Long time no see." He grins devilishly, then sweeps a finger across my cheek with a bandaged hand. I grumble in disgust. "Oh, and nice job taking Melody down the other night. You're stronger than I've given you credit for, baby girl."

Everything freezes. My body. My thoughts. My heart.

Did he just call me...baby girl?

Once I come back down to reality, I watch him as he walks away, laughing with a couple of his friends. The god-awful sound is like nails on a chalkboard. How dare he laugh after he...

No! It couldn't have been him. Could it?

My legs give out from underneath me and I grab the door.

"Sorry," I say to a girl coming out. I slide my hand across the outside wall, bracing myself against the structure. My nails embed in the stone as I try to get a grip. On the wall. On myself. On what I just heard.

He definitely called me baby girl. I heard him correctly. He's drugged girls in the past. Why didn't I see this? How could I have been so wrong?

I spot Ridge in the distance, but everything around him is a hazy cloud; he's all I see. His eyes lock with mine as my stomach swims with grief.

I'm gonna be sick.

In an instant, I tear open the door and haul ass to the bathroom on the right.

As soon as I'm in a stall, I click the lock and my knees hit the floor, not caring about the potential filth I'm kneeling in. Nothing can make me feel as revolting as the knowledge that I let Cade into my bed, underneath my clothes. I kissed him. He put his fingers inside me and I came around them, all the while thinking it was Ridge. Then I assumed it was Zeke. But all this time...it was Cade.

Leaning over the toilet, everything comes out. I gag and cough and throw up until I've emptied my stomach completely. Then I drop down on the floor with my back pressed to the stall.

I break down. A mess of tears and snot and regret. When the bathroom door opens, a light breeze hits my back from the gap in the stalls. I pay no mind to whoever just entered. I sob uncontrollably, not caring who hears me on the other side of this stall.

"Angel?"

His voice hits my ears and I never could have anticipated the sense of relief that washes over me. My head lifts. "Ridge?" I cry harder, getting to my feet so I can tear open the door, and when I see him, I collapse in his arms. "Ridge." My head rests on his shoulder that catches every tear that falls down my face. His arms wrap around me and I feel safe.

"You're okay. I've got you, Angel. I've always got you."

We stand like this for several minutes. Even as two girls walk in, only to walk right back.

Ridge doesn't press for answers or shy away from my hold. He just keeps his arms wrapped around me, not letting go until I'm ready.

Another minute passes, maybe two, and I rub my face on the shoulder of his coat. When I take a step back, his thumbs sweep under my eyes, and the solemn look on his face is endearing. No judgment. Just him being here for me. "You ready to talk about it?"

I nod. "I think so."

He takes my hand and leads me over to the sink before turning on the water. Running his hand under it, he adjusts the cold and hot a couple times, then positions me directly in front of the sink. "Lean down."

I'm not sure why, but I do. Then he splashes some lukewarm water on my face while holding my hair from behind. In a swift motion, he seizes some paper towels from the holder and pats my face as I straighten my back. "Tell me what happened." He keeps dabbing and patting, drying my face and wiping the tears that continue to spill.

I swallow hard, feeling like a ball is resting in my throat. Then I choke out the words, "It was Cade."

"I know. I saw him touch you when you entered the building. I tried to catch him in time, but came after you instead. Don't worry, Angel. I'll take care of him."

"No," I correct him, "it's not about him touching my face earlier. Cade is the one who came into my room that night.

248

He's the guy I thought was you. He must have killed Zeke, too."

It all makes sense now. Cade took advantage of me. Then he lured Zeke to my room, while I was knocked out from the pill he gave me. Then he somehow framed me by stealing my phone.

His fists clench. The corded veins in his neck protrude and he grits his teeth. "You're sure?"

"Mmhmm. Pretty sure. The guy that night kept calling me 'baby girl.' It's how I came to the realization it wasn't you. Earlier, at the door, Cade called me baby girl, and it was the same voice. Same cockiness."

"Where's Scar?"

"In class."

He reaches into his pocket and pulls out his phone. "I'm calling her. Telling her to leave class. I don't want you to be alone."

"Why? What are you doing?"

Completely ignoring my question, his fingers hover over the dial pad on his phone. "What's her number?"

I grab it away from him and hold it behind my back. "What are you planning to do, Ridge?"

"What do you think I'm going to do? I'm gonna torture the fuck out of him." The seriousness in his tone is unsettling.

"No," I blurt out. "You can't do that."

"Sure I can."

"You can't just go around hurting people just because they've hurt me. You're going to get yourself in serious trouble."

"You think I care what happens to me, Angel? I don't fucking care. As long as you're safe and happy, I'm living my best life." He reaches behind me and takes his phone back. I'm too weak to fight him for it and too mentally drained to argue. "What's her number?"

"Who's going to protect me when you're banished? Huh? Who is going to keep me safe and happy once The Elders destroy your life for bringing harm to another member?"

"Maddox. He'll make you happy. He'll keep you safe."

"That's why you told him to go be with me, isn't it? Because you're planning to get kicked out of The Society? You know what's coming?"

His voice rises to a near shout and my limbs quiver. "Give me the damn number."

"We'll never be together if you do that. You know the rules —no outside relationships. Is that a risk you're willing to take?"

I've already told him we can't be together, but I know in his head one day we will. If anything will change his mind, it has to be that.

"Number. Now!"

"Fine. Do what you want. I don't care anyways." It's a lie. Probably the biggest I've ever told, but I try to convince myself it's true. So, I cave and I give him the number, so Scar can come to me and he can go ruin his life.

He sends a text then says, "She'll meet us out front."

A minute later, we're walking out the doors of the school to meet Scar. His hand rests softly on my hip as he leads me to the picnic table out front. "She said she'd be here in five minutes."

We wait in silence. There is so much I want to say, but this time, I'm the one who can't speak. I gnaw on the inside of my cheek so hard that a metallic taste seeps onto my tongue. My nerves are fucking shot.

Scar comes running out the front doors, straight toward us. "What the fuck happened?"

Ridge jumps up, ready to flee, but I grab him by the back of the coat. "You don't have to do this. You don't always have to be the hero."

He takes a moment to stare longingly into my eyes, as if he's reading a page in our future, then he smiles. "See you around, Angel."

And just like a superhero flying away, he's gone.

CHAPTER 32
RIDGE

ANY MINUTE NOW, he should be walking out this door, probably with his arm thrown around the shoulders of one of his whores. I could be dumb about this, not give a fuck and let everyone see. But I need to play this one safe. This will be my most important task thus far—the most personal, anyway.

My skin itches with red-hot anger. Adrenaline pumps fiercely through my veins in anticipation of making this fucker pay.

I glance at my phone, checking the time.

Five. Four. Three. Two...

The classroom doors open, and there he is.

Allowing him to lead the way, I follow behind with my black hood lifted.

A girl joins his side. Cade smacks her ass and she giggles, then nudges her side against his.

Stupid fucking guy.

She scurries away then blows him a kiss, and the second she turns her head, he flips her off and laughs with his friends.

Stupid fucking girl.

As I step outside, I slide on a pair of shades. It's a cloudy day—in fact, I'm pretty sure they're calling for snow. But the insanity I wear on the outside matches what I feel on the inside. I feel fucking crazy.

I jog up to his side, then throw an arm around his neck. "What's up, Cade?"

He ducks and tries to free himself from my arm, but I squeeze tighter. I retrieve my gun from the pocket of my coat and dig it into his rib cage. "Make a scene. I dare you."

I don't look at his face as we walk side by side, my new friend and me. He's likely pale. Probably a little horror-stricken. That thought excites me.

Cade mumbles off words, begging for mercy, but all I can think about is the fact that this son of a bitch dipped his fingers into *my* pussy.

We hit the pavement of the parking lot and keep walking, weaving through parked cars, almost getting hit by a couple moving ones.

"What drug did you feed her, Cade?"

"Who? What drug? I don't know what the hell you're talking about. I swear, man. I didn't do anything."

I dig the gun deeper as we approach the woods. "Fluni-trazepam? GHB? Or was it just your everyday sleeping pill?"

"I don't even know what those pills are. You've got the wrong guy."

Taking a shortcut down the trail, I keep him close with the gun engaged. "I don't think I do. Tell me, how tight was her pussy? You touched it before I did, so I'm curious. How many fingers were you able to get in?"

"Who are you talking about?"

"I don't like games, Cade. You know exactly who I'm talking about. Do you remember the day I broke that nose of yours? As I was leaving your room, you said, *'I've always craved what I'm told I can't have. Challenge accepted.'* Did you or did you not say that?"

"I...I don't remember."

I click the safety on the gun with a sweep of my thumb and he trembles. "Maybe that'll jog your memory."

"Okay. Okay. I remember saying that, but I was pissed. You'd just broken my nose. I didn't mean anything by it."

"I'm gonna be honest with you, Cade. We can do this the easy way. Or we can do it the hard way. But either way, it's getting done."

Maddox is parked right where I told him to be. He's wearing a black ski mask, being more inconspicuous than I am. He's not a fan of this shit. Maddox is a good guy. But he's beating himself up for letting this happen. After all, his assignment was to keep an eye on the Kappa Rho brothers, and one of them fucked up royally. His saintly ass will probably never forgive himself. I'm not sure I'll forgive myself, either. I should have been there. Should've protected her from this dipshit.

Maddox gets out of the car when he sees us approaching and opens up the back door with his glove-covered hands.

Cade panics, crying like a little bitch. "Who's that? Where are we going? Please. I didn't do anything."

Dislodging the gun from his side, I throw him in the back seat, then point it right back at him before sliding in beside him.

Maddox slams his foot on the gas, leaving a trail of black smoke behind us.

I keep the gun pointed at Cade as I press for answers that I know he won't give. "When she called you by my name, what went through your head?"

His head jerks and trembles, and I'm sure he's in a state of shock right now, which makes him useless to me.

A couple short minutes later, we pull up to the old brick building that will be Cade's home for a while. At least until he decides to cooperate. It's only a short walk from campus, but considering I'm kidnapping a guy, I figured a ride was necessary.

The old structure sits at the end of a desolate industrial drive, but while it appears abandoned from the outside, one small space on the inside is frequently occupied.

Lev comes walking out the door, making no attempt to hide his identity from his cousin. We're alike in that way. Both don't give a fuck. Both fucked up.

Maddox opens the door for us, then we part ways for now. He agreed to be our driver. He refused to handle weapons and was adamant about not entering the building.

Lev joins me and aids in getting our new buddy inside the building. He's been prepping for Cade's arrival since I made the call.

Being the dick that he is, Lev shoves Cade, who's trying to drag his feet. When we catch up to him, Lev shoves him again.

"He really is a little bitch," Lev says. "I've been waiting a long time to rock this fucker's world." Another shove. "Still think you're fucking stupid for defending that girl's honor, though. She doesn't deserve it."

I give Lev a look of warning. "She's more than worth it." My voice rises so Cade can hear me. "Ain't that right? You touched that pussy, you know it's gold. Don't ya?"

Head held low, he just keeps walking.

Once we're inside, Lev leads the way to the basement. He rented the entire building, only to occupy a small space in it. It was the only one available within walking distance to campus and he needed somewhere to meet with his therapist. Things get intense during his meetings, so he wanted to ensure he'd have privacy. I'd say this building is perfect. For his appointments, and for what we need to do now.

Lev has a chair all set up for Cade. Rope, duct tape, and tools laid out neatly, as if we're preparing to perform a heinous type of surgery on this fucker. There are pliers, a hammer, hand-held clamps.

Excitement swims inside my deranged mind.

I shove Cade down on the chair, as he begs for his life. "Please. You've got the wrong person. I didn't do this. I swear to you."

"Shut the fuck up." I slap him hard across the face while Lev ties him to the chair. "You just thank your lucky stars I haven't killed your ass yet. Told you I would if you touched her again. Killing you is too generous, though. First, I'm gonna torture the fuck out of you while you describe in detail every inch of her body you touched."

Speaking of...

I pull out my notepad that has all the names on my list checked off, then I add another...

Dennis Mathers

Robby Nelson

Andy Porter

Eric Mathers

Cade Pemberley

Cade fucked with the wrong girl, and pissed off the wrong guy. Once he's out of the picture, Riley will be safe again.

EPILOGUE
RILEY

MY HEART IS LITERALLY in my throat as I pace in front of Ridge's dorm room. I've knocked a dozen times with no answer, so I can only assume no one is here.

At first, I was hesitant to return after my encounter with Lev the last time. Then, I put on my big-girl panties and...

"Oh. Hi," I say to a very grouchy-looking Lev, who's approaching his door.

Of course, he's alone. I would put a nail in my foot before I'd enter that room with him. At least out here, people can come out of their rooms if I scream loud enough.

Then again, they could hear me from inside the room, too, but they wouldn't be able to save me. Lev could drown me in a bathtub by the time they got in.

Why am I thinking like this? He's just a guy. Only a couple years older than me. Sure, he's intimidating and a straight-up asshole, but he's not a killer.

"Go the fuck home, Trouble." He sticks his key in the door and turns it.

"Actually. I came for Ridge. Or Maddox. Whichever I see first."

He turns around, leaving the key stuck in the door. "Is that how it works with you? You fuck with whatever one is around when you need them?"

"No. I didn't say that."

"You don't have to. I see you for what you are. A home-wrecker."

My arms cross over my chest and I lift my chin. "Your names don't hurt me, Lev."

He closes the gap between us, breathing down my neck. "My names don't have to when my hands can get the job done."

His eyes sweep left, then right, before his nose rests mere inches from mine. "I don't like you. I've got no idea what my friends see in you, but to me, you're everything that's wrong with The Society. You might have them fooled, but you're not fooling me."

"You keep saying that, but I have yet to understand how I am trying to fool anyone."

The corners of his lips tug up in a grin and it's a look that unnerves me. Chills shimmy down my arms and I hug myself tighter.

"I'll tell you what. I'll let you live to see another day as a Blue Blood by keeping your dirty little secret."

I open my mouth to speak, but he shuts me right back up.

"I'm not finished. You're going to do exactly what I say. You're my little pet now and my pets *will* obey. And if you tell a single soul about any of this, your secret will be the least of your worries."

"I'm not scared of you, Lev."

"You should be. I'm your worst fucking nightmare."

"I don't have any secrets." My voice cracks, breaths shaky. "So good luck trying to tattle on me."

"Is that so? I happen to know, and have proof, that you

killed our former state governor. Is that not a secret you're trying to keep?"

My chest rattles as I fight to fill my lungs. "You have nothing."

Lev reaches into the pocket of his jeans and pulls out his phone. A second later, he's holding it up. I gasp at the video playing and the sounds that ring out."

I choke up, my words barely recognizable. "Where the hell did you get that?"

"Next time you kill someone, you might want to make sure there's no video evidence lying around."

Jagger. He told us he recorded the whole thing. Said he would keep it safe and only use it if we needed proof of how the whole thing went down.

"That proves it was self-defense. You've got nothing."

"That's where you're wrong. At least four local Elders are fighting to clear the governor's name. A lot of people didn't like him, but a few did. This video shows a member killed him. That's all they care about. So, Trouble," he jerks down the zipper of his jeans, "do you spit or swallow?"

My feet don't stop as I take off down the hall as quickly as I can. Tears drip down my face and I mentally prepare myself for one of two options: turn myself in or do exactly what Lev tells me to do.

One problem was solved today, but an even bigger one arose.

Snowflakes coat my lashes as I walk at a leisurely pace, in no hurry to face Scar, or anyone for that matter. I can't tell her. Lev threatened me, and I take him to be a man of his word. He wants to destroy me and I've got no doubt he will if I don't do everything he asks of me.

My phone buzzes in the pocket of my jacket so I pull it out

and read the text message, while seeing I have two unread ones.

> Maddox: I'm sorry I couldn't walk you home after class. Everything is over. The planted evidence. The bodies. Zeke. It's over, babe. We know who it was and he's being dealt with.

Not responding, because I'm not sure how to, I read the next one.

> Scar: Staying with the guys tonight. Think Maddox will want to stay with you?

I don't respond to her either. I've got nothing to worry about back at the dorms. Zeke is dead. Ridge and Maddox have handled Cade. I'm still not sure what they'll do to him, but I'm sure I'll find out tomorrow if he's sporting more broken bones.

> Ridge: You're safe, Angel. I've got you!

I should feel relieved. Should be grateful that the nightmare has ended. But how can I be when another has begun?

Dragging my feet up the stairs and into my room, I collapse on the floor and lose it. All the pain from the last couple weeks spills onto my pink shag rug.

I lie there for what feels like hours, and when I finally force myself up with my hands pressed to the rug, my index finger rolls over something. I pick it up and get a better look, only to realize it's a pill.

I must have dropped it at some point, so I pull open the drawer of my nightstand and take out my prescription bottle. But when I go to drop it in, I realize it's not the same color. My pills are light blue, and this one is yellow.

Then it hits me. I didn't drop this because it isn't mine. Cade must have dropped it when he was in my room. This has to be the drug he gave me that knocked me out.

With my drawer open, I take out a ring box that's empty and I set it inside. It won't be long before I'll know exactly what he put in my system that night.

The guys might be handling Cade, but when they're done with him, I just might finish him off for good.

The End.

Read a steamy bonus scene from Ridge and Riley HERE
https://BookHip.com/VNQSWJB

Book Two, *You Will Bow*, is coming in May: Preorder Now
http://mybook.to/youwillbow

ALSO BY RACHEL LEIGH

Bastards of Boulder Cove

Book One: Savage Games

Book Two: Vicious Lies

Book Three: Twisted Secrets

Wicked Boys of BCU

Book One: We Will Reign

Book Two: You Will Bow

Book Three: They Will Fall

Redwood Rebels Series

Book One: Striker

Book Two: Heathen

Book Three: Vandal

Book Four: Reaper

Redwood High Series

Book One: Like Gravity

Book Two: Like You

Book Three: Like Hate

Fallen Kingdom Duet

His Hollow Heart & Her Broken Pieces

Black Heart Duet

Four & Five

Standalones

ACKNOWLEDGMENTS

Thank you so much for reading We Will Reign. I hope you enjoyed the start of this wicked series!

A special thanks to my wonderful team for all the hard work you put into helping me create this book: My dedicated PA, Carolina Leon. All my girls for your support, friendship, and advice. My Street Team, the Rebel Readers for your help in getting the word out.

Thank you to my beta readers: Amanda, Erica, & Drita. I appreciate you ladies so much!

A BIG thanks to...

Y'all That Graphic for the amazing cover and graphics!

Fairest Reviews Editing Service for the editing and putting up with my craziness.

Rumi Khan for proofreading and being so patient with me.

Greys Promo for PR Services.

Amanda Anderson for helping with my release plan & schedule.

Thank you to my family for your support and for giving me grace and still loving me when I'm holed away in my writing cave for weeks on end.

XOXO Rachel

ABOUT THE AUTHOR

Rachel Leigh is a USA Today and International bestselling author of new adult and contemporary romances.

She loves to write—and read—flawed bad-boys and strong heroines. You can expect dark elements, a dash of suspense, and a lot of steam.

Her goal is to take readers on an adventure with her words, while showing them that even on the darkest days, love conquers all.

Rachel lives in Michigan with her husband, three little monsters (who aren't so little anymore) and a couple of fur babies. When she's not writing or reading, she's likely lounging in leggings, with coffee in her hand, while binge watching her favorite reality tv shows.

Rachel Leigh is represented by SBR Media. For all subsidiary rights, please contact: stephanie@sbrmedia.com

Printed in Great Britain
by Amazon

21809963R00160